Angela Bull was born  reader from childhood, University and later Victorian children's bo young people, one of w The Other Award in 1 phies of Anne Frank, N gale, Marie Curie and Elizabeth Fry. Researching the lives of these famous women gave her an insight into women's place in history. A supporter of the Movement for the Ordination of Women, Angela Bull is married to a clergyman. They live in Bingley, West Yorkshire and have two grown-up children.

Virago Upstarts is a new series of books for girls and young women. Upstarts are about love and romance, family and friends, work and school – and about new preoccupations – because in the last two decades the lives and expectations of girls have changed a lot. With fiction of all kinds – humour, mystery, love stories, science fiction, detective, thrillers – and nonfiction, this new series will show the funny, difficult, and exciting real lives and times of teenage girls today. Lively, down-to-earth and entertaining, Virago's new list is an important new Upstart on the scene.

UP THE ATTIC STAIRS

Angela Bull

VIRAGO UPSTARTS

Published by VIRAGO PRESS Limited 1989
20–23 Mandela Street
Camden Town
London NW1 0HQ

British Library Cataloguing in Publication Data

Bull, Angela
 Up the attic stairs.
 I. Title
 823'.914 [F]

 ISBN 1-85381-060-60

Typeset by CentraCet, Cambridge
Printed in Great Britain by
The Guernsey Press Ltd. C.I.

In creating this story of women through the last eighty years, there have been times when I have needed assistance, and I would like to thank those of my friends and relations who made suggestions, wrote me letters, and lent me useful books. My thanks go also to Lennie Goodings for her careful and sympathetic editing.

The early part of the book is a tribute to my mother and her sisters, whose enthralling recollections of their romantic girlhood lie somewhere behind the story of the Floods. But my most especial gratitude goes to my daughter Priscilla, who helped and advised, criticized, encouraged, and in places coscripted this work. To her, *Up the Attic Stairs* is affectionately dedicated.

The letter arrived in January, two days into the university term. There was a Sudanese stamp on it, and it was addressed to *The Occupants, 1 Marlborough Street, Wortley Hill, Crosthwaite, Yorkshire, England*.

Fortunately for the sender of the letter, Marlborough Street was still standing. Many Wortley Hill houses had been pulled down. They were slums, disfiguring Crosthwaite; which, with a university, a polytechnic and a new shopping centre, was trying to shrug off its dark, industrial image. Marlborough Street remained, a relic amongst tower blocks and modern housing developments; and, since it was shabby and old-fashioned, it made suitably cheap student accommodation. The three girls who lived there were all students.

Lucy picked up the envelope from the handful of circulars and advertisements which had been pushed through the door, read the address and called to the others, Elizabeth and Gabriel. By the time they joined her in the kitchen, she had ripped open the envelope and pulled out a letter and a photograph.

The photograph showed a long, low building, half roofless and holed by shells. Beside it stood a little group of women, one or two white but mainly Sudanese, with staring, frightened faces. On the back, someone had written – *This was the Amy Whittingham Hospital*.

'How awful,' said Elizabeth.

'There's civil war in the Sudan,' said Lucy, checking the place again from the stamp.

Gabriel, the newcomer to the house, gazed silently over Elizabeth's shoulder, seeing the distress, seeing too the yellow-browns and dusty whites and the hot blue sky.

'They're appealing for help,' announced Lucy, who had been reading the letter. 'One of those women in the picture has written. She's on the medical staff, and she says they desperately need money to rebuild and re-equip.'

'So why ask us?' said Elizabeth.

Lucy took the photograph and turned it over. 'Yes; it says "Amy Whittingham Hospital". Apparently someone called Amy Whittingham once lived in this house. She was a doctor, who went out to the Sudan in – Lucy referred back to the letter – 1912. She founded the hospital for women and children.'

'She can't be still alive, surely?' Elizabeth exclaimed.

'No; but she's still remembered, they say. That's why they risked writing to her old address, in the hope that people living there might know about her. They're appealing to aid agencies, of course, but every penny they can get will count. They'd be really grateful if we could make even a bit of money for them.'

Lucy was mad, thought Elizabeth, for how could they raise money, the three of them, penniless students with hectic schedules? She'd like to, of course. She felt for those lost, victimized women, facing the tragedy of the shattered hospital. But life was such a hassle. There was her degree. There was her ambition to get something – an article or review – published in the student paper, *Cross-Questioning*, as a forerunner of all the influential pieces she would one day pen for national magazines. There was the Students' Union Women's Group.

The Women's Group . . . She looked at Lucy, for the message from the Amy Whittingham Hospital seemed almost calculated to twang the heartstrings of feminists, as she and Lucy considered themselves to be. Indeed a

2

meeting of the SUWG had brought them together, a summer ago.

Lucy, curly-haired, untidy and lively, had been leaning over a table, arguing for a free issue of rape alarms to all women students, when Elizabeth first noticed her.

'Anything could happen! We're not safe,' Lucy had announced. 'Wasn't one of the Ripper's victims a student? And think of the attacks there've been lately. We've a right to protection.'

Elizabeth had supported her whole-heartedly – though the university authorities, with their usual excuse of 'cuts', hadn't. Elizabeth had got chatting to Lucy afterwards and they'd found themselves fixing up to share a house for the next academic year, with a third girl, Suzanne, who was on the SUWG too.

It should be good, Elizabeth had thought during the summer vacation, cheering herself with the prospect as she trogged round the streets near her home, trying – and generally failing – to find news stories which would be accepted by her local paper. She'd seen herself, Lucy and Suzanne as serious, single-minded feminists, a close unit in a university environment dominated by men, their ideas and habits. But she had been disappointed. Suzanne had spent her summer falling in love, and at Christmas she had left Marlborough Street and the university forever; while Lucy, it turned out, was a campaigner for a thousand causes, amongst which feminism alternately flickered and faded. She wore a 'Free Nelson Mandela' badge; she stuck CND and 'Save the Whale' posters round her room; and, in the Religious Studies Department, she joined the struggle for the ordination of women as priests – which was all right in its way, thought Elizabeth, but a side issue compared with the really degrading ways in which some women were treated.

3

Now she glanced at Lucy; and Lucy ran her hand through her hair, thinking of the hospital, but remembering Steve, who was coming for the weekend, and Robin and Alec whom she'd invited to supper that evening, and her Student Nightline shift the following evening, and the SUWG, and the Christian Union, and the Schools' Assembly team . . .

'I'll put on a fashion show.'

It was Gabriel Klavir who had spoken. The flare of excitement in her voice startled Lucy and Elizabeth.

'I'll design a whole collection. I've always wanted to. We could show it to raise money, and sell the clothes afterwards.'

And she looked round, hopefully.

As yet, Lucy and Elizabeth hardly knew her. She had answered the advert they had hastily sent into *Student Newsround* when Suzanne so abruptly left; but she wasn't a university student. She was in the first year of a fashion course at the Poly; eighteen, fragile, beautiful, with thick dark hair that had shone blue-black under the hall light when she came to enquire about the room, and widely-spaced eyes which were vividly blue between blackly mascara'd eyelashes. Just seeing her made Elizabeth feel instinctively dowdy, and Lucy overweight.

'Oh, I'd love to do it!' she went on.

'Can you?' Elizabeth felt doubtful. 'It sounds like a lot of work.'

But Lucy interrupted, her imagination fired.

'That's great! That's really great! We'd help you all we could. I don't mind setting up a show, selling tickets. I've done it before.'

'Oh, come off it! They need money now. Gabriel can't possibly design a whole collection of clothes in a few

4

weeks,' Elizabeth couldn't help objecting. 'Besides, who'd pay for the materials?'

'I've plenty of material already,' said Gabriel. 'Market-stall people often let you have the ends of their rolls for next to nothing; and shops sometimes do on the last day of a sale. I've even picked up fabrics from jumble sales – gorgeous things; and friends have given me bits they don't want. That's how I've been able to start a collection. D'you want to see some of my designs?' Gabriel flew out of the room, and was back in a moment, tossing things over a chair, or holding them up separately.

'There's a skirt, a jacket. I got some gorgeous buttons. And I loved the way the collar went. I kept drawing and it suddenly happened.'

She was alight, and the clothes glowed too – raspberry, turquoise and cream. They were gemlike, magical. Lucy remembered how she had heard that people said Gabriel Klavir's talent was something special.

'Do all your designs just "happen"?' asked Lucy.

'Yes.'

'Honestly,' said Lucy, 'you must be a genius. Let me try one on.'

She tugged the raspberry jacket over her sweater; wondering, as she did so, why Gabriel, with her sense of colour, invariably chose to wear black.

But Elizabeth had complicated feelings about clothes, which she was reluctant, just then, to express.

'Wear a tight skirt, and lots of make-up,' a friend in the English Department had advised when Elizabeth had spoken about seeing the editor of *Cross-Questioning* to ask for an assignment.

'I'm going to use my mind, not my body,' Elizabeth had protested.

5

'He's a man, after all, and you want to impress him, don't you?'

'Not like that.'

There was so often this stupidity to contend with. As an escape from her thoughts, Elizabeth picked up the letter and read it for herself.

More than seventy years ago, a woman doctor had lived at 1, Marlborough Street; used the very kitchen they were standing in; slept upstairs in either hers or Lucy's bedroom; worried – perhaps? – over a range of matters about which they were quite ignorant. And surely, thought Elizabeth, she must have been something of a pioneer. There couldn't have been that many women doctors in 1912. What was she like? Why did she leave Crosthwaite?

I wonder, thought Elizabeth, if I could find out about her. And then write my great feminist piece . . .

'We could call your show Fashion-Aid!' Lucy was exclaiming. Already she could see, in her mind's eye, posters up everywhere, crowds arriving. 'You'll be famous, and we'll make loads of money.'

I'll leave them to it. I'll research into Amy Whittingham on my own, Elizabeth decided.

For the next three weeks, when Lucy had time to spare from all her friends and commitments, she dashed about, promoting Fashion-Aid. She discovered a hall that was cheap to rent and had a large changing-room. She mulled over catwalks and programmes and posters. She worked out relative prices for printing or photocopying tickets. And she talked to everyone she met about Gabriel.

'There's this girl who's into fashion design. She's really brilliant. She's putting on this show at the end of term. Hope you can make it.'

'Is it free?' people asked.

'You've got to be joking. We're doing it in aid of a women's hospital in the Sudan.'

The cause was important, Lucy reminded herself, for Gabriel's talent sometimes seemed to eclipse it; and she wrote 'Remember Amy Whittingham' at the top of a page of lecture notes and highlighted it with a textliner.

While Lucy's life was a hectic round of activity, Gabriel's was concentrated and intense. She stayed in her room with her sketching-pad and the pieces of material which she shaped and folded and cut.

She seized the opportunity to miss her classes at the Poly for a while. 'Of course you must get some qualifications,' everyone had told her; and so she had obediently applied for the course. But she found it a strain. She had never been good at adapting and conforming to the ratpack. She relied on her own, untrammelled inspiration.

How out of the ordinary she was, Lucy and Elizabeth were gradually finding out. Her room, to begin with, was unconventional. She had covered the walls with a bright patchwork of pictures, haphazardly Blu-Tacked, crowded and overlapping. Many were portraits, illustrating clothes of every period. There were Elizabethan ladies in brocaded farthingales and gauzy ruffs; Regency girls wearing airy muslins; and Pre-Raphaelite beauties swathed in silken draperies. Scattered amongst them, abstract prints beamed out vibrant colours or blocks of startling whiteness.

'Don't they make you dizzy?' asked Lucy, staring in amazement.

'No. I like them.'

'It's a fantastic pattern,' agreed Lucy. Yet she was puzzled as she contrasted the glowing walls with Gabriel's stark black clothes.

'I can't really suss Gabriel out,' she admitted to Elizabeth in the kitchen one day.

'Don't expect me to, then.'

'She's just so odd, and I can't understand her not having a boyfriend when she's so attractive.'

But Elizabeth replied that Gabriel had a right to live as she liked, and not hamper herself with unnecessary status symbols, which boyfriends often were; and Lucy, who had learned to expect a certain sharpness in Elizabeth, didn't argue. All the same, she was still curious, and it wasn't only about Gabriel's apparently anti-social nature. She had never known anyone live quite so single-mindedly for her work. Elizabeth, of course, worked hard, and right now she was spending a lot of time researching into the background of Amy Whittingham too. But at least she gave herself breaks. Gabriel never did. Lucy made a couple of mugs of coffee and took them into Gabriel's room.

'I thought you might need this. You're working so hard,' she said.

'Oh, thanks.'

Gabriel put the mug on the table and went on with her drawing. Lucy peeped over her shoulder.

'That's amazing; but don't kill yourself. We've only booked a provisional date for Fashion-Aid. There's no need to give up your whole social life.'

'This is my life. I *want* to do it. OK?'

Gabriel's pencil swirled over the paper, checked, and swirled again.

'Would you like to come to a party tomorrow? A crowd of us are going along – Robin and Alec and John and Sue –'

'Not tomorrow,' said Gabriel.

'But you need time off.'

'Not at a party. Not with tons of people. That's why I left the hall of residence last term – to get away from people.'

She must be a genius, Lucy decided. Only a genius would behave like Gabriel.

'What d'your family think of your work?' she asked.

Gabriel shrugged.

'Sarah's not interested in clothes.'

'Is she your sister?'

'No. My mother.'

That was almost the first personal detail Lucy had learned about Gabriel.

'Have you got any sisters?'

'No.'

'Lucky you! I've always had to share a bedroom at home with mine, and she spreads her things all over the place. Mum and Dad are both teachers, you see; so we can't afford a house with lots of room. Did you have loads of space to yourself?'

'Springfield!' The name jangled silently in Gabriel's

9

head. 'Springfield!' Her eyes on her paper, her coffee cooling, she sketched rapidly, without answering. It struck Lucy suddenly that there was something frenetic in the movement of her hand; a hint of tension gathering and rising.

'Do come with us tomorrow,' she urged again.

'No, thanks.'

Lucy picked up the mugs and left. The door closed and Gabriel stood rigidly by the drawing-board, her pencil clenched in her fingers.

It frightened her how quickly she reacted to dangerous subjects like Springfield; how her nerves tightened like wires. Whether it was a twist in her own personality, or a legacy from her Eastern European ancestors she didn't know. 'Highly strung,' her mother's friend Josie labelled her, meaning to be kind but sounding patronizing.

Only my work matters, Gabriel told herself, as she had done many times before. Work could save her from remembering her parents' divorce, or the irritations of life in Sarah's flat, or the problems of relationships that she could never sort out, or the black depressions that sometimes overwhelmed her. It would be nice to be like Lucy – friendly, untroubled. But she couldn't be. She was like a prisoner in a shell which yet wasn't tough enough to withstand the pinpricks chance brought along.

Or not chance. She had been mad to choose the fashion course at Crosthwaite Poly.

What she hadn't told Lucy, what she hadn't told anyone, was that the first eight years of her life had been spent in Crosthwaite, in the old house she had instantly recalled when Lucy spoke of loads of space. She had lived there, at Springfield, with her parents before they separated. It was only up Wortley Hill, hardly twenty minutes' walk from Marlborough Street. She had pretended that she had forgotten it since she went away; but she hadn't. And some buried longing had tricked her into applying – with Sarah's enthusiastic support as well – to Crosthwaite Poly.

Soon after she started her course, she nerved herself to visit the house again. She had walked along the high hilltop road and seen, beyond the wall and the waving trees whose exuberant growth had annoyed her father, Springfield's familiar chimneys and picturesquely irregular gables. And such a sudden pain of loss, of exclusion, had stabbed her, that she found herself running away, as fast as she could.

She hadn't mentioned the experience to anyone. Perhaps she should have confided in Sarah at Christmas – but everyone confided in Sarah. The small flat was full of people, pouring out their stories. So she worked to forget. Now, with Fashion-Aid ahead, she was in top gear, going faster and faster, shutting out the thought of Springfield up the hill.

≫ *3* ≪

When darkness fell, time lost its meaning in Marlborough Street. The scattered lamps shone faintly on stone housefronts, unchanged since Amy Whittingham opened her surgery, and began to think about women and society.

In this very house, Elizabeth reflected.

Pen in hand, she sat at her desk, imagining the life of eighty years ago. She saw a bare room – Gabriel's room –

11

with linoleum on the floor, plain cupboards, upright chairs and a scrubbed table on which lay a few papers and basic medical instruments.

~

'Only one left,' said Ruth, looking round the door.

'Show her in then,' said Amy.

Clogs rattled in the hall, and the last patient, a young woman, came into the surgery. A brown shawl framed her haggard face and half covered the baby cradled in her arms.

'It's the little 'un, doctor,' she began hastily, as if time pressed. 'It's his stomach. He keeps being sick.'

'Sit down,' Amy invited, and she took the baby onto her lap; a pitifully thin child, too listless to mind a stranger's touch.

'I can't feed him myself, you see, ma'am. I don't know why –' The woman shook her head in despair at the difficulties of life.

'Do you get enough rest?' asked Amy, though she really knew the answer.

'Does anyone, with a husband and four bairns? Taking rest never paid for a hot dinner. I go out scrubbing every night when Alf gets in, down at one of them big High Street shops. That's after I've done all my own work at home. I should be there now. I'm losing good wages, but I had to bring the baby. He can't keep down his milk.'

'What sort of milk do you give him?'

The woman looked surprised.

'Condensed, ma'am.'

'But you see,' said Amy gently, 'condensed milk can harm babies. They need fresh milk, boiled, with a little sugar.'

'There's no fresh milk to be had on Wortley Hill. And if I'd the time to go looking for it, it's tuppence a pint and I can't afford that. Condensed's fivepence a tin, I know, but it goes ever such a long way, if you water it down.'

Amy studied the little pallid face leaning exhaustedly against her dress, the shadowed eyelids and matchstick limbs.

'It's so unjust. Children have the right to a good start in life,' she murmured.

12

But the woman only shook her head. Rights meant nothing to her. Rather doubtfully she took the free milk tokens Amy offered her, and shuffled out into the night.

'Supper's nearly ready,' called Ruth from the kitchen; but for once Amy didn't answer. She sat motionlessly at the table, her thoughts running over their familiar track. Why were poor mothers forced to work until their natural milk dried up? Why were babies allowed to be undernourished so that they could only grow into frail, sickly children? Even as she asked the questions, she knew the answers. Nobody understood the lives of the poor; or, nobody who mattered. The government in London, those men with the power to legislate for all the social improvements that were so desperately needed, were complacent in their ignorance. If women elected governments, they would ensure that only people who knew the sufferings of the poor were given power. If women had the vote . . .

Ruth appeared in the doorway with a tray.

'Seventeen patients tonight – you'll be ready for this! Who was the last one?'

'An infantile colic case,' said Amy, rousing herself to clear a space on the table, and taking plates and knives from Ruth. 'Another baby who's not getting a proper diet. I gave the mother some milk tokens, but I doubt if she's the time or the energy to find a dairy selling fresh milk. There should be some on Wortley Hill, or better still a milkman who delivers, but I suppose there wouldn't be enough customers. We'll have to change the system, Ruth. Things can't go on like this.'

'Oh, we'll change it!' cried Ruth, cutting bread with a flourish. 'Votes for women – that'll be the way.'

~

Returning late from her party on the following evening, Lucy saw that the light in Gabriel's room was still on. She might have looked in, only several friends were with her, crowding into the kitchen, sobering up with Nescafé, and she hadn't a chance. They were making excited plans for another party.

13

'Here, if you like,' offered Lucy.

'OK; great! When?'

'How about Valentine's Day? People'll be in the mood then.'

'Yeah. Why not?'

There was light behind Gabriel's curtains when the last friends finally vanished into the dark; and a line of light under her door the next morning when Lucy tottered downstairs, cursing the impulse that had made her volunteer for the Schools' Assembly team, with its eight o'clock breakfast meeting. But there was no time to think of Gabriel. Later, there were lectures and seminars, and the business of designing and photocopying party invitations and distributing them far and wide, to occupy Lucy's day. A supper invitation, with a drink at a pub afterwards, filled her evening. When at last she got back to Marlborough Street, Gabriel's light still shone.

Elizabeth was in the kitchen. She was sitting at the table, drinking tea, with a book propped up in front of her.

'I'm reading about Amy Whittingham,' she began, the moment Lucy came in. 'It's really interesting. Apparently she was a suffragette.'

'A what?'

'You must know. Those women who wanted the vote and kicked up a fuss till they got it.'

'Oh, yeah. I know.' Lucy was tired, and vaguely irritated at the spectacle of Elizabeth being scholarly and calm.

'I was chatting to one of the librarians,' said Elizabeth. 'She's given me the address of someone whose mother knew Amy Whittingham well; a woman called Anne Cropper. She's a doctor too. I'm thinking of contacting her next. There's tons of stuff to find out still.'

'So the past's more important than Fashion-Aid?'

Elizabeth was instantly defensive. 'Don't be so sarky. Fashion-Aid's Gabriel's concern.'

'And mine. Have you seen Gabriel today?'

'No.'

'Not at all?'

'I said not, didn't I?'

With a queer presentiment of disaster, Lucy tapped, and opened the door of the front room. Gabriel, poignantly thin in her black sweater, was hunched over the table, her head in her hands. Her face, when she lifted it, was white; her eyes dark-ringed with exhaustion.

'Whatever's the matter?' exclaimed Lucy, forgetting her own tiredness.

'Everything's gone wrong. Wrong! Wrong! Wrong!'

'What?'

'My designing. I haven't been able to do a thing since yesterday. I can't do it any longer.'

'Don't be stupid. Of course you can.'

'I can't. It's all useless. My mind's gone blank. Just suddenly blank.' And she screwed up a sheet of paper with violent fingers, unable to understand what had happened, why the flow of inspiration had, without warning, blocked itself off. No, not quite without warning. For the last few days she had been snatching at ideas, seeing half of them fail, but snatching hopefully at others. There was a collection to design; a whole collection. Fashion-Aid was a fantastic opportunity. She might not have another one like it for years. Her mind had spun, raced – and, all at once, gone dead. 'That's the end of Fashion-Aid,' she said.

'Oh, rubbish!' cried Lucy, remembering all the preliminary arrangements she had made. 'I've half booked the hall, and done all sorts of things. I've told loads of people

15

about you. You've been working yourself into the ground. What you need is a break. You'll soon be ready to start up again. You can't just pack it in.'

'I'll have to.' Gabriel unscrewed the paper and stared at it with hatred. 'That's supposed to be a dress, a sophisticated sheath; and it's more like a shopping bag. I've never seen anything so grotty and cheap-looking. I can't bear it.'

'For heaven's sake – '

But it was no good. Swamped with gloom, her confidence gone, Gabriel put her head down on the table and burst into tears.

⇒ *4* ⇐

The rain slanted against the little house in Marlborough Street, streaking the windows and darkening the kitchen where Lucy and Elizabeth were having breakfast. At least, Elizabeth was having breakfast. She ate her muesli silently, concentrating on the pages of a long letter which she had propped against the packet. There had been no Valentines for her.

Lucy, having opened a pile of cards, was trying to do several things simultaneously – make toast, drink tea, clear out the fridge, plan a shopping list and count the plastic cups, rattling about in a Co-op carrier, which someone had lent her.

'Twenty-nine. We'll need more than that. I wish I could remember how many people I've invited.' She began to run through names, checking them off on her fingers. 'It'll be more than forty. Oh, and there was that boy I spoke to in the Old White Horse. I wonder if he'll come? I'd better get another twenty or so cups.'

She scribbled on her list.

The toaster pinged up, hurling two slices onto the table. Elizabeth read on impassively.

'Someone's got loads to say,' remarked Lucy, buttering her toast and looking at the closely written sheets.

'It's Dr Anne Cropper. She's telling me all about Amy Whittingham and the suffragettes.'

Lucy groaned. Amy Whittingham meant Fashion-Aid; and that meant Gabriel, who was staying in her room, pale and uncommunicative.

'I wish Gabriel would snap out of it,' she said abruptly. 'I know it must be awful, having this creative block or whatever; but the longer she lurks by herself, the worse it seems to get.'

'Wasn't she seeing a doctor yesterday?' said Elizabeth, glancing up from her letter.

'Yes; about not sleeping. But I didn't have time to ask how she got on. I did the counselling course for Student Nightline, only I never seem to get round to counselling Gabriel.'

'She wouldn't want an agony aunt,' said Elizabeth.

'No, I don't suppose she would.'

And Lucy dropped on her knees in front of the fridge again.

'What on earth are all these yucky little bowls doing? How come there are so many? I'm sure they must breed, or something.' She peered under the damp, clingfilm covers. 'Old mashed potato. Dead kidney beans. You don't really want to keep them, do you Liz? They're taking up loads of shelf space.'

17

'So's the trifle you made for Steve.'

'Oh, I'm chucking that out.' Lucy scooped a soggy mess into the bin. 'OK; I can fit in a couple of wineboxes now.'

Elizabeth let her chatter on. She wasn't enthusiastic herself at the prospect of the evening's party. There were sure to be lots of 'cute' couples and the usual gossip would be regurgitated over and over again. Whether John was going out with Sue still. What Dave had done when he was drunk. If it was true that Bella had got twenty red roses through Interflora. How many Valentine cards – that was an awkward topic. She suddenly noticed that Lucy was speaking to her again.

'What?'

'Shouldn't we do something to revive Fashion-Aid? That hospital – '

Elizabeth looked at the cork board, hanging over the fridge. Pinned beside a copy of Lucy's party invitation, edged with its border of pierced hearts and toppling bottles, was the photograph of the shattered hospital.

'They certainly need help,' she said, 'but I don't see what we can do.'

'I wonder if Gabriel – ?' Lucy jumped to her feet. 'I'll go and find out. She might be feeling better.'

Gabriel was dressed, but lying on her bed. Her hair was black against the pillow, her eyes hollow in her white face.

'Did you manage to sleep?' asked Lucy.

'Not a lot.'

'What did the doctor say?'

'He just suggested hot baths, and milky bedtime drinks.'

'Couldn't you try a bit of designing again? Just for Fashion-Aid.'

18

'I don't want to even think about designing,' said Gabriel. 'Ever. I told you my mind's gone blank.'

'But if you just – '

Gabriel closed her eyes.

'Well, why not come to my party?' said Lucy. 'It might cheer you up.'

Francis Ashwell, the boy Lucy had spoken to in the Old White Horse, drove his car slowly down Wortley Hill, trying to make out, through the rain-splashed windscreen, the names of the side-streets. At a corner, his headlights picked out the words 'Marlborough Street'. He turned the wheel and drew up outside number 1.

The dashboard clock said half past ten. He'd spent the evening wondering whether to go to the party. He remembered Lucy clearly – curly-haired, bright-eyed, lively. She and a couple of friends had sat down at his table and a few exchanged remarks had led into quite a conversation. He'd been glad to talk. He'd spent most of the last weeks on his own because he didn't know many people in Crosthwaite.

He'd come down from Springfield, the old house on the moors above Wortley Hill. It was his home, though he'd never spent much time there. A settled life was impossible when his father was an actor, living in London or travelling round the world. Now Francis was alone at Springfield, with just a housekeeper to look after things, and he felt lonely and resentful.

He'd told Lucy about his father, but not the other things. She had taken the invitation out of her bag and pushed it across the table to him. She probably thought he was a Crosthwaite student. He sat in the car for a moment; then made up his mind, slammed the door and dashed through the rain to the house.

19

Somebody let him in and he pushed his way down a narrow hall to the kitchen. Candles flared in bottles, cut-out hearts swung from the ceiling, drops of condensation ran clammily down the walls, crisps scrunched underfoot. Dim figures, mainly girls, were moving to loud disco music. Boys with beer-cans leaned against the damp walls. 'Come on, you lot. Dance!' a girl called to them, but nobody responded. A couple locked together swayed against Francis. The kitchen was far too small for such a crowd.

'Oh, hi!' That was Lucy. 'I didn't know if you'd make it. Have a drink.'

He took one, standing conspicuously alone. Snatches of talk bounced across him.

'Apparently those red roses were from Dr Saunders.'

'Oh, come off it. Not really!'

'Well, you know his reputation.'

'Yes, but I mean – roses! They're not exactly his style.'

'Acshually, I am responsible for those roses.'

'Oh, shut up, Dave. You wouldn't know a rose if you saw one, the state you're in.'

'Rubbish! I've never been more sober in my life. And roses are the red prickly ones.'

'I'm sorry.' Lucy was beside Francis again. 'Don't you know anyone? I thought you might. This is Alec –'

'I can't stay long,' Francis stalled. He gulped wine from his plastic cup.

Lucy looked at him, standing in the candlelight, tall and thin with indeterminately fair hair, indeterminately long, flopping over his forehead, and a striped shirt with a narrow tie. Lucy stared incredulously at the tie. It marked him as different from most of the Crosthwaite students. She had a sudden idea.

20

'Hang on, Alec.' She disentangled herself from the arm round her waist. 'I want Francis to meet Gabriel.'

He followed her into the hall and through a door which she knocked on and opened. The extraordinary colours on the walls arrested his attention. For a moment he didn't even notice the room's occupant.

'Gabriel Klavir,' Lucy was saying. The name sounded vaguely familiar. Then he turned and saw her.

She looked as if she had dressed for the party, but lost her nerve. She was wearing a white shirt with a fine black line, and a long slender black skirt. Silver earrings swung against her neck. He had never seen anyone so beautiful.

But instinctively he knew that she didn't want to meet him. She was tensely, exhaustedly remote. Lucy chattered brightly.

'Have a drink with Francis. Or would you like a coffee?' Gabriel shook her head.

'Lucy!' someone called. 'I can't find the bottle-opener.'

'Try Dave,' suggested another voice.

'Coming,' said Lucy.

Francis was left, facing Gabriel.

'You must like historical costumes,' he ventured inadequately, gesturing towards the walls.

'Yes.'

The word fell like a little cold pebble. She stood there, black and white against the riotous colour, fragile, ill. What was the matter? He felt a mad longing somehow to get through to her.

'We've trunks full of clothes in our attics; old ones, collected years ago, I suppose.'

She looked straight at him for a moment. There was a faint gleam of interest in her eyes.

'You know,' he went on, trying desperately to recollect what exactly the trunks contained, for the sake of holding

21

her interest; 'twenties' things of my grandmother's, and Edwardian dresses – '

Lucy looked round the door.

'I've just put the kettle on.'

And Francis saw the gleam in Gabriel's face die away.

'I can't stop,' he said quickly. 'I only looked in for a minute. You should come up to Springfield some time.'

'Oh, thanks,' said Lucy. They were in the hall now. 'I might some time. Sorry to land you with Gabriel,' she added. 'She's not like that really. She's going through a bad patch.'

So am I, thought Francis, but he didn't speak. They squeezed past a couple entwined beside the door. Alec hovered.

'See you,' said Francis, and went.

Hours later, the front door slammed for the last time. Guttering candles showed the hall strewn with peanuts, cigarette ends and trodden plastic cups. Elizabeth had long since disappeared upstairs, but a line of light glinted from Gabriel's room.

Lucy couldn't face the kitchen. She tapped on Gabriel's door and went in. There was a sheet of paper on the drawing board and Gabriel was standing beside it, sketching a baby's dress – long, voluminous and elaborately trimmed.

'What on earth are you doing?' cried Lucy.

At first Gabriel didn't answer. With intense concentration she outlined a tiny frill.

'Is this a new line, or something?' asked Lucy.

'No. Something I remembered.'

'At this time of night?' For clearly Gabriel hadn't been to bed, though she hadn't shown up at the party either. She was still wearing her elegant black skirt.

Gabriel looked up from her drawing at last.

'That boy you brought in here. He said something about clothes in an attic. And then he said to you – I think he said – he lived in Springfield.'

Through a haze of exhaustion and wine, Lucy tried to recapture Francis's final words.

'Yeah. That's right.'

'You see, I used to live there,' said Gabriel. 'And there *were* clothes in the attic. Some of them were my great-grandmother's. And there was this baby's dress. I'd forgotten all about it, but I loved it when I was little, and it suddenly came back to me.'

'Honestly, Gabriel! Why didn't you tell us this before?'

'I don't know.'

With a sudden return to her old uncommunicative self, Gabriel bent over her drawing.

'I suppose,' guessed Lucy, 'that you'd like to go back; see the clothes again.'

'Oh, I really would.'

Lucy leaned on the doorpost, yawning.

'OK. Tell you what. You help me bung all this rubbish in the bin and I'll ring Francis for you.'

'Don't make it sound as if I want to see *him*! It's only the clothes.'

'Fine. Have it your own way. On second thoughts,' added Lucy, 'let's leave the clearing up for now. Let's leave the whole lot till the morning.'

⇒ 5 ⇐

'I know this'll sound awful, but could you sort of leave her to herself? She'd rather be alone,' Lucy finished; and heard a mumble of agreement from Francis at the other end of the line. She put down the phone, satisfied.

'It's all OK,' she reported, bouncing into the kitchen, where Gabriel was stuffing rubbish into a bin-liner. 'Francis says his parents aren't there. His father's acting in London, or something; but there's this housekeeper who looks after things, and she'll probably let you in. I can't make out why Francis is stuck there on his own. Anyway, you'll have the attic to yourself.'

'Oh!' said Gabriel. She looked up, and Lucy saw the first hint of a smile on her face for days. 'You're a star!'

'Any time. Did you sleep better?'

'Yes, thanks.'

For, thinking of the clothes in the attic, she had fallen instantly and easily asleep as soon as she got into bed.

They had always comforted her. As a tiny child she had run up to the attic to escape the arguing voices of her parents, as they clashed in the rooms below; her desperate mother – 'You're a real tyrant!' her coldly scornful father – 'Shut up, you silly little pussycat.' Crouching on the floor, she had examined an exquisite, long, baby's gown, gently touching its minute pearl buttons and dainty frills, its pintucks and inset bands of lace, while calm seemed to flow from them, through her fingers to her tense body. Could these clothes work the same spell now when she was so depressed by the failure of her creative imagination?

'You see,' she began, suddenly wanting to confide, since Lucy had been so kind, 'it's not just that I used to

24

live at Springfield myself, but my great-grandmother lived there too when she was a girl. Some of the clothes belonged to her, and the others in the family – sisters, maybe; I'm not sure who.'

'Really?' Lucy stared in amazement. 'Fancy having an ancestral home and proper ancestors.'

'Their surname was Flood,' said Gabriel dreamily.

'Definitely out of the Ark, then,' said Lucy. 'Hey, hang on! You're chucking out a perfectly good packet of Chocolate Hobnobs. They cost me all of 62p.'

There were the waving trees! Gabriel having walked up Wortley Hill and along a high road winding towards distant moors, saw the bare branches clustering above a grey stone wall that still, irrationally, meant home.

After her parents' last quarrel, when her mother had whisked her away to the new life in London, she'd minded leaving Springfield more than her father. She had forced herself not to think about it. Now here it was, with its low gables and deep-set windows, and the projecting porch where she used to imagine Victorian ladies tying their bonnet strings and unfurling their umbrellas, for it was often wet and windy at Springfield.

Inside the porch she rang the bell, hoping that *he* wouldn't answer it; and, to her relief, the housekeeper opened the door.

Immediately, she forgot him in the delight of rediscovering the three steps down into the hall. Going down into the house, instead of up, had always seemed magical. The hall looked glorious, no longer dim and faded as she remembered it – though she had loved its ancient shadowiness – but with the walls painted strawberry red and the doorframes and waist-high panelling white. A Chinese carpet, in reds, creams, purples and blacks, covered the dipping flagstones. Gabriel's spirit soared at such colour.

'This way,' the housekeeper directed.

'Yes.'

For the staircase, as she knew, climbed sideways from a passage beyond the hall, up between panelled walls to a window looking towards the road and back to a creaking, sloping landing with many doors. Through one of these the attic stairs led on, into a great, cavelike room lit by a narrow window in the gable end. Dustiness; tranquillity. It still smelled the same.

'All right?' said the housekeeper, and left her.

Near the door was expensive luggage, belonging to the Ashwells. At the window end of the room, older relics – some feather mattresses, a broken-stringed harp – were jumbled together. The real treasures were in between.

The trunks and boxes, where the clothes lay hidden, were neatly arranged, each one labelled, each – though Gabriel didn't realize this – dusted for her by Francis. It was dawning on her that someone, sometime, had sorted a whole family's belongings, packing each person's things separately. Who could have done it?

The handwriting on the labels answered her question. That black, spiky lettering was recognizably Dorothy's – great-great-aunt Dorothy Flood, an octogenarian ex-headmistress. Gabriel's mother, Sarah, had told her that Gabriel was coming to Crosthwaite, and Dorothy had written last term, inviting her to tea. I never replied, thought Gabriel, feeling vaguely guilty. But she hadn't wanted to get involved with an elderly relation. Her work was too absorbing.

She looked at some of the labels. 'Mother'. 'Iona'. 'Lettice'. 'Dorothy'. 'Family'. The baby-clothes were in the family box. She remembered its brassbound corners.

26

She opened it, and there, in soft tissue-paper bundles, exuding mothballs, were the tiny dresses of silk and lawn which had been handed down from one Flood baby to the next. Such delicacy! Such fairylike stitching!

Under them were harder parcels. Gabriel took out a photograph album with sepia portraits mounted on brown cardboard; and then a stiffbacked notebook. Her great-great-aunt's writing appeared again on the first page. *A Memoir of the Flood Family, 1888–1911, by Dorothy Mabel Flood.*

~

I have decided, *Dorothy's spiky script began,* to tell the story of my family in a semi-fictitious way. I didn't take part in any of the dramatic scenes which so greatly affected my sisters' lives. I, the youngest child, was the audience, to whom all was gradually told. It always seemed to me more like a novel than reality, so I shall write it as a story, though the events I shall record are all perfectly true.

Lionel and Mary Flood married in 1888. They had five children. Iona was born in 1890, Lettice in 1891, Harry in 1893, Phyllis in 1895 and Dorothy in 1899.

~

Shall I ever remember which is which, wondered Gabriel. She opened the photograph album and found a family group, dated 1909, and posed in the garden at Springfield.

Mary Flood, seated in an oak chair and wearing a high-necked dress and a hat piled with roses, was the centre and focus of the picture. On one side, her husband displayed his dignified profile. On the other, smiling Harry had his hands in his pockets. The two elder girls occupied low stools. They looked very slender and grace-ful. Lettice had a dreamy, delicate face, framed in a cloud of fair curls. Iona looked out with intelligent, luminous eyes under strongly marked brows. A tam-o'-shanter sat picturesquely askew on her dark coils of hair. By contrast, the younger sisters, kneeling on a rug at their mother's feet, were plain. Phyllis was thin, with eyes screwed up short-sightedly against the light. Dorothy's hair was dragged back from a bumpy forehead, into a pigtail.

The younger girls adored the elder ones, wrote Dorothy.

No wonder, thought Gabriel.

She opened the trunk marked 'Lettice'. Its contents reflected a dream of Edwardian girlhood. There were pretty silk blouses, chiffon and taffeta evening dresses, and something heavy in white satin, which Gabriel guessed might be a wedding dress. The colours – misty greens and greys, rose pinks – seemed ideally chosen for the fair girl in the photograph.

There were more things in Iona's trunk than Lettice's, as if the contents of a whole set of drawers and cupboards had been bundled away together. The evening dresses were there, in creams and apricots; the blouses with whalebone stiffeners inside their high collars; the long, slim skirts. But there were underclothes too.

'Oh!' exclaimed Gabriel, lifting out a petticoat with flounces of ribbon-threaded broderie anglaise; and 'Oh!' again, at a white camisole with fine embroidery round the neck. Even more than the dresses, they seemed to bring the girl of long ago very close.

Fired with interest, Gabriel turned back to Dorothy's *Memoir*.

⇒ 6 ⇐

The five children at Springfield were close companions. They played hide-and-seek round the rambling old house, scurrying with shrieks and flying hair up and down the staircases and in and out of the panelled rooms. They clustered around the drawing-room fire to roast chestnuts, glossy heads silhouetted against the rich, crimson wallpaper, white pinafores smudged with ash from the burnt shells. In winter they painted Christmas cards and glued pictures onto the nursery scrap-screen. In summer there was French cricket in the garden.

The girls were at home more than Harry. He had a long day at his preparatory school, studying maths and classics to prepare him for his public school at thirteen. The girls only went to school in the mornings, and spent leisurely afternoons with books, music and dancing lessons – or simply dreaming in idleness, which was Lettice's favourite occupation. Mrs Flood declared that girls should not overtax their bodies or their brains. When what was delicately called 'the time of the month' came round, Iona and Lettice were encouraged to lie down in a darkened room.

Lying down was a familiar habit at Springfield, for Mrs Flood was often in bed. No name was given to her illness. It was mentioned only in the vaguest terms – 'Mother is unwell' – and it never occurred to the girls that there might be some psychological cause for the headaches and the inexplicable 'tiredness'. Besides, they had learned, from their nursery days, that it wasn't polite to talk about illness: just as it wasn't polite to talk about money or food, or anything that their nurse labelled 'vulgar'. Reticence was the habit at Springfield. It was one of the rules which made a stiff framework to life beneath the fun and leisure, like the boned bodices the girls wore from childhood under their frocks and pinafores.

Of course they were a happy family. None of them doubted that. It never crossed their minds that parents might not invariably be kind and loving, and children – in intention, at least – good and obedient. They grew up in unruffled security. A month at the seaside or a trip to the pantomime were the rare pleasures that broke their placid routine. 'As it was in the beginning, is now, and ever shall be, world without end,' they sang on Sundays in church; and it seemed a true reflection of their own state.

Girls were not encouraged, either at home or at school, to think for themselves. There seemed no need for them to do so. They could echo the values and opinions of their parents and teachers. But it was Iona's misfortune to be intelligent, and the eldest – a dangerous combination; and when she left school and found herself at home with nothing to do except help her mother, she began – silently and guiltily at first – to question this state of affairs. Once started, she couldn't stop. The questions and criticisms nagged more sharply. Weren't there more stimulating things in life, she wondered, than the daily round at Springfield?

She was sitting in her bedroom one afternoon when she was nineteen, her dark head bent over the stocking she was darning. Lettice, who shared the room, lay on her bed. Her fair curls were scattered across the pillow and she was reading a novel.

'I finished my darning this morning,' she remarked.

'I had so much to do for Mother,' said Iona.

'Poor you.' And Lettice yawned.

She might offer to help me, thought Iona, wearily weaving her needleful of black wool.

'Isn't life trying?' she sighed.

'No,' Lettice murmured, turning a page.

Iona glanced through the window at the grey sky and tossing trees. Why did she feel so dismal and downcast and bored? Perhaps today had been unfortunate in its succession of small chores. Her mother, who had stayed in bed for breakfast, had summoned her to answer various letters and then sent her off to post them, match some embroidery silks and buy two yards of ribbon for a camisole. When she got home she had to sort out a basket of clean stockings and see which needed darning, water the house plants and wash the leaves of the aspidistra.

'Can't Letty do something?' she'd asked.

'Letty's lying down.'

'The time of the month,' Lettice had said complacently. It seemed sometimes to Iona that Letty's 'time of the month' came every week.

'I depend on you, dear,' said Mrs Flood; 'my eldest daughter.'

She spoke as if it were a privilege, but just then, to Iona, it meant slavery. Remembering, she stabbed her stocking with the needle.

'What are you reading?' she asked Lettice.

'*Lady Maud's Secret*. Bertha lent it to me.'

'Would Mother like you borrowing books from the maids?'

'I daresay not, but it's nice talking about them when Bertha's washing my hair. The hero has black eyes – like Rufus Orme.'

The parlourmaid tapped on the girls' door.

'Mrs Flood wants you in the drawing-room, Miss Iona. There's company.'

Mrs Johnson and Mrs Beaumont were sitting by the fire with Mrs Flood, exchanging stories about their cooks. Mrs Johnson's middle-aged spinster daughter, who was known to be eccentric, had settled in a distant corner, aloof from the gossip.

'And when I opened the tureen,' exclaimed Mrs Beaumont, 'the cabbage looked like wet mackintosh.'

'Cabbage,' Mrs Johnson pronounced, 'needs shredding, very finely.'

'Make sure you have a good cook when you marry, Iona,' said Mrs Beaumont. 'It's the best way of keeping your husband happy.'

How oddly people talked of marriage, thought Iona. That marriage – and the earlier the better – was a girl's main object, had long since become clear to her. Harry was educated to make his way in the world. Girls, with their music and dancing and careful avoidance of anything intellectual, were educated

31

to attract men. Not that this was said openly – reticence prevented candour – but it was understood. Girls were like ornaments displayed on a mantlepiece, waiting to be chosen.

Real friendship between the sexes was difficult, for a girl was seldom allowed to be alone with a man. It might compromise her, and that would finish her chances of marriage. Girls and men must meet publicly, in company, and only through her accomplishments could a girl properly draw attention to herself.

Very possibly you would hardly know the man you were marrying, thought Iona; and if you hadn't much in common, you might be dependent on well-shredded cabbage to please him. How terrible!

'I may not want to marry,' she said.

There was a moment's pause. Such a remark, the silence declared, was in very poor taste.

'Ring for tea, Iona,' said Mrs Flood coldly – and there she was, back in her usual role of doing her mother's bidding. She felt dragged down; hopeless.

When the parlourmaid brought in the tea, Iona carried cups to Mrs Johnson and Mrs Beaumont. They were talking about hats now, and the latest models in Madam Logan's hatshop. Lost in her discontent, Iona took a third cup across to Miss Johnson, and jumped, almost spilling the tea, when a hand touched her arm. Brown eyes were looking keenly up at her from Miss Johnson's sallow face.

'I heard what you said about marriage. You *are* an independent girl!' Miss Johnson whispered.

'Oh, I'm not,' Iona answered. The words seemed desperately ironic when she thought of her day. 'I'd like to be independent, of course, but it doesn't seem possible.'

'It could be,' said Miss Johnson.

'What do you mean? How?' asked Iona, feeling puzzled. No one had ever said a thing like that to her before.

'Well.' Miss Johnson glanced towards the fireplace, but the hatshop was still occupying the ladies. 'Have you heard of the suffragettes?'

'The women who want the vote?' Iona responded uncertainly.

32

'They want more than that. They want to be free agents, not slaves.'

'Do they?' A sudden interest, almost a sense of identification, welled up inside Iona.

'Perhaps the suffragettes might have something to offer you. They certainly need intelligent girls.' Miss Johnson dropped her voice even lower. 'Try visiting number 1, Marlborough Street, if you'd like to know more. You needn't tell your mother, you know.'

~

Gabriel closed Dorothy's notebook with a bang. The suffragettes! Their name had recurred endlessly in discussions at her mother's flat in Warburton Street.

'Votes for women. If only we had a clear-cut cause like that!' she had heard Josie sigh.

'We have. Greenham Common,' retorted Nina, who had once cut the wire at the Greenham base, and dashed through to spray slogans of peace on the American warplanes.

'No – something that concerns every woman, that unites us all.'

'Greenham Common should.'

'I grant you're following in suffragette footsteps, but they came first. They were the real heroines,' declared Josie, alight with enthusiasm.

Women and their causes! I'm bored with them, thought Gabriel. I like clothes – or rather, I did.

To stem the worries which threatened to sweep over her afresh, she picked up Iona's petticoat – and caught sight of her watch. After twelve. She'd been in the attic all morning. It was time to go. But I'll come back, she promised herself.

Could she – possibly – borrow the petticoat? It would be fascinating to take it back to Marlborough Street and examine it properly. She didn't want to ask – but surely no one would mind. It belonged to her family, not the Ashwells. She folded it carefully and tucked it under her arm.

'Fool!' muttered Francis Ashwell to himself. From his window, he watched Gabriel disappear down the drive. He had been wondering whether to ignore Lucy's instructions and offer her coffee. Now it was too late. But he couldn't forget that image of her, frail and pale against her brilliant walls. It had haunted him all night.

His eyes lingered on her black leather jacket, her black skirt and her scarlet boots – an unexpected touch which pleased him. Then he noticed the petticoat under her arm. Relief! Surely that meant she would have to come back.

≫7≪

With the petticoat under her arm, Gabriel hurried back down Wortley Hill, past a jumble of shops and pubs, takeaways and launderettes. Tower blocks rose like high-rigged sailing ships behind them. 'Not a nice part of Crosthwaite,' people said of Wortley Hill, as they'd been saying for more than a hundred years. Gabriel liked it – the Asian shops with their glowing piles of fruit and vegetables and their rolls of gauzy material; the angles of old terraces, jostling new ones.

She turned into Marlborough Street, opened the door of number 1, and met Elizabeth in the hall.

Elizabeth didn't usually come home for lunch. She had

a quick snack near the university and worked in the library all afternoon. But since she had begun researching into Amy Whittingham, her English course had faded into the background. She couldn't be bothered with Wordsworth and Coleridge, when there was this fascinating story waiting to be uncovered. For Amy Whittingham wasn't just a pioneering woman doctor, up against the inevitable opposition of the conservative medical world. She was a suffragette too. Elizabeth approved of the suffragettes.

With growing excitement, she had hunted through local history books and old newspaper files, putting together a narrative. There had only been a handful of Crosthwaite suffragettes, but they had been active and articulate. Then the long letter had come from Anne Cropper, the woman – she was a doctor too – whom Elizabeth had contacted with reference to Amy Whittingham. Anne Cropper's mother had been one of the suffragette group, and the letter was packed with the sort of detail that gave personality to the women Elizabeth had read about.

As she read and studied, Elizabeth felt more and more certain that this was the raw material for the really interesting magazine article she had always intended to write. She tried over titles: 'The Doctor and the Vote', 'Trail-blazers for the Women's Movement', 'The Cause in Crosthwaite'. The day before, with the letter beside her, she had started writing, resenting the noisy interruption of Lucy's party; and that morning she had dashed back from her lectures, meaning to settle down to an afternoon of roughing out her piece. It would be a success; she was sure it would.

She had dropped her books in her room and run

downstairs again to get some lunch, when the front door opened and Gabriel came in.

'Hi!' said Gabriel, surprisingly cheerful, clutching an armful of white flounces against her black leather jacket.

'Hi. What on earth have you got there?' Elizabeth was intrigued enough to pause for a moment.

'An Edwardian petticoat. D'you want to have a look?'

Edwardian – the time of the suffragettes. Elizabeth let herself be tempted, although she had no real interest in clothes.

'Well – if it'll only take a minute – '

In her room, Gabriel laid the petticoat across a big bare table, switching on an anglepoise, so that lamplight fanned over the edging of feather-stitched frills.

'It belonged to one of my ancestors, Iona Flood,' she explained.

'Iona Flood!' It was a bit of a shock. 'What – really? I've just been reading about her. She was a suffragette. She used to live round here, didn't she?'

'That's right. At Springfield.'

Elizabeth touched the white muslin almost timidly.

'I'm going to write about her. There's this article I want to do, perhaps for *Cross-Questioning*. People should know about the Crosthwaite suffragettes.'

'You reckon?'

The fervour in Elizabeth's voice had turned Gabriel off. She began to smooth out and pore over the hand-stitched seams which ran from the waistband of the petticoat down to the frills.

Elizabeth saw that their moment of contact was over, but she never expected to get close to Gabriel. There was no point in going on about Iona Flood.

'I'm just going to stick a potato in the microwave for

dinner. D'you want one? There's some cheese left, I think.'

'Maybe later.'

OK, thought Elizabeth; be like that. She went into the kitchen, found a potato and got a lump of cheese out of the fridge. From the cork board above it, the ruined hospital beamed out its silent message.

'Oh, what a pain!' sighed Elizabeth. The hospital was Amy Whittingham's legacy and something should be done to help. There was Fashion-Aid, but would Gabriel ever get it off the ground? Elizabeth felt doubtful.

Anyway, she decided, I'm far too busy right now; and, with her back firmly to the photograph, she grated cheese. The frothy petticoat had given her a new angle on the Crosthwaite suffragettes. She had thought of them as plainly dressed, in coats and skirts of brown or navy serge. But, of course, Iona Flood was different; a bit of an outsider. She could stress that when she wrote about the personalities.

Back upstairs, she sat down at her desk, opened a file, found her notes on Iona, and added the word 'petticoat'. Then she flicked on to the draft of her introductory paragraph, and re-read it carefully:

~

The Women's Social and Political Union, popularly known as the Suffragette Movement, was founded on 10 October 1903, at a meeting in the Manchester home of Mrs Emmeline Pankhurst, its leader and inspirer. The membership was limited to women, and the aim was to achieve for every woman the right to vote in parliamentary elections. To be refused this right was a slur on women's dignity and humanity. It branded them as second-class citizens. A programme of public rallies, lectures and street corner meetings was initiated to draw attention to the cause. Small committees planned local action.

Petitions were presented, deputations met the prime minister, and the subject was debated inconclusively in Parliament. The cause was just; yet, after campaigning for five years, the women were no nearer their objective. That was why peaceful demonstrations began to change into violent ones. Violence was not the wish of all the women. Those who called themselves suffragists wanted to remain within the law. But others, the suffragettes, came to believe that violence was their only option when men refused to recognize the justice of their cause.

~

It was all right, thought Elizabeth; a bit dry, but she could brighten it up later. Basically, she wanted to set the scene for the Suffragette Committee, formed in Crosthwaite in 1909, whose personalities and activities she was researching. She tried to visualize them now – the little band of women who used to meet, nearly eighty years ago, in this very house where she was sitting.

Amy Whittingham had gathered them together, which was why – as Elizabeth had learned – they customarily met in Marlborough Street. In 1909 Amy was thirty, gentle in manner, and clever. A photograph Elizabeth had seen of her showed a tired face, too lined for its youth, but lit by visionary eyes. She had trained at the London School of Medicine for Women, and chosen to practise among the slums of Wortley Hill. In those days the hillside was netted with dark, narrow streets of back-to-back houses which had no running water, no lavatories, no gardens and hardly any light, so closely were they packed together. Disease of every kind flourished. Amy burned with compassion for the women who lived there, battling to maintain decent homes while endless pregnancies wore them down and dirt and malnutrition ravaged their families.

'Women,' Amy Whittingham wrote in a letter to the local paper dated 12 February 1909, which Elizabeth had read, 'are the most deprived, defenceless, exploited and enslaved section of society. They come to my surgery, desperate with poverty, sick in their minds from the strain of trying to cope on inadequate means, and from sacrificing themselves daily for their husbands and children; and there is no one in authority who understands how much these women need help. That is why women must have the vote. They must be given power for the benefit of their own sex. They must crowd into Parliament and legislate to make the lives of themselves and their children happier and healthier. Votes for women could lead, not just to a political revolution, but to the greatest social revolution the world has ever known.'

Such letters made enemies. The Crosthwaite Hospital Board, who paid half Amy's salary, began to consider her a dangerous woman who must be ousted. The husbands of Wortley Hill resented her already because she told their wives to allow themselves plenty of time to recover from childbirth. Yet, despondent as she often was, her gentle kindness never faltered; and whenever there was an accident on Wortley Hill, or a sudden illness, hostility was forgotten, for if a life could be saved, Amy Whittingham was the doctor to do it.

Ida Johnson, the second member of the committee, was, Elizabeth knew, a spinster in her forties. While Amy Whittingham shone with tired benevolence, Ida Johnson glowered angrily at the world from her photograph. She was an eldest daughter who had seen younger sisters marry and leave home, while she seemed bound by duty to her mother. As a girl, she had despised spinsters; now she was one of the despised herself. It was the unfairness of things which had made her a suffragette – the feeble education most girls received, and the middle-class prejudice against women who earned their living, which made any career except marriage impossible. Yet it was a stark fact that there were not enough men for every girl to marry. While Amy fought for the downtrodden married women of Wortley Hill, Ida Johnson remembered those superfluous old maids, dependent on their parents for every handkerchief, every stamp they needed. The vote might embolden them to stand up against the domination of their families.

In the acrimonious correspondence which had followed Amy's letter in the *Crosthwaite News*, Miss Johnson too had her say. 'Women must be recognized, not merely as the equals of men, which of course they are, but as human beings in their own right, who won't be moulded into particular shapes by the whims of men and society, but are free to do as they please. The vote is the symbol of this freedom, and win it we shall, even if we suffer imprisonment or death for our cause. It was said that the blood of the martyrs was the seed of the church. Let the drops of blood, which we may be called upon to shed, be the seeds of a fairer society.'

Reading these letters in faded old newspapers, Elizabeth had thrilled in response. She was less thrilled by the third of the leading suffragettes, Jane Hawkins. Jane was a genuine militant, ready to shatter windows or plant bombs to draw attention to her demands. Elizabeth disliked militancy. Perhaps that was why she felt little warmth towards Jane Hawkins; that and the appearance of Jane in a photograph Elizabeth had seen. She seemed to have made herself – deliberately or defiantly – into a sort of caricature of a 'liberated woman'. If there was pain behind the image, she refused to show it. Her hair was cut short and she stared fiercely at the world through pince-nez spectacles. But she was a rich spinster whose money was useful to the cause. Unlike Miss Johnson, she had no family ties.

The last of the leaders was Ruth Kennett, and Elizabeth knew most about her because she was the mother of Anne Cropper who had written the long letter. What she knew, she liked. Ruth was a country girl, whose intelligence frightened and embarrassed her parents and the teachers at her village school. She was a clever girl, stuck in a labourer's cottage; but, at seventeen, she was lucky enough to be taken on as a maid by Amy Whittingham, and her drab life changed to glory. She and Amy were not a conventional mistress and maid. They shared their meals and sat together – when they had leisure to sit down. Amy let Ruth help in the surgery too, and the girl's hopes grew that, one day, she might pass the qualifying exams for a medical school herself. Ruth had lively eyes and curling dark hair. She was enthusiastic, attractive and ready for anything.

Pen in hand, Elizabeth stared into space, picturing the four women in the downstairs room, where Gabriel was now studying Iona's petticoat. She imagined Amy, hollow-eyed and idealistic, seated at the head of a table used indiscriminately for meals and medical consultations. She saw Miss Johnson and Miss Hawkins on either side of her, and Ruth at the table's foot, ready, if necessary, to jump up and answer the doorbell.

But what would they have been saying as they sat there? Elizabeth tried to guess the sort of things which might have been said, as they discussed their hopes and aims. 'We must raise the consciousness of the poor,' Amy might begin. 'We must embarrass the middle classes,' Ida would suggest. 'We must show that we mean business,' Jane would declare. 'We must try everything!' Ruth would cry, whisking in and out, making tea, fetching papers.

Amongst them, one day, came Iona Flood, with her

elegant clothes; doubtfully, not sure what she was letting herself in for. She had said nothing at home, not even to Lettice, about Miss Johnson's invitation. She arrived, prepared to listen and hurry away.

It was Amy Whittingham who captivated her. Amy was that rare thing in Crosthwaite – a woman with the courage to make herself a career. Of course, women by the hundred had menial jobs as servants or factory hands; but for a middle-class woman to work was almost unheard of. 'She must be a battleaxe!' Iona could imagine her father snorting. How wrong he would be! Just by sitting in her bare room with oilcloth on the floor and medicine cupboards along the walls, Amy presented a new, appealing model. She wouldn't fret about cabbage or the washing of aspidistra leaves, thought Iona. She didn't seem worried by her lack of a wedding ring. Something about her drove Iona to speech.

'Is there anything I could do – something quite modest? And it will have to be secret, I'm afraid. My parents would never approve.'

'That's true,' said Ida Johnson. 'I've heard the suffragettes called harpies in the Springfield drawing-room. And your mother goes along with the view that girls' brains are too weak to tackle political issues. I don't suppose you've read a newspaper in your life?'

Iona shook her head.

Amy made the suggestion which involved Iona. With Jane Hawkins's money, the women had rented a small shop, where their literature could be sold. They wanted eye-catching banners to decorate the window, embroidered in the suffragette colours of green, purple and white. Could Iona make some?

Grateful for such a manageable task, Iona agreed; and

so, shyly and uncertainly, she committed herself to the cause.

⇒ *8* ⇐

Slowly, luxuriously, Gabriel woke. She lay in bed, savouring the thought of Springfield. Iona's petticoat was still on the table. She would take it back that morning, climb the panelled stairs, peep into the trunks of rustling silks and taffetas, and go on with the story in Dorothy's notebook. But there was no hurry. Snuggling under her duvet, she felt wrapped in contentment.

The front door banged as Lucy came in from her shift on Student Nightline. Voices drifted muzzily through the kitchen wall, behind the head of Gabriel's bed.

'. . . this bloke who thought he'd got AIDS. He wasn't sure – he hadn't even seen a doctor. He'd just panicked. I really had to force myself to keep calm, he was in such a state. He kept saying over and over again – "I'm finished, aren't I? I'm finished."'

Elizabeth chimed in soothingly.

'Coffee? You'll feel better.'

'Thanks. What a sweetie.'

'Shouldn't he go to the Health Centre?'

'That's what I told him. I gave him the number, I don't know how many times. He probably knew it anyway.'

Lulled into drowsiness, Gabriel was suddenly jerked awake again.

'Yes, that hospital!' she heard Lucy exclaiming. 'We're

43

getting nowhere with our money-raising – and that's the understatement of the century.'

'Fashion-Aid?' Elizabeth seemed to be querying.

'What do *you* think?'

Why did they have to remind her? Gabriel buried her head under the bedclothes to shut out the voices, concentrating ferociously on Iona's underwear, imagining the camisole top coming down tightly to meet the petticoat's waistband, and the petticoat flaring out into its ruffle of frills. There would have been stays underneath; and, underneath those, combinations.

Lucy's footsteps dragged wearily upstairs. Elizabeth's heels tapped down the path, brisk and businesslike. I'll get up now, thought Gabriel, go back to Springfield, take out Dorothy's *Memoir* . . .

~

High on its hilltop, away from the dark streets of Wortley Hill, the old grey walls of Springfield encircled and protected the Floods. They lived in the comfortable style of the Edwardian middle class. The dining-room was furnished in gleaming mahogany; the drawing-room upholstered in crimson velvet. In the world outside, women campaigned and struggled for their rights. At Springfield, only the girls' social engagements fluttered the placidity of life.

One September evening Iona and Lettice were upstairs, getting ready for a dance. It was to mark the twenty-first birthday of Rufus Orme, the handsome son of a Crosthwaite banker. Phyllis and Dorothy sat on Iona's bed, watching, as Bertha, the housemaid, brushed the girls' hair and helped them into their evening dresses.

Iona was excited, but Lettice was in a twitter of nerves. She changed from one pair of silk stockings to another, thrust in her hairpins and tweaked them out again, and looked so pale that Iona felt worried.

'It's only a small dance. We're not going to Buckingham Palace,' she said.

'I know,' snapped Lettice, rummaging through her jewel case.

'Don't wear those earrings,' warned Iona. 'You know they pinch.'

'They look nice,' responded Lettice, feverishly screwing the pearl drops into her ears.

'You don't need them. You couldn't look prettier.' For now a pink flush coloured Lettice's cheeks, rivalling the pink rose she had pinned in her hair, and the pink sash ringing her tiny waist. And it *was* tiny! Lettice was almost too thin.

The Ormes' house wasn't Buckingham Palace, but fairy-lights, hothouse flowers and the seductive throb of a string band touched it with magic. Young men, elegant in black, thronged to sign Iona's and Lettice's dance programmes.

Iona – forgetting the suffragettes, the idealism which had fired her, and the banner she had left, half embroidered, in the attic – abandoned herself to pleasure; but occasional glimpses of Lettice troubled her. Now flushed, now pale, Letty whirled from one partner to another, exclaiming hysterically as she juggled the names on her programme. It was mainly done, Iona suspected, to catch Rufus Orme's attention. She was standing with him still on the dance floor, though the twostep had ended, laughing on a high, unsteady note, gazing at him with bright, enormous eyes.

'These earrings! They're agony! Why did I put them on?'

There and then she unscrewed them, and tucked them provocatively into Rufus's waistcoat pocket.

Then it was supper – lobster mayonnaise, trifle, lemonade and coffee, with champagne for the toast. Lettice was a centre of attention. She looked white now, and kept pressing her hand to her pink satin sash, but still she sparkled, and fluttered her long eyelashes.

People will say she's a flirt, thought Iona despairingly. Crosthwaite society could be merciless to girls who pushed themselves forward, or attracted attention with their behaviour. They should wait, quietly and modestly, like ornaments on a mantlepiece, until a man noticed them.

45

After supper, the dancing resumed. Through the gay music of a waltz, there was a cry and a crash, and Iona spun round to see Lettice on the floor, an insubstantial drift of rose and white.

Exclamations rang out.

'Letty's fainted!'

'Get some brandy!'

'Try fanning her!'

Mr Orme scooped up the unconscious girl and carried her to a bedroom, with Iona anxiously following. Windows were opened, a maid was sent to fetch smelling salts, and at last Lettice's eyelids flickered.

'My stays – so tight!' she gasped, and fainted again.

With the maid's assistance, Iona partly undressed Lettice, but the stay laces were inextricably knotted. Iona needed scissors. As the pressure loosened, Lettice's eyes opened again.

'You silly girl! How did you lace yourself so tightly?' asked Iona.

'I didn't. Bertha – '

'Bertha?'

'I called her early, to brush my hair. You were in the bath.'

'And – ?'

'I needed an eighteen-inch waist. I made Bertha pull and pull.' Lettice smiled wanly. 'Rufus likes slim waists.'

'Yours is slim enough already, Letty.'

Lettice shook her head.

~

Gabriel put down the notebook and opened Iona's trunk. Amongst the underclothes, she found a pair of thick, white cotton stays, fitting from bust to hips, and fastened with crossing laces at the back. Whalebone stiffeners were seamed into the cotton and angled to compress the waist, while shaping curves above it and below.

Torture, thought Gabriel.

~

A growing passion for Rufus Orme obsessed Lettice all autumn. Whenever she was invited out, a glance round the room for Rufus dictated the evening's happiness or despair. With no real occupations, Lettice sank into an endless daydream about Rufus's black eyes, glossy hair and square white hands.

Her dreams were virginal and innocent. She barely distinguished between Rufus and the heroes she read about in novels, who led their brides to the altar on the last page. It delighted her to look at him; she loved dancing with him; but she never imagined kissing him. He lived on a pedestal – the pedestal reserved for the fantasy figure she would marry. A husband was a man who bought you presents and gave you a ring; who paid you compliments and looked after you. That was all Lettice knew; but it was enough to fuel her dreams.

Iona, by contrast, had plenty to think about. Following Miss Johnson's advice, she had visited number 1, Marlborough Street, and found that it was the home of a woman doctor, Amy Whittingham, one of a small group of Crosthwaite suffragettes. Iona began to learn about the Women's Suffrage Movement, reacting with fascination, sympathy and alarm. Of course women must be given their proper rights; it was only fair. But how could she raise the subject at home? It was far too controversial for her mother's drawing-room; and neither her character nor her upbringing made her a ready disturber of the peace. But she worried about her own feebleness.

There was one thing she could do. The suffragettes needed banners to carry at demonstrations and to decorate a shop they had rented; and Iona was asked to make them. She began to get up early every morning and sew in the attic with candles to supplement the latening daylight.

She didn't mean anyone to know, but she couldn't entirely hide what she was doing from Lettice. They shared a room, and when Iona woke, Lettice often woke too. Her feelings for Rufus made her tense and restless. She slept badly, and sometimes she followed Iona to the attic and paced about amidst the lumber, seeking reassurance and encouragement.

'Does he like me?'

'I think so.'

47

'Have you noticed him looking at me?'

'Oh, yes.'

'How long did Mother wait before Father proposed to her?'

'I've no idea.'

'Girls always have to wait, don't they? Poor us!'

Fortunately she never once asked what Iona was doing. She was lost in her own thoughts. And although, one day, Iona intended to tell her about the suffragettes, the right moment never seemed to come. Iona heard, in Marlborough Street, that women were being imprisoned and going on hunger strike for the right to vote. At Springfield, they talked about Christmas parties.

The greatest event in Crosthwaite's social calendar was the Charity Ball, held on New Year's Eve. Iona and Lettice were going with their parents. To whirl round a ballroom with Rufus was the ultimate ecstasy for Lettice. Her heart raced when she alighted from a cab at the Town Hall, where the Ball was held, and saw Rufus on the steps, waiting for her. He looked wonderful, his black hair shining, his starched shirt fastened with gold studs. He bent towards her.

'Will you give me the first dance? And – Letty – don't fill up your programme.'

Obediently, in the ballroom, she held her pasteboard programme shut.

'I'm afraid I've no dances to spare,' she told the clustering young men.

The band played a waltz. Rufus gripped her hand. They spun over the polished floor.

'Quick, Letty!'

He pulled her through a door and up a staircase to a dim ante-room where two chairs waited in an alcove. He took her hand and, before she knew what was happening, he was unbuttoning her glove and kissing her fingers.

'We're never alone, and I must have you to myself. Letty – suppose I told you I loved you?'

She felt herself trembling, blushing.

'Do you?' she faltered.

'How can you ask? You know I do. But, Letty, what about you?'

'I might – a little – '

She could say no more, for his arms came round her in a fierce embrace. His mouth pressed hard against her cheek. Suddenly Lettice was frightened. Snatching herself away, she ran out into the red-carpeted corridor.

'What's the matter?'

He'd followed her, but Lettice felt safe again – although it was impossible to answer his question. She smiled instead.

'Let's dance here, since you won't allow me any other partners,' she said; and if the carpet was lumpy, and the band far away, dancing with him was still more perfect than ever.

'Would you like an ice?' he asked presently.

'If you would.'

His clasp round her waist tightened. She stifled another wild pang of fear.

'Where shall we have the ices?' she exclaimed.

'Up here, so that nobody can see us.'

She didn't know what to answer.

Suddenly all his fierceness melted. He gave a look which she thought she would never forget.

'Oh, Letty, I'm so clumsy; but haven't you realized yet? We're in love.'

The silence in the homebound cab made Iona quake. Lettice never noticed it. Only when, back at Springfield, her father gravely asked to see her programme, did Lettice understand her appalling crime. No respectable girl danced more than three times with the same man. To spend the evening alone with one was utterly disgraceful.

The only help was to repeat what Rufus had said. 'We're in love.'

But that was worse still. Girls didn't admit love before an engagement.

'Rufus can't marry,' said Mr Flood. 'He's only twenty-one. His father doesn't allow the bank clerks to marry before they're twenty-five, and he can't make an exception of his son.'

49

'But that's years!'

Overcome by all her emotions, Lettice collapsed in hysterics.

Stiff notes passed between the two families. Rufus was sent to work in a bank in Egypt, and Lettice was left to suffer alone.

~

⇒ 9 ⇐

Gabriel closed Dorothy's notebook on her finger, to mark the page she'd reached, and leaned back against Iona's trunk. Men! It was a problem she hadn't cracked yet. Other people seemed to know what to do. She felt helpless.

She relaxed, as best she could with the trunk's hard edge sawing her back, and pondered.

The difficulty was Sarah, her mother. Gabriel loved her, of course. Who wouldn't, with a mother as warm and happy as Sarah? But Sarah made it very clear that her happiness dated from the moment when she left Paul, Gabriel's father, to throw in her lot with the women who ran a feminist magazine together in London. Happiness, for Sarah, meant liberation from men.

And Gabriel understood. Bitter memories lingered from her childhood. There was her mother crying – 'I want freedom to do my own thing'; and her father sneering – 'I thought "your own thing" was pleasing me. It has been for most of your life.' No wonder Sarah needed to escape.

She had been lucky. She had found friends and companions who satisfied her totally, and one, Josie, whom she loved. They gathered in Warburton Street – that band of women – enthusing over ideas, laughing and joking, sharing their troubles, always mutually supportive. They didn't seem to need men.

From the security of her relationship with Josie, Sarah had, over the years, tossed out a shower of warnings. If you loved a man, she said, you were sucked, willy-nilly, into his life. You lost your own identity. It was usually that way round. Men were the dominant sex. Women were willing to submerge their personalities for men and get nothing in return. 'Women can be dreadfully passive. I was,' said Sarah.

She was so sure – that was partly why Gabriel felt separated from her. Gabriel found it hard to be confident about anything except her designing – when it was going well. She'd always felt an outsider in the excited, purposeful, confidential, feminist atmosphere of Warburton Street, with its defined hopes and objectives.

She had had an odd position as the only child in a grown-up world. She didn't like being treated as a pet, yet she could never feel one of the crowd. At first she missed Springfield agonizingly, and, because that too had divided her from Sarah, who was delighted to have got away, Springfield had turned into a bottled-up secret. Her passion for clothes, colours and fabrics cut her off as well. None of these things interested Sarah or her friends. They were content with a casual, downbeat scruffiness, left over from the 1970s, which Gabriel hated. The sheer awfulness of Sarah's clothes was often beyond belief – and it made a barrier.

To express her feeling of alienation, Gabriel began to wear only black. She couldn't exactly remember when she started, but the habit soon became fixed. Occasionally she allowed herself white, or a touch of red, but that was all. Yet somehow her relationship with Sarah remained strong, though their views on almost everything differed.

Except, Gabriel reflected, men and love. She suddenly realized how much she had let Sarah put her off. It was time for rebellion. She was eighteen. She couldn't go on drifting, not so much heart-whole as heart-blank.

Why shouldn't I fall in love with a man, she argued with an imaginary Sarah. There are all these films and stories where fulfilled love is the climax of the heroine's life. You'd probably say it was sickly rubbish, but it might just as easily be down-to-earth reality. What about Lettice, for instance? After all, thought Gabriel, I am her descendant. (So is Sarah.) Lettice believed in love; and though she suffered for it – those stays, and now Rufus's banishment – I'm sure she was right. I even feel envious of her.

What a pain it all is! I wish I was in love.

Footsteps made her jump and drop the book.

'Sorry. Do you remember me? Francis Ashwell. I saw you in your room, at Lucy Summers's party. I've brought you some coffee.'

Men! And all the thousand familiar complaints, learned from Sarah, sprang up instinctively in Gabriel's mind, obliterating Lettice. He hadn't even asked if she wanted coffee; if she minded being disturbed.

'No coffee, thanks,' she answered coldly.

He didn't hear. He was lifting the creaking lid of a cabin trunk.

'I'm sure you'd like these clothes. They were my grandmother's.'

Gabriel picked up the notebook, rose – and saw in the trunk the shimmery, mermaid-green silk of a folded dress. But she wasn't going to be enticed.

'You see,' Francis continued, 'my grandparents bought Springfield from the Floods.'

In the shadows of the attic, Gabriel missed the anxious pleading in his face.

'I shall have to go,' she said stiffly.

Then she noticed the coffee tray. He had found two old Crown Derby cups, gold-rimmed, patterned in scarlet and blue; and removed the everyday cups which the housekeeper had put out, because he remembered Gabriel's walls. The cups almost swayed her, but not quite. She brushed past him and ran downstairs.

⇒ *IO* ⇐

Elizabeth ate half her lunchtime salad, popped the rest into the fridge and ran upstairs. The notes about the suffragettes were stacked tidily on her desk. She picked up Anne Cropper's letter, found a page about Ruth Kennett, Anne's mother, and lost herself again in the world of the Crosthwaite suffragettes.

~

Ruth's position in Amy Whittingham's house was quite unconventional. People gossiped about the maid who sat down to meals with her mistress, but Ruth took gossip in her stride. She was always brave. Not many girls would have stood on a soapbox at street corners, arguing for women's rights with passers-by, but Ruth enjoyed the experience. She had enough wit and determination to deal with anyone. Or, she thought she did, before life got on top of her.

She used to talk about the first time she let herself be flattered into taking tea with Jack Cropper. He was a greengrocer's assistant, who delivered vegetables in Marlborough Street; pale and undersized, like many young men on Wortley Hill, with gingery hair under his cloth cap. Every time he rang the doorbell, with his basket of vegetables, he had some jaunty compliment for Ruth. He meant to melt her heart.

Unfortunately, Ruth didn't melt easily. As soon as she had accepted Jack's invitation, she regretted it. She didn't want to get friendly with him. But he was on the doorstep punctually the next Sunday, to escort her to his home.

Ruth eyed the Croppers' house sternly. It was full of fussy things she couldn't stand – antimacassars, crocheted table-runners, and dust-collecting, draped net curtains. But the manners of the Cropper family were even worse than the furnishings.

Jack, it seemed, was a sun round whom his widowed mother and two unmarried sisters revolved like deferential planets. Although Ruth was the guest, the refrain of the tea-party was: 'Fill Jack's cup, Lily'; 'Give our Jack the last sausage, Ma.'

Ruth grew rigid with annoyance. Such grovelling to a gingery shrimp! The Cropper women needed the vote to instil a proper sense of self-respect. At the earliest possible opportunity she stood up, and said a chilly goodbye.

'Give us a kiss!'

Jack, walking her home, edged her towards a dark doorway.

'Certainly not!'

'Go on.'

'Mr Cropper,' said Ruth, 'will you kindly take me home, or – ' her temper was beginning to flare, as still he edged and grinned under a gaslamp – 'I might spoil your beautiful face, and then what would your ma and sisters say?'

Jack looked suddenly downcast.

'Is it yon lady doctor who's taught you to be so high and mighty?'

'I'm not high and mighty. But I'm a woman with feelings, not a walking doll to amuse you on Sundays.'

'No,' he agreed, 'you're not a doll. You're more of a spitfire. I could be scared of you, if you want the truth. You're different from other girls I've walked out with.'

'Good,' said Ruth, appreciating the compliment.

'I bet there's dozens after you.' He sounded wistful.

'Not really.'

There was only Joe Linton, her old sweetheart in the village where she'd spent her childhood. Pressed under the fly-leaf of her Bible were some primroses he'd picked for her as they walked entwined down a flowery lane one April evening before she went to Crosthwaite. The faded petals and pink stems still caught a little at her heart.

~

Elizabeth folded up the letter. Faded relics tucked into Bibles didn't really appeal to her; or long-ago love affairs. She glanced at her watch. It was two o'clock, and she'd promised to wake Lucy. She went and banged on her door.

'Time to get back to your action-packed life,' she said, as Lucy lifted a tousled head from the pillow.

'Oh, no! I can't face it.'

'SUWG tonight'

'Women's Group. So it is.' Lucy sat up, suddenly eager. 'There's something I want to raise at the meeting.'

'Rape alarms again? Tampax in every loo?'

'No. Fashion-Aid.'

'Oh,' said Elizabeth. Her voice was not encouraging.

'Well, why not? I've gone and booked the hall and told people about it. We've got to do something.'

'Fashion design's so specialized. Who on earth in SUWG would know anything about it?'

Lucy did a quick mental review of the members. Against them she set Gabriel, in her beautiful, exotic black clothes. She sighed.

'You're right – unfortunately. Nobody'd know a thing.'

55

'I don't think there's any point even raising it,' said Elizabeth. 'I mean, we could tell them about Amy Whittingham and the hospital, but I don't see any of them designing clothes.'

'Could we ask a shop to put on a show for us? They do,' said Lucy.

'But what'd we have to pay? And how much commission would they want? We could end up losing money. I just wish,' added Elizabeth, 'that Gabriel hadn't started the idea, the way she's let it drop.'

'I like Gabriel, though,' said Lucy. 'She's interesting.'

'I never seem to get through to her. Did you know one of her relations was a Crosthwaite suffragette? I bumped into Gabriel in the kitchen last night, so I just casually suggested she might come along to the SUWG with us, in case it was her kind of thing, but she said she had enough of feminism at home.'

'Oh, yes,' said Lucy. 'I saw that magazine *Boudicca* in her room the other day, when she was feeling really low. I asked her if she'd bought it to cheer herself up, but she said her mother had sent it, because she works on it. Gabriel's home is a flat above the office, I think she said.'

But the mention of a magazine was a reminder to Elizabeth.

'I can't stay here chatting, I'm afraid. I've loads of work to do on my article.'

Thoroughly upset by Francis's interruption, Gabriel flew back down Wortley Hill. Yet, through her exasperation, she kept seeing, in her mind's eye, the deep reds and browns of his sweater – did Francis love colour too? – and the pleasingly spidery shape of his thin hands on the lid of the trunk. Attracted, repelled, she just felt completely mixed up.

So it was a relief to get back to her room and retreat into Dorothy's story. The world of the Floods closed round her, shutting out problems of relationships and creativity. Reading it, she felt as if she were living at Springfield again; or perhaps crossing the barrier of time into an older Springfield with which she had always been half in touch. She remembered her childhood awareness of other presences – those ladies in the porch, tying their bonnets and opening their umbrellas; the babies whose dresses she had fingered, carried by nursemaids up and down the panelled stairs; excited children whisking past her on the landing. She had never told Sarah about them; Sarah would have been sceptical.

But I'm sure I didn't imagine them. I'm sure they were there, thought Gabriel as, stretched out on her bed, she devoured Dorothy's pages.

~

Bereft of Rufus, Lettice grew ill with misery. She stayed in bed, refusing to eat. It was the best thing she could have done, for her illness alarmed her parents and the Ormes; and, within a few weeks, they capitulated, promising that if, in a year's time, Lettice and Rufus still felt the same, they might marry, despite the bank's rules.

'Damn it all, he is my son,' said Mr Orme, who thought Lettice very charming.

Lettice revived like a watered flower; and when an aunt volunteered to take her abroad for a long convalescence, she left in a state of joyful anticipation.

Poor Iona – she wasn't offered a foreign holiday. It was her duty to stay with her mother; and duty was taken seriously in those days. Mrs Flood wasn't well. Lettice's collapse had affected her, and Iona had never known her so constantly indisposed and so demanding.

She let herself neglect the suffragette banners, at least for the time. It was hard enough to get up in the morning and face the round of petty tasks lying ahead. Why prolong the day with a cold, early session in the attic? She often thought of the half-embroidered banner, folded inside an old sheet, and scolded herself for her feebleness; but getting through the reading and answering of her mother's letters, the mending, the errands and the little games of cards her mother enjoyed, seemed to take all her will-power.

One day I'll do something really heroic for the cause, she promised herself; one day. But the weeks ground monotonously and unheroically past.

Presumably her parents noticed her depression; for when Lettice and her aunt arrived back in London, in November 1910, Mr Flood took Iona with him to meet them. Coincidentally, it was Black Friday; and a contingent of Crosthwaite suffragettes was joining the protest in London. Iona blushed when she saw them at the station. She dared not speak to them. She wasn't ready to betray her sympathies to her father.

~

Gabriel stopped reading. What was Black Friday? Why were the suffragettes going to London? It was frustrating not to know.

Suddenly she remembered Elizabeth, coming into her room to look at Iona's petticoat. 'People should know about the Crosthwaite suffragettes,' she had said. So –

Do I really want to go and ask her, Gabriel wondered. She felt awkward with Elizabeth. Anybody could get on with Lucy. Elizabeth was different. She was rather like the Warburton Street feminists in her ideas, but she didn't share their relaxed lifestyle. She was – not exactly uptight, Gabriel decided, but a bit stiff, and offputtingly clever. She was attractive, in a way, to look at, with fair hair falling in a neat bob round her oval face; though she didn't make the best of herself, with chainstore clothes in unadventurous colours, and dull, pale lipsticks and eye-shadows. People who deliberately underplayed their appearance didn't appeal to Gabriel.

So why bother? And she turned back to the notebook.

Then, immediately, she changed her mind. She had begun to identify with Iona and Lettice. She liked them. She wanted to understand them as well as she could. It would be mad not to discover as much as possible about them, just because Elizabeth made her feel embarrassed.

Without giving herself time for further thought, she ran upstairs.

Elizabeth listened in amazement.

'A journal about Iona Flood and the suffragettes! Proper source material! That's really great. Have you finished with it?'

'Not yet,' said Gabriel, 'but I soon will have. It's not that long. I just wanted to ask you about the suffragettes going to London for Black Friday? I thought you'd probably know. And what was Black Friday, anyway?'

Instead of answering, Elizabeth opened one of her local history books.

'Look,' she said; and Gabriel saw a blurred photograph of women in tight skirts, and top-heavy hats, standing on a station platform, holding up a banner which proclaimed 'VOTES FOR WOMEN'. 'There they are, on their way to London – the Crosthwaite lot. Not Iona Flood, of course, and not Amy Whittingham. She couldn't leave a dicey confinement. But that's Ida Johnson, and that's Jane Hawkins, and that one's Ruth Kennett.'

'She looks nice,' said Gabriel, meaning Ruth, who was the youngest and prettiest of the women. She wore her hat at a dashing tilt and she grasped the banner-pole with a look of amused determination. Clearly she regarded the journey to London as an adventure.

'I like her too,' agreed Elizabeth, 'more than any of the others, except Amy Whittingham. It was November 18th, 1910, and they were setting off to join a big demo. That's what Black Friday was – or what it turned into. You see, Parliament had been considering a Bill to give some women the right to vote; but then the Commons and the Lords got stuck in a quarrel about the Budget, and Prime Minister Asquith threatened to dissolve Parliament without bothering to get the women's Bill passed. Obviously the suffragettes were horrified. They converged on London from absolutely everywhere, with a petition demanding that the legislation was rushed through. They held a rally in Caxton Hall first, and then they set off in groups to lobby Parliament. They meant to be peaceful, but the police – it's quite incredible! – got hold of a rabble of louts from the East End, and together they blocked the way. The women tried to push through, and there was chaos.'

'Push through – in those clothes?' protested Gabriel, eyeing the hampering skirts and unwieldly hats.

'Oh, clothes never stopped the suffragettes, though they must have been a problem. And their hair! I read somewhere that shovelfuls of hairpins were swept up afterwards. The police were really awful. They knocked the women down and dragged them into Black Marias. Both Ida Johnson and Jane Hawkins were arrested, though they were freed next day. Naturally the suffragettes got blamed for what had happened. They would, wouldn't they? And, in spite of their efforts, Parliament was dissolved, so the Bill went too.'

'All that for nothing. What a waste,' sighed Gabriel, seeing the eager faces in the photographs.

Elizabeth looked at the notebook.

'I suppose you couldn't read me a bit?' she asked. 'I mean, it's just the sort of thing I want for my article.'

~

'Absolute lunacy!' snorted Mr Flood, from his first-class seat, as the train puffed towards London. 'Those suffragettes should take a leaf out of Letty's book. She's got her way without a vote. Feminine wiles – that's all a woman needs.'

The Floods had booked rooms for the night in a hotel near Victoria Street, where there was a delighted reunion with Lettice. But, as they talked, Iona could hear uproar nearby – shouts, screams, running feet.

'What's happening?' she couldn't help asking.

'The hotel manager told me that Mrs Pankhurst is trying to take a petition to Parliament,' replied her aunt; 'and right along Victoria Street too. It seems a noisy affair.'

'The less we know of it, the better,' said Mr Flood.

They sat calmly with their teacups, while Lettice rhapsodized over mountains. Iona sprang up.

'Excuse me,' she murmured, and flew down into the street.

The dusk was punctuated by glowing gaslamps. Beneath them, people stood staring towards Victoria Street, where a mob swayed and battled. A banner was flaunted aloft and torn down with an angry roar. Involuntarily, Iona moved towards the affray. Groups of women, arms linked, were trying to pass onwards, while men, with distorted faces, hurled them back.

'How can they?' gasped Iona; and then, 'Ruth!'

A girl had been dragged from her companions, manhandled and flung bodily into the side-street. Her clothes were torn and her hat was missing so that her hair spread in a dark tangle over the pavement. Iona rushed up to her.

'Ruth!' she exclaimed again, for she had recognized the pretty girl who was Amy Whittingham's maid and friend.

Ruth raised a ghastly face, where a bruise was already darkening her cheek. Blood dripped from a cut lip.

'My handkerchief,' said Iona. 'No, let me. Keep still.' For Ruth was struggling to get up, dazed though she was.

'We must get through. The petition – Oh, my God! Look what they've done!'

As she moved, her clothes fell apart, ripped from shoulder to waist. Little more than a cotton bodice covered her.

'They want to humiliate us. Pigs!'

She sank back; and, throwing her own coat over Ruth, Iona looked round desperately for help.

The baying, trampling horde fought on. Other victims lay huddled on the ground. Thrown horse dung spattered beside Iona, and there were wild guffaws.

Then a dignified woman, the suffragette colours pinned to her lapel, touched Iona's arm.

'We've made a temporary hospital at Caxton Hall,' she said. 'I'll take your friend. There's a cab waiting down the street. Are you hurt too?'

'I wasn't in the demonstration,' said Iona; and the confession seemed more humiliating than anything Ruth had suffered.

~

'How fascinating! I must make some notes. Can you hang on?' asked Elizabeth.

But Gabriel couldn't bear to stop. She curled herself deeply into Elizabeth's armchair and went on reading. Below her, through the window at her elbow, was the old terraced street, with its phantoms of sickly women trudging to Amy's surgery, and of suffragettes in long skirts, plotting subversion. They seemed as real as anything in Elizabeth's neat, booklined bedroom.

Rufus was home for Christmas, the engagement was announced, but Iona couldn't forget her own feebleness. She escaped one day to a suffragette meeting, and found that Black Friday had already receded in importance. There was bitterness in Crosthwaite. Opponents were scheming to have Amy Whittingham barred from the hospital.

'It'll halve my salary, but we must make sacrifices, I suppose,' said Amy wearily.

'The blood of the martyrs,' quoted Ida Johnson.

Jane Hawkins giggled.

'Pardon me. I was thinking of the little burnt sacrifice you're preparing, Miss Johnson. You'll be a real martyr soon.'

Iona felt out of things, depressed, a failure. They discussed matters she knew nothing about. Nobody told her what Miss Johnson was planning. She suspected it was something Amy didn't approve of, though Ruth was eager. She left them, still plotting.

'I've just been out for a walk,' she explained, rather drearily, to Letty.

'Have you heard the news?' exclaimed Mrs Beaumont, positively hurtling into the Springfield drawing-room next day. 'Miss Johnson set fire to a letterbox in the High Street this morning! She was shouting "Votes for women!" when she was arrested.'

Miss Johnson, convicted of arson, was sent to prison.

What can I do for the cause, Iona wondered desperately; but there was no time to do anything. Rufus and Lettice were to marry at Easter, and days vanished under avalanches of guest-lists and invitations, and calls at florists and dressmakers, which neither Mrs Flood nor Lettice could manage without Iona.

Then it was the afternoon before the wedding. Lettice's satin dress, embroidered with seed pearls, hung in the wardrobe. Guests were coming. All was bustle. Iona, whisking through the drawing-room on some errand, found Lettice unpacking her latest presents – a silver cakebasket, a crystal rosebowl.

'Won't we have a lovely home?' Lettice said; and she gazed dreamily into space, seeing herself and Rufus having tea together, picking flowers . . .

Fury swept suddenly over Iona. Lettice, with no claims except a pretty face, was showered with gifts, while idealists like Amy and Ida were suffering poverty and imprisonment. And she dissociated herself from their sufferings by her silence. Angry, ashamed, she rushed into the garden.

'When Letty's married, I'll speak out,' she vowed.

A woman stepped from under a tree near the gate. She was yellow-faced, emaciated.

'Miss Johnson!' exclaimed Iona.

'I was looking for you.' Miss Johnson swayed and clutched a branch. 'They released me this morning. I went home – my mother won't have me back. I tried the suffragette shop – and Marlborough Street. No one was there. There's Miss Hawkins – but her home's the other side of town. You were near. I'll try Miss Hawkins tomorrow, but I need shelter. Just for tonight. And food. I've been hunger-striking.'

Relief surged through Iona. Here was the opportunity she had longed for to help the cause!

'You can stay the night in our attic. It's got mattresses and blankets, and the house is stuffed with food. Letty's getting married, so it's not a good time to explain things to my parents. There'd be a row. But – '

'You'll harbour me secretly?'

'Exactly,' said Iona.

She smuggled Miss Johnson up the attic stairs – miraculously nobody was about – and settled her on an old mattress. Then she hurried to the kitchen, but her parents were giving a dinner party that evening, servants swarmed everywhere, and it was impossible to take any food unobserved. So she collected biscuits from the dining-room sideboard, filled a toothglass with water and returned to the attic.

Miss Johnson was lying down. Grey hair straggled round her

face. Her eyes were pits of shadow. She gulped the water but winced when she tried a biscuit.

'I was force-fed in prison,' she mumbled. 'They gouge out your teeth to get the feeding tube into your mouth.'

'You need some soup,' said Iona.

'Soup!' echoed Miss Johnson longingly.

'But I'm afraid you'll have to wait. They're so busy in the kitchen.'

'I can rest.'

'Was it worth it?' asked Iona, looking at Miss Johnson's gaunt face.

'Oh, yes! Men see we're in earnest when we damage their property. That letterbox I burned was full of business letters. And our cruel sentences show that men are frightened. They fear we'll win. I heard in prison that suffragette premises may be searched.'

'What for?'

'Incriminating papers; pamphlets. Anything they can use against us. That's why I removed all these from the shop today.'

She took a bundle of leaflets from her pocket. The words *Crosthwaite Women's Social and Political Union* were written on each.

'Could you read for a bit?' Iona suggested. 'I'll light a candle. I'd better go down before I'm missed. I'll bring some soup when I can.'

She returned to the world of the wedding. In her best apricot silk dress she sat at the dinner-table, hearing the laughter, drinking the toasts. Flower garlands trailed over the tablecloth. The looking-glass centrepiece mirrored smiling, ignorant faces. In the attic, Miss Johnson suffered . . .

The party dragged to its close. For the last time, Iona and Lettice went upstairs together, to their shared bedroom.

When Letty's asleep, I'll creep down, and warm some soup, thought Iona.

Mrs Flood opened her bedroom door.

'Letty!' she called. 'I'd like a word with you.'

Iona undressed and got into bed. Still Lettice didn't come. Iona switched off the light; and, when at last the door opened, she pretended to be asleep.

'Iona,' whispered Lettice, an odd note in her voice.

Iona didn't answer. Miss Johnson was more important just then than Letty. She counted five hundred, once Lettice was in bed, and stole out of the room.

In the kitchen, she faced unexpected difficulties. There was no soup to be seen. The larder was full of elaborate wedding food, sealed under aspic or cream. Can I make some tea, Iona wondered. She had never made any in her life, but she could try. The fire was banked up for the night beneath a crust of coal. She tried to stir it into a blaze for the kettle.

Lettice lay rigid in bed. If she moved, she was afraid she might scream. The terrible things her mother had said beat in her brain like caged birds. She had been so ignorant of marriage! She had dreamed of daytime pleasures. She had never thought about the nights.

The mother who summoned her to talk looked very different from the dignified hostess of the dinner party. She was flushed; she twisted her hands nervously; for this was the moment she had long dreaded, and it had taken every scrap of will-power to bring herself to it. A mother should tell her daughters what to expect in marriage and give them good advice. But, so far, she had shirked her duty; and if she had known any good advice, she would have followed it herself. Her own mother had never said a word to her, abandoning her to a traumatic wedding night. She would have to say something to Lettice – but what?

'Letty,' she began, 'there's something you must know.'

Lettice stared, astonished.

'What is it?'

'There's more to marriage than you may realize.' Mrs Flood picked up a hairbrush, examined it, but found it no help, and put it down. 'You have to give yourself to your husband – bodily.'

'How?' asked Letty.

'Oh!' Flushing still more hotly, Mrs Flood fumbled for words. 'In bed – he'll want – It may seem like an assault, Letty dear. Men have this overpowering desire – I can't explain, but you'll soon discover. You must just be prepared.' She bit her lip. 'Letty, he'll want to see you naked – '

'He can't! Not Rufus!' cried Lettice, appalled.

'He will. Oh, Letty, it's the price of marriage; the price a woman pays for security. Distasteful though it seems, it has to be endured. I try to detach my mind – think of other things. One gets used to it, in the end.'

Or one escapes, thought Mrs Flood, into the merciful harbours of vague ill health where husbands, with luck, may hold back.

She made herself go on.

'It's to do with babies – planting the seed. From him to you. Perhaps I should have explained before, Letty, but why should girls know about these things before they have to?'

'Must I just – let him?' faltered Letty; still not quite understanding.

'After a while, possibly not. But on a honeymoon there's not much choice. I wish it didn't have to happen, Letty.'

'But you wanted me – you want us all – to marry.'

'Yes. There's no status, no respect, for a spinster. It's a failure not to marry. And, in time, you'll get used to the ways of men. Try to consider it as – a sort of animal passion.'

Rufus's kisses had been frightening enough, but there was worse to come! Lettice lay in bed quaking, digging her nails into her palms.

'Iona!' she sobbed aloud.

There was no answer. Iona, she suddenly remembered, had left the room. Perhaps she had gone to the attic. She sometimes did. Trembling, Lettice crawled out of bed. If she could tell Iona what their mother had said, she might feel calmer. She stumbled up the attic stairs.

Candlelight gleamed under the gable. A witch, with tangled hair and a face like a skull, reared up from an ancient mattress.

67

Then the house rang, as Lettice screamed and screamed and screamed.

~

⇒ *13* ⇐

What a start to a wedding day! Gabriel felt quite shattered as she turned the pages. She hardly needed Dorothy's words to imagine all the stresses – Lettice in shock, Iona in disgrace, Miss Johnson bundled away. But nothing was said to the guests. The conventions were properly observed. Brides, even bridesmaids, were allowed to look pale. Speeches were made; champagne corks popped.

~

'Don't wear those pearl earrings. You know they pinch,' begged Iona tremulously, as she helped Lettice into her going-away dress.

'They'll take my mind off – ' Lettice shivered, and screwed in the earrings. She adjusted her hat, forced a ghastly smile and ran downstairs.

~

Mr and Mrs Flood left Springfield next day for a holiday. Harry returned to school. Iona, Phyllis and Dorothy were left with the maids; and, in the last pages of the *Memoir*, Phyllis sprang into prominence. While Dorothy – accurately or not, Gabriel didn't know – presented herself as shy, dull and bookish, she revealed an unexpected streak of independence in Phyllis, a trait which, in Iona, had been nearly smothered by a sense of duty.

Gabriel remembered the younger sisters in the photograph, outshone by their prettier elders. In focusing her story on Iona and Lettice, Dorothy had reflected her childhood adoration of them. But Phyllis was growing up too. She was sixteen, and, in the lull after the wedding, she began to share confidences with Iona.

~

For the first time in her life, Iona had neither her mother nor Lettice to claim her. This would be the moment to help the suffragettes, but she was exhausted. She was sitting alone in the drawing-room, trying to recover her energy, brooding over how she had let Miss Johnson down – when Phyllis came in.

Abruptly, awkwardly, Phyllis explained that, when she had finished at school, she wanted to go to university. She loved studying. Science, in particular, fascinated her. But how would their parents react, and what did Iona think? Would education make a girl the unmarriageable blue-stocking everyone predicted? And did it matter?

Iona was full of admiration and encouragement. There seemed, at that moment, nothing more appealing than life away from Springfield. Girls needed freedom; and, as they talked, she described her own, woefully inadequate, support for the suffragettes.

'I should have acted differently,' she sighed. 'If I'd had the courage to speak, I might have been able to invite Miss Johnson openly. But I was afraid of what Father and Mother would say. They tied me down, somehow.'

'I won't be tied down!' declared Phyllis.

Three nights after the wedding, they were woken by a deafening explosion. Rushing to the windows, they saw the sky streaked with flame. News of what had happened came with the milkman next morning. A derelict farmhouse, on the moor nearby, had been blown up by a bomb. A note was found tied to a stake: '*Uninhabited houses now. Inhabited houses soon. Votes for women!*'

'Hooray for the suffragettes!' triumphed Phyllis. 'But who planted it? Miss Johnson?'

'I don't think she'd be strong enough yet.'

'Dr Whittingham?'

Iona hoped not. Tired out by the events of the last few days, she set off for a long, solitary walk. Dusk was gathering when she got home. Phyllis met her in the hall.

'The police have been here.'

'The police! Why?'

'Because of that bomb. We're near the farmhouse, and they've heard you sheltered Miss Johnson. They want to know if another suffragette was here last night. They're coming back to question you.'

'I don't know anything.'

'I told them that, but it wasn't enough. And they're bringing a warrant to search the attic.'

Those papers Miss Johnson had brought! What had happened to them? Iona tore up to the attic, pulled aside the mattress, and saw a scattering of leaflets, white against the dusty floor. Their titles proclaimed *Justice for Women, Women Demand their Rights* and, with incriminating clarity, *How to make a Bomb*.

Iona stared, aghast.

'They belong to the Crosthwaite suffragettes,' said Phyllis, who had followed Iona, and seen the writing on each.

'Yes,' said Iona.

'Shall we burn them?'

'Or should I take them back?'

'You might meet the police.'

'Oh!' exclaimed Iona. 'I'm sick of being a coward. I'm going to take them to Dr Whittingham's house. She'll know what to do. I'll go on my bicycle. It won't take long. If I see the police, I'll just dash past.'

Stuffing the leaflets into her jacket pocket, she ran down to the barn where her bicycle was.

'If the police come, say I haven't got home,' she directed; and, with a wave to Phyllis, she rode off into the gloom.

She was happy, thought Phyllis. She was doing something active for the suffragettes at last.

Rain, spattering down from the dark clouds, made Iona pedal as fast as she could. She turned into Wortley Hill, the bicycle quickening, and bouncing over the cobbles. I mustn't slip, she thought, as the rain fell harder, lashing her face.

She was alerted to danger by the clatter of hooves. A cart came charging at her from a side road, the horse out of control, the driver tugging at the reins and shouting.

I shall be run over, thought Iona, panic-stricken.

She pulled the bicycle sideways and the front wheel caught in a tramline groove. It shuddered, the back wheel reared and, though she tried to cling on, she was catapulted, head first, over the handlebars and onto the black and murdering cobbles.

And family life, *Dorothy's story concluded*, was never the same again.

~

⇒ *14* ⇐

Iona dead! Gabriel was shocked. Soon after beginning Dorothy's story, Gabriel had realized that she was a descendant of Lettice's – her mother had reverted to her maiden name of Orme when she left Paul Klavir – but she had thought Iona too would have married and had children. It had never crossed her mind that Iona might be killed. Yet out there on Wortley Hill, where lorries crawled and cars meshed themselves into impatient knots, was a patch of ground where Iona had died alone.

'How awful – about Iona, I mean,' she said.

'Yes.' Elizabeth looked round. 'Wasn't it dreadful? She wasn't much older than us.'

'Twenty-one.'

'And she seems to have been only loosely linked with the Crosthwaite suffragettes,' said Elizabeth. 'I've been trying to find out more about her since you showed me the petticoat, but there's not a lot. She made one or two banners, but I don't think she took part in any of their demos.'

'She blamed herself for not getting more involved,' said Gabriel.

'It's a shame.' Elizabeth paused and then tossed out a theory she had formed. 'Iona's death meant the end of the Suffragette Movement here.'

'How come, if she wasn't important?'

Elizabeth tried to assemble her pieces of evidence neatly.

'Amy Whittingham was the key figure, as you know; and it looks as if Iona's death pushed her into leaving Crosthwaite for the Sudan. I'll tell you why in a minute. When she went, Ruth lost her home, so that finished things for her. Ida Johnson never got over her ordeal in prison, and Jane Hawkins took off for London, where the action was.

'But even before Iona died, Amy was in a dilemma. She lost her hospital job after the letterbox was burned, because people connected her with Ida Johnson. The hospital committee evidently grabbed the chance to throw her out. And her private practice was dwindling. She put people's backs up with her new ideas, like hygiene and rudimentary contraception. They thought she was a wild revolutionary. Poor Amy. I feel really sorry for her.'

'Yeah; me too,' Gabriel agreed.

'Anne Cropper wrote all about it in her letter to me,' Elizabeth went on. 'She said that, as things got worse,

Amy started making inquiries about going abroad, perhaps working in one of the mission hospitals that were being opened all over Africa. In fact Anne says that she was being interviewed in London the day Ida Johnson came out of prison and didn't find anyone here in Marlborough Street. Anyway, Amy was offered a post, but she couldn't decide whether to take it, so she asked for a few days to think it over. There was Ruth to consider, though she'd heard that Ruth had this old boyfriend in the country, whom she might marry.' Elizabeth skimmed over her papers. 'Yes; he was called Joe Linton. If they were going to get married, Amy wouldn't have to worry about Ruth's future. She could suit herself. She was mulling it all over, when the police suddenly arrived for the big interrogation.'

~

'Are these papers yours?' asked the police sergeant.

'Not mine personally.'

'Don't try to wriggle out of it, ma'am. They belong to the Crosthwaite suffragettes, and you're known to be their leader.'

Amy stared down at the leaflets, so boldly labelled in another's writing. *How to make a Bomb*. She'd never seen it before.

'Where did you find these things?' she asked.

'In the dead girl's clothes.'

At the word 'dead', Amy, used though she was to tragedy, shivered.

'How are Mr and Mrs Flood?' she asked.

The policeman ransacked his vocabulary.

'Shocked. Horror-stricken. Heartbroken.'

Amy wished she hadn't asked. A violent death was often harder to take than death from illness. Some families never recovered from the blow.

She was told that Phyllis Flood said Iona had died bringing the papers to her. Indirectly, the disaster seemed her responsibility. Failure after failure. She tightened her lips so that their trembling wouldn't be visible.

73

'I was asking about the papers,' said the policeman.

Knowing nothing, Amy didn't answer.

'This one here.' His voice rose indignantly. 'It's called *How to make a Bomb*.' He directed at her the outraged stare which had cowed many people on Wortley Hill, but her eyes were lowered. 'It seems connected,' he said heavily, 'with that bomb at the old farmhouse.'

'You can't accuse me of that,' said Amy. 'I was in London.'

'I'm not accusing you, ma'am, yet. Though there is an offence of incitement. At present I'm merely seeking the truth.'

'I've told you all I can. If you'll excuse me, I have patients to see.'

'I must warn you that the Inspector may not be satisfied, ma'am. He knows your reputation.'

'In that case' – Amy made her lightning decision – 'you may tell the Inspector that I shall be leaving Crosthwaite for Africa, very shortly.'

~

'It sounds as if Amy definitely didn't plant the bomb,' said Gabriel.

'She couldn't have; she just couldn't,' said Elizabeth. 'I mean, even if she'd been around, she wasn't that sort of person. The one thing I've got against the suffragettes is the violence they used; but I'm a pacifist. I'd rather remember them, in your room downstairs, talking about the ways they could help other women. I know there were reasons for the violence. I can understand them, if I'm fair. They were afraid that, if they didn't make trouble, nobody would bother with them. And they were shocked by the sort of treatment women got when they were hunger-striking. Think of people you knew and liked, being held down by great enormous prison wardresses, having feeding-tubes forced down their throats, and food pumped into them till they were sick. Yuck! All the same, when Mrs Pankhurst incited them to more

74

violence so that they really went over the top with their smashing and burning and bombing – well, I wish she hadn't.'

'It must have worked, if they got the vote,' said Gabriel.

'Yeah, but it was in a kind of delayed-action way. They hadn't got it when the First World War started, but they gave up campaigning as a patriotic gesture. Mrs Pankhurst was really into patriotism then, in spite of the way men had behaved to her. She guessed how vital women were going to be; and she was right, because women just had to do a lot of the jobs men usually did, since men were off in the trenches, fighting. By 1918 the government had decided that women deserved the right to vote, but it wouldn't have happened without the suffragettes and perhaps even without their violence. I can't go into it all, though,' Elizabeth finished. 'I'm worried that my article's going to be far too long, as it is.'

Taking the hint, Gabriel left her. She went back to her room, put on a tape of Handel's *Water Music*, and lay flat on her bed. The suffragettes and their affairs were Elizabeth's concern. She meant to think about Miss Johnson hiding in the Springfield attic – wasn't the mattress still there? – about the terrible enlightening of Lettice, and Iona's appalling death. Instead, she found herself thinking about families.

An odd yearning seized her for the family life glimpsed beneath the drama of Dorothy's pages. How lovely for Iona and Lettice to share a bedroom. What fun for Phyllis and Dorothy to huddle on a bed and watch their glamorous sisters dressing for a dance.

I've missed out on family life, she reflected.

When she was small and living at Springfield, she was

usually solitary. Her mother, though kind, was preoccupied, her father was busy with academic work, and she had no siblings or nearby children to play with. The rift between her parents drew them still further from her; so she had begun visiting the attic, and finding an odd companionship in the trunks of clothes.

Springfield itself had been a companion too. She'd always felt that. She would shut the front door, jump down the three magical steps into the hall, and sense the walls closing softly round her, protecting her as a shell protects the kernel of a nut.

By association, her mind threw up a picture of real nuts. They were sweet chestnuts, piled on the stone hearth of what Sarah called the sitting-room, and the Floods, evidently, the drawing-room. She remembered pricking the nuts, pushing them into the glowing embers, and seeing their smooth brown skins wrinkle and blacken as they roasted. She had felt then that other children were in the room. She had almost heard their dresses rustling as they clustered round to share the nuts. They must have been the Floods when they were young and untroubled by suffragettes and suitors – just as Dorothy had described them!

I'd love a family of my own with lots of children, thought Gabriel; and another picture – dreamlike this time – flashed through her mind, of children scampering over the dipping floorboards at Springfield, and herself watching, drinking coffee from a Crown Derby cup, with Francis Ashwell.

'Stop it,' she told herself with a twitch of annoyance. What a stupid fantasy! Probably she was just feeling guilty about Francis. She shouldn't have rushed out of the attic in that childish way when he came in. Because it might be possible to like him . . .

No. Think about families, she urged herself; and, all at once, it occurred to her that a lack of family had been her mother's tragedy. Like herself, Sarah had been an only child; and, unlike herself, an orphan. A grandmother had been involved in her upbringing – Lettice, surely! Could it have been? Yes; Lettice, the pretty, volatile innocent of Dorothy's pages, had changed into the rather frigid grandmother Sarah had talked about. How strange!

'I never minded not having brothers and sisters,' Sarah declared lightly sometimes. 'I spent every second I could with Paul.'

She had married Paul, Gabriel's father. He was now Professor Klavir, living far away in Australia. He sent Gabriel a generous allowance, but he never asked her to visit him.

The group of women who now surrounded Sarah must be a sort of substitute family, Gabriel decided. Sarah might not think she'd missed anything, but unconsciously she had been pining for sisters. So she had provided herself with some; the women who ran their feminist magazine, *Boudicca*, from the offices below Sarah's flat. Gabriel knew them so well! There was Josie Crewe, the editor, who was warm-hearted and romantic about her mission to save women; Nina and Fleur, the business manager and the art editor, a couple; and Lyn and Diana, and several others, who hovered on the fringes. They were not unlike the Crosthwaite suffragettes in their closeness and unity.

Elizabeth had mentioned a name – Mrs Pankhurst. Gabriel sprang up and examined a section of picture-blanketed wall. There, sure enough, was an old, brown poster, labelled 'Mrs Emmeline Pankhurst'. Gabriel loved it, not for any feminist reasons but simply for the sumptuous Edwardian clothes. A lace hood, tied with broad, glossy ribbons, covered Mrs Pankhurst's head. A theatrical cloak, with cartwheel buttons, hung from her shoulders.

Mrs Pankhurst was a heroine in Warburton Street. Josie had found the poster and passed it on to Gabriel. Perhaps she had hoped it would be inspiring. But Gabriel had never been interested in women's causes. The suffragettes and the feminists could carry on in their own way, as far as she was concerned. She – and she raised her eyebrows in surprise at the discovery – she wanted a family.

What had happened to Lettice after her marriage? How many children had she had? And what about Harry, and Phyllis, and Dorothy? Dorothy . . .

Gabriel got out a sheet of notepaper.

1, Marlborough Street

Dear Aunt Dorothy,

I'm very sorry I never answered your letter last term. I'd love to have tea with you. Sunday is a good day –

The *Water Music* tape clicked off. Gabriel looked up in bewilderment. She had put on the tape without thinking. Handel, her favourite composer, was linked in her mind with designing. She tried to recreate his elegance, his clear lines, in her clothes. Normally, when she was depressed, she didn't play Handel. It was too painful. But now she had done, and it hadn't hurt.

How odd, thought Gabriel, licking up her envelope. She realized that, for several hours, she hadn't thought about the problems of designing once.

15

'You mean Lettice's marriage didn't work out then?' said Gabriel. She was disappointed.

'Letty was a silly girl,' Dorothy grunted, 'and pathetically ignorant. Our mother was to blame. She warned Letty to expect hell in the marriage bed, and Letty believed her. What chance had poor Rufus after that? I daresay he was pretty ignorant himself. People just weren't taught the facts of life. I've sometimes thought the suffragettes should have campaigned for compulsory sex education. Most girls would have found that quite as useful as the vote.'

They were sitting in the living-room of Dorothy's flat. The walls were beige, the carpet brown, and Dorothy herself wore a shapeless old brown suit. That poor quality tweed always goes baggy, thought Gabriel; and blue nylon blouses are hideous and terribly old-fashioned. She glanced thankfully at the soft wool of her own black-and-white skirt, and the crisp linen cuffs of her white shirt, fastened with black links.

As if suspecting criticism, Dorothy glared through thick spectacles. She looked very old, with thinning hair above her bumpy forehead, sunken cheeks, and legs – like a hen's, Gabriel decided. But she was a great-great-aunt, a real relation; and there were few enough of them; so Gabriel smiled determinedly.

'Did Lettice and Rufus stay together?'

'Yes. People did in those days. And then the war started and Rufus volunteered, which gave Letty a breather – until he came back gassed and ill. Letty couldn't cope with that. But there weren't many situations she could cope with. Girls were trained for the wrong things.'

'Like what, for instance.'

'Fiddle-faddling needlework. Pointless social calls. Iona had them worse than Letty. She let herself be tied down. I've thought, since then, that she might have been pleased to go in such a blaze of glory. Not that we considered it a blaze of glory at the time. We were all, except Phyllis, thoroughly ashamed of Iona's being involved with the suffragettes. Nice girls didn't get mixed up in that kind of thing – or so we thought. Even when she hid Miss Johnson, nobody realized how committed she was. Well, we were thinking more about Lettice at the time. My mother supposed Iona had foolishly sheltered Miss Johnson out of pity. But we couldn't ignore those ghastly leaflets that were found in her pocket.'

'I got the impression you admired her,' said Gabriel.

'I came round to that in the end, but it took years. I had to acquire some self-respect before I could sympathize with her. When I was young, I thought she'd had everything she could want, and thrown it away. I'm sure that's what my parents always thought. We overlooked her longing for independence. All except Phyllis.'

'Tell me about Phyllis,' said Gabriel.

'Phyllis?' The eyes behind the glasses closed, remembering, and opened again. 'She was strong-minded. She knew what she wanted and she got it. When Iona died, Phyllis begged to go to boarding-school; and though Mother called her unfeeling, she gave way and allowed it. Phyllis wanted to escape from the misery at Springfield. We were dreadfully miserable; Iona gone in that appalling manner, Letty like a ghost.'

'But hadn't Letty been in love with Rufus?'

'Yes, in a romantic sort of way. But he wasn't real to her – just a dream figure. She wanted to fall in love, but she'd never thought beyond that. And she hardly knew him. He was sent to Egypt and, when he came back and they were engaged, she was usually chaperoned. You're lucky nowadays, you girls. You know your boyfriends much better than Letty's generation did.'

Boyfriends reminded Gabriel of her musings in the Springfield attic, which Francis Ashwell had interrupted. It was weird how often her thoughts ran back to that moment; how she saw him in her mind's eye; how she – almost – wished to see him again . . . 'Go on about Phyllis,' she prompted.

'She passed her exams for London University. She planned to read Sciences. Then the war broke out and she shelved the university and joined the volunteer nurses. VADs they were called. I can see her now, in a blue uniform dress, and a white apron with a red cross on the bib.'

'Did your mother let her?'

'Yes. Old rules were relaxed. It seemed patriotic for girls, as well as their brothers, to help the war effort. Girls' work was safer, of course. Poor Harry was killed in 1915.'

'How awful!'

'Yes, another dreadful blow. He was a jolly person – not clever, like Iona and Phyllis were, but nice. Phyllis thought it unfair that he'd automatically got a good education, while she had to argue and fight for hers, but that's the way things were. Boys were favoured. My mother was shattered by his death. She died herself next year, from ulcers caused by all the stress. They couldn't treat them in those days.

'Phyllis was sent to France to nurse wounded soldiers. It was a primitive hospital, wooden huts crammed from end to end with mangled, mutilated men. The wounds were unspeakable, but the nurses just had to manage as best they could. Phyllis said the smell of gangrenous dressings nearly knocked you down. They used to play records, very loudly, on a wind-up gramophone, to drown the cries and moans. She often worked sixteen hours a day, feeding, bandaging, even helping with operations; but, in a strange way, she enjoyed it.

'I remember when she'd been home for Mother's funeral, and I saw her off at Crosthwaite station. A troop train had just left, and some girls we knew had been serving coffee to the soldiers. They came mincing along the platform on their high heels. They were doing so much for our gallant boys, they told us complacently. They'd sent them off to the trenches with a nice hot drink inside them. I could see the incredulity on Phyllis's face. She couldn't believe girls could be satisfied with doing so little.

'"What's nursing like?" they asked, giggling, and longing to hear about romances with officers, and horrific amputations.

'"It's freedom," Phyllis answered.

'They looked baffled.

'"How can it be? Don't you have to do what you're told?"

'"Yes, but I've chosen the situation for myself. I'm not bound by Crosthwaite rules. That's my freedom."

'They tripped away, shaking their heads, thinking she was as mad as Iona. But really,' Dorothy finished, 'there were plenty of opportunities during the war for a woman of spirit to seize; more than the suffragettes had ever dreamed of. Women were in munition factories, making shells. They were working in offices and on the land. Some actually put on trousers.'

'How about you?' asked Gabriel.

'Me?' Dorothy grimaced. 'That's an awkward question. I was only fifteen when the war began, and for the next four years I – well.' She paused. 'I rolled myself up like a hedgehog and stayed that way. I can find excuses for myself. There was the shock of Iona and then Harry and Mother dying. Lettice was unhappy, Rufus was ill, Phyllis was abroad, Father was sunk in gloom. I just curled up in a corner of the attic and buried myself in Angela Brazil's school stories. It was peaceful there – '

Behind the glasses, her eyelids drooped.

'I like the attic too,' said Gabriel, and saw that Dorothy had dozed off. She sat quietly, studying the room. It was dismal. It gave the impression that Dorothy couldn't cope any longer, and didn't care. She needs people to look after her, thought Gabriel – which might, she suddenly realized, mean herself. Or Sarah.

'Did you see the harp?' demanded Dorothy, opening her eyes.

'What harp?'

'Miss Cassia's harp, in the attic. Iona and Letty thought it very romantic.'

'Oh, yes,' answered Gabriel, remembering the dusty instrument with its broken, coiled strings. 'Who was Cassia?'

'Miss Cassia Hardcastle. The Hardcastles owned Springfield before us; three elderly spinsters. When Cassia was young she had pretty arms, so she learned the harp to display them. That was the way of things. Girls with pretty throats sang; girls with pretty arms harped. But poor Miss Cassia fell in love with the harp master, so that was the end of her music.'

'How come?'

'He was the wrong class. Girls shouldn't love the lower orders. Letty used to get the maids to tell her about Miss Cassia's broken heart. The maids knew everything.'

'Poor Miss Cassia. How unfair!' said Gabriel.

'You needn't pity her. A broken heart was a respectable possession in those days. That frantic, we-must-get-a-husband came in later, with my mother's generation, when so many men had disappeared to govern the Empire that husbands were thin on the ground, and needed grabbing. Back in the 1850s, spinsters from good families still had status. I'm sure Miss Cassia lived very comfortably with her sisters, once she'd got over her disappointment.'

'I think I used to see their ghosts in the porch!' Gabriel began excitedly; and saw that Dorothy's eyes had closed again. For a moment she closed her own, considering those shadowy figures, who had seemed to haunt the porch. They could have been the Miss Hardcastles, with their bonnets and umbrellas, setting out on some social or charitable errand and sensibly leaving the harp to moulder in the attic.

Dorothy sat bolt upright.

'I nodded off. D'you want some tea?'

'Well – ' Gabriel stalled.

'There's a tray in the kitchen. You'll have to boil the kettle.'

Gabriel boiled the kettle in a musty, mouse-smelling kitchen. I ought to take her to stay with Sarah, she thought, and then come back and redecorate all this for her. It's such a dump, and not very clean. She decided not to risk the digestive biscuits lying limply on a saucer.

'I like a drop of whisky in my tea,' said Dorothy, reaching a bottle from the shelf at her elbow. 'It's warming. Does that shock you?'

'No. I'm used to women drinking, like I'm used to women who don't mind not being married.'

'What?' Dorothy glared through her glasses. 'I minded. God, I minded!'

84

Her bitterness alarmed Gabriel. She changed the subject quickly.

'What happened to you all after the war?'

'Father died. That was the first thing. Influenza. Phyllis came home from France and found me mewed up with *The Madcap of the School*. She was pitiless. Mind you, she was right. People used to talk about "arrested development" in those days. I was a case in point. Phyllis had a place at London University. She sold Springfield, dragged me to London, found me a crammer's, chivvied me through Higher Certificate and into college with her. She did Chemistry; I did English. Then she said that, since I liked school stories, I should train as a teacher.'

'Did you want to?'

'Certainly not! I loathed the idea. But Phyllis was very bossy. She told me girls had to earn their living. It wasn't what Mother had said. Mother – ironically, I suppose – said girls should marry. She believed you were nothing if you didn't.' Dorothy sighed crossly. 'Don't go chasing men, Geraldine – what's your name? I'd blush over my chasings, if I wasn't too old. But so many men had been killed in the war, and they were still governing the Empire too. There were three million surplus women, we used to read in the papers. You had to fight.

'I bought cigarettes for other girls' boyfriends. I laughed uproariously if any man within earshot made the feeblest joke. I bought eye-catching clothes. I put some away in the Springfield attic as reminders of past stupidity. Black-and-white striped suits, green cloche hats – I must have looked a freak. And nothing worked. No one gave me a second glance, let alone a kiss. So – I had to teach.'

'Was Phyllis teaching?'

'Not she! She intended to be a world-famous scientist,

and win the Nobel Prize, like Marie Curie. This whisky's jolly good. Try some.'

'No, thanks,' said Gabriel, gulping her tea with difficulty. The cup didn't look very clean.

'Yes, Phyllis dreamed of research, but it was a privileged field. "Men Only" signs all over the place. She got a job as a lab assistant eventually, but the pay was poor and the prospects nonexistent. If she tried to discuss the work with the men in the lab, they walked away. She was kept in a cubby hole, washing test tubes. "At least you're *seeing* men," I used to say. "I'm stuck with a crowd of schoolgirls." But Phyllis wasn't the marrying sort.

'Then she saw an advertisement for a chemistry demonstrator's job in an American women's college. She sent in an application, explaining how frustrated she was, and got the post. Up till then we'd shared digs – rooms in a dreary boarding-house. I was furious at being left there alone. Phyllis told me to stand on my own feet. She would!'

'So what did you do?'

'I came back to Crosthwaite, got a job in a piffling girls' private school and moved in with Letty. She was a widow, by that time, with a little girl. Funny thing,' Dorothy yawned. 'She'd kept Rufus at arm's length for years. She'd go nearly hysterical if he touched her. Then she learned he was dying; his lungs – something had happened in the war. I can't remember details.' She yawned again. 'Letty suddenly went soft, when it was too late. Silly girl! But at least, when Rufus died, she had her baby. I – '

Dorothy's voice blurred, and her head jerked forward in sleep.

16

Elizabeth's article was nearly finished. She had recounted how Amy Whittingham arrived in Crosthwaite and was drawn into the Women's Movement by her experiences among poor families. She had described Amy's associates, their meetings and activities, Miss Johnson's arson, the bomb for which nobody claimed responsibility, and Iona's death when she was carrying compromising papers.

Anne Cropper, whose letter had been so useful, could tell little about Amy after she left Crosthwaite. She knew that Amy had made such a reputation in the first mission hospital where she'd worked that she was asked to establish a new one for mothers and children. ('Oh, my God; Fashion-Aid!' Elizabeth groaned when she thought about it.) In 1930, Amy died of polio, contracted from a patient. She never went back to England to vote.

The Suffrage Movement in Crosthwaite, as Elizabeth had told Gabriel, petered out. London, in any case, was always the centre of action. But, at the end of her letter, Anne outlined a last, rather touching example of co-operation between her mother, Ruth Kennett, and another former suffragette, which showed that old links were not forgotten.

~

During the two years Ruth lived with Amy, campaigning for women and dreaming of a medical career, an inner security warmed her. If everything failed, she could marry Joe Linton. As the hostility and the financial troubles mounted, threatening Amy's livelihood, Ruth found herself gazing at the faded primroses and remembering kisses she hadn't valued.

While Amy agonized over whether to go to the Sudan, Ruth was away. She had gone back to the village of her childhood, to see Joe Linton again. She went, sure that he would propose to her, and determined to accept. Instead, he told her he loved someone else.

'You left me. You never wrote. I thought you'd forgotten me,' he said, justifying himself.

She returned the evening following the bomb blast. She found Amy, just back too, shattered by the news of Iona's death, and committed to Africa. Ruth was too proud to show that the world was disintegrating under her feet.

'I can't go unless I'm sure you'll be all right,' said Amy. 'Does the young man still – care for you?'

Ruth nodded, unable to tell a direct lie, knowing it was best for Amy to go. She helped with the packing and saw Amy off. She locked the house for the last time and gave the key to the agent; and then she paced the streets of Crosthwaite, wondering what to do. She might take another job as a maid, but there'd be no other employer like Amy and she couldn't face the dull drudgery most servants endured. Her reputation as a suffragette would count against her if she asked for work at one of the mills. People would remember her militant speeches from soapboxes. They would think her a troublemaker. As she pondered despairingly, she ran into Jack Cropper.

Well – he'd always wanted to marry her.

But she wasn't in love with him. She married – as countless poor women did – from financial necessity. She admitted quite clearly to herself that she was trading her body for food and a roof. She didn't know that security would mean slavery.

Jack Cropper, once he had married her, meant to master her. There was to be no more dodging of embraces. He couldn't afford a home of his own, so Ruth was taken to live in the small terrace house with his mother and sisters, Dora and Lily, amongst the antimacassars and dusty drapery. A secondhand double bed was squeezed into Jack's narrow bedroom, its every creak greeted with giggles from Dora and Lily in the attic above. Ruth tried to resist, but Jack held her down with all his puny strength. Between 1912 and 1915 she had four babies, all boys, filling the tiny house to bursting point.

Amy, she remembered bitterly, had refused to discuss one

subject with her – birth control. She had said Ruth was too young to know about such things. Now there was nobody to turn to. She and Jack's family were soon on bad terms; and though she sometimes thought of writing to Amy for help, she would have had to ask Jack for the price of a stamp, so dependent was she, and he would have demanded to see the letter. Often she thought of running away, but she couldn't leave her children to the Croppers.

The adulation of Jack continued. Nearly every day Mrs Cropper made a stew, but the women only got the suet dumplings and turnips, while Jack had the meat. Amy had shared everything fairly. But if Ruth protested, there was uproar. 'Nay, rob our Jack of his shin beef! Hark at her, Ma.' Even when she was pregnant, Jack took the only armchair of right. 'Sit yourself down, lad; you're tired,' his mother would say, although it was Ruth who had walked the kitchen half the night, soothing a teething baby.

'How can you be such toadies?' she cried to them once.

'Hark at them fancy words!' they whooped, shrieking with laughter.

She racked her brains for a means of escape; and suddenly the war, which, embroiled in her troubles she had hardly noticed, provided one. Jack was conscripted into the army. In sheer relief, Ruth was almost cordial to Dora and Lily, but she knew the respite might be brief. Jack – if he wasn't killed – would return when the war ended, and her subjection would begin again.

She was pushing a wheeled cart, loaded with babies, through one of the darkest alleys of Wortley Hill, when she found her salvation. A 'To Let' board hung outside a run-down greengrocery. It was hardly a proper shop, just a pinched, cabbage-smelling hole, with a lop-sided window and dank flags underfoot, but that didn't matter. She'd learned something from Jack about vegetables; and there was a kitchen-living-room behind the shop, two tiny bedrooms and a cupboard-room under the stairs. If she could rent it, she would be independent. She would turn it into a profitable business before Jack came home; and, if he didn't like it, he could go back to his precious Ma.

But rent would be asked in advance and where could she get it? She'd never saved a penny from her meagre allowance as a soldier's wife. The old idealism about women, reviving in her jaded mind as she glimpsed this chink of light, supplied an idea. As soon as the babies were in bed, she smartened herself up as well as she could and, ignoring squawks of 'Where are you off to, lass?' she made her way to an address she remembered – Miss Johnson's.

Mrs Johnson had died, grudgingly reconciled to her daughter, and Miss Johnson lived in sickly solitude. The force-feeding had wrecked her digestion, and yellowed her face. She sat, shawled and hunched, by her fireside, but she managed a gap-toothed grimace of a smile when she saw Ruth.

'After all these years,' she mumbled, stretching out a bony hand.

'I'm not the sort of company you're used to,' said Ruth.

Miss Johnson shook her head.

'I can't often do with company of any kind. But for old times' sake – '

'What do you think we achieved?' asked Ruth, as they talked over the suffragette days.

'Not much. We haven't even got the vote yet, though they say it may come.'

'The movement hasn't really helped the poor, as Amy hoped it would,' sighed Ruth. 'We should have demanded state wages for wives, so that they could be independent of their husbands.'

Miss Johnson eyed Ruth's thin face and shabby clothes.

'Are you short of money?' she asked. 'I could spare a little.'

Miss Johnson insisted that the landlord had the shop white-washed and painted. She paid three months' rent and added a sum for Ruth to buy basic necessities. By the beginning of 1 917 Ruth had snapped her fingers at the Croppers and moved into the shop.

The work was tough. She got up before dawn to visit the

market and buy potatoes, turnips and cabbage – the only vegetables cheap enough for Wortley Hill. But she wasn't a mere shopkeeper. She made it known that she had once been Dr Whittingham's assistant, and Dr Whittingham was remembered with gratitude in many homes.

Soon Ruth was an unofficial medical adviser to the neighbourhood. She even learned the secret of contraception. 'Sponges!' a midwife whispered; so Ruth kept some, beside the embrocations, loaned out for a farthing a rub, and the big bottles of cod-liver oil and Scott's Emulsion, dispensed over the counter – three days' doses for a halfpenny, to be paid in advance. She persuaded Miss Johnson to subsidize a milk bill, for Amy's sake, and supplied healthy milk at nominal rates to Wortley Hill babies.

She was well established when Jack came home at the end of the war.

~

⇒ *17* ⇐

The tailpiece to the suffragette story was interesting but, Elizabeth decided, it would overload her article. She wrote up Amy's departure, and leaned back, satisfied. The only thing she hadn't yet settled was what the title should be.

She was rather pleased that she'd been able to concentrate, for Sunday afternoon in Marlborough Street hadn't been exactly peaceful. She would have escaped to a library if one had been open.

Lucy's boyfriend, Steve, had turned up, after hitching the forty miles from his own university. He was cheerful and noisy – and the wall between Lucy's room and Elizabeth's was thin. He had hardly arrived when Emma, a Christian feminist, rang the bell, wanting to discuss with Lucy the opposition to women's ordination and what they should do. Then Robin and Alec dropped by, because they always did on Sunday; and a distraught Sue landed on the doorstep after her latest row with John. They all crammed into Lucy's room and Lucy rushed up and downstairs.

'How many teas?' she yelled from the kitchen.

'Oh, we all tease,' Alec shouted back.

Well, perhaps the laughter proved that Sue was feeling better.

And, through it all, Elizabeth worked resolutely on; telling her story to present Amy the idealist, Amy the committed feminist who had tried to change the world; a real heroine.

The history of the suffragettes, it seemed to Elizabeth, starkly illustrated the struggle between good and evil. On the evil side were the prime minister of 1912, Mr Asquith, and his all-male Government, who repudiated women's rights; the Crosthwaite Hospital Committee, who banned Amy; conventional citizens, like Mr Flood, who shut their eyes to reality; the police; the magistrates who handed down harsh sentences to women who wanted *true* justice; and the prison doctors involved in force-feeding. On the side of the good were Amy and her friends, suffering for the sake of their sex, as martyrs.

Suddenly she knew what her title would be. She wrote it boldly at the top of her first page. *Heroines and Martyrs.*

Her sympathies were strongly engaged because of the conflicts in her own life. Her father was aggressively masculine, a garage-owner, who went motor-racing and drinking with 'the lads'; while her mother devoted herself to growing herbs and preparing pot-pourri which she sold in dainty muslin sachets. Elizabeth longed for an alliance with her mother; yet it was her father who took the most notice of her; who joked with her, and at her expense; who told her that her legs were super but that she should get her hair permed; who alternately hugged her and shouted at her; and made her life a misery when he tried to teach her to drive. Elizabeth's mother was cool, detached and clever. She'd written a couple of books on English herb gardens. She was the parent Elizabeth identified with – and knew least.

And that, it seemed to Elizabeth, was the pattern of life. At school, the boys and male teachers hogged the limelight, were deferred to and placated. The novels read in English classes were chosen to interest the boys because the girls, it was said, would read anyway. History was the brutal record of men, grabbing power and lands, fighting to keep them. Such violence had turned Elizabeth into a pacifist. Why was school history never about things women did – the households they cared for while men were slugging it out elsewhere; the quiet skills they passed on to their daughters; the loyalty they showed each other; the humanitarian causes they pursued; and the foreign journeys and adventures which a few of them, in laughably unsuitable clothes, had risked and enjoyed.

Gradually, Elizabeth formulated her own feminism. She wrote essays to prove that Jane Austen's heroines preferred their sisters and women friends to their suitors; and that Heathcliff, in *Wuthering Heights*, was not the world's great lover but a vicious oaf. She annoyed the male teachers but the women praised her originality.

Things were more enlightened at the university. Women were elected to office in the Students' Union and ran their own Women's Group. The Vice-Chancellor and most of the professors were – naturally – men, but Women's Studies could be followed as an option in many of the Arts courses. What Elizabeth really minded was the way the boys seemed to control most university journalism, filling student magazines with sports reports and tediously vulgar jokes. Except for *Cross-Questioning*. That, Elizabeth considered, was a serious magazine; the right setting for 'Heroines and Martyrs'.

She had tried her luck with *Cross-Questioning* before. Every two or three weeks, the editor – a man, needless to say, called Nick – summoned hopeful critics to his office and handed out free tickets for any plays or concerts to be reviewed. Only it wasn't a case of handing out. The noisiest, most aggressive people snatched. The less assertive were left ticketless.

For a long time, that was Elizabeth's fate. Then, one day last autumn, Nick said, 'Ballet?'. There was a perceptible pause – and Elizabeth got the ticket.

She wrote and rewrote her review, polished every sentence. The following Friday, she rushed to buy *Cross-Questioning*. Her article wasn't there.

She geared herself to go and ask what had happened. Bella – of the red roses – was in the outer office; and – yes – she had a tight skirt and carefully applied make-up; and her hair was an incredible blonde waterfall. Elizabeth brushed past, and faced Nick across a table littered with clippings and printouts.

'That ballet thing?' he said. He had a long, sneering face, pale as a mushroom above a stalky neck. 'Gutless. No bite.'

He'd get 'bite' this time; a long, enthralling article, which any editor would be proud to publish. It would

94

take male citadels by storm and establish the claims of feminism.

Lucy's mob was dispersing. Feet clattered downstairs. Steve alone lingered. There were fond goodbyes on the landing. Elizabeth closed her ears and reread her draft. Amy Whittingham's name should ring round the university.

'Oh, Lucy! I've left my scarf in your room, and it's freezing.'

Steve was by the front door at last.

'I'll get it.'

Lucy raced back upstairs. And she called herself a feminist – ! Except, of course, that she called herself a dozen other things as well. Not like Amy. Amy was single-minded; committed.

Lucy pounded down again and the front door slammed.

Later, Lucy stood in the kitchen feeling defeated. There were moments – and this was one – when she regretted her hospitable impulses. That Chinese takeaway she'd shared with Steve had spread rice and sauce over an incredible number of dishes. She gazed despairingly at unwashed mugs, the pot of herb tea she'd made to calm Sue's nerves, the plates with sticky cake crumbs, the unexplained apple core, the carton of milk knocked over among the debris, the meat-pie Steve had kindly brought with him, in case she didn't fancy a takeaway . . . Well, that could go in the fridge. Lucy opened the door and groaned at Elizabeth's little bowls of half-eaten salad spreading everywhere again.

The photo of the Amy Whittingham Hospital looked down at her, and Lucy groaned again. What *were* they going to do about it? She still had a provisional booking on the hall, but Fashion-Aid seemed as dead as the limp carrot gratings Elizabeth apparently cherished. And she herself had so much on, as usual.

Elizabeth came in, looking pleased, murmuring about making some tea, and then registering dismay at the sight of the kitchen.

'They *will* come,' said Lucy.

'Well, don't be such a doormat. Make them do their own washing-up.'

'I s'ppose.'

Lucy ran water into the sink.

'I've started worrying about Fashion-Aid again,' she said.

Elizbeth felt a bit annoyed.

'You keep going on about it. If Gabriel won't do it, we'll have to drop it.'

'Isn't that a shame, when it's a feminist cause?'

'Fashion's not specially feminist.'

'What d'you mean? Isn't it?'

'No; it's all about female stereotypes. It's saying that women are only proper women if they make themselves look what's considered attractive; if they wear the right clothes and do the right things with their hair. Because a certain sort of appearance is supposed to be vital if women are to justify themselves in the conventional way by catching a man – '

'Hang on,' interrupted Lucy. 'That's a bit OTT.'

'I bet it's what Amy Whittingham would have said.'

'Fair enough; but that was centuries ago.'

'Only seventy years. And what the suffragettes stood for is still valid today. Don't you see?' Elizabeth snatched up a teatowel and began drying mugs. 'Amy wanted women to be valued in their own right and not by the standards of the male world. For centuries – for ever, almost – women had been accepting men's views of things as if they were iron laws; but, you see, Amy was just longing for them to recognize their own, independent worth. I've thought about all this while I've been researching into her, and it's frightening how many of the suffragette insights and opinions were forgotten. There's a whole suffragette culture which could tell us a lot, I'm sure, about women's quest for their own individuality – their freedom to be themselves, not the slaves of fashions and conventions – if only it was uncovered again. I've heard there are novels of theirs waiting to be dug out of libraries; and I know they wrote plays, if only people would revive them.'

The passion in her voice surprised Lucy, who'd thought of Elizabeth as cool.

'Well, there's this hall I've booked. If Fashion-Aid doesn't come off, maybe we could try one of their plays. I'd rather like to – '

The doorbell rang.

'It'll be for you,' said Elizabeth, taking the dishcloth from Lucy.

'Er – is Gabriel in?'

Francis Ashwell, tall and thin, in a loose, flapping coat, was standing on the doorstep.

'Hi!' said Lucy. 'No, she's not in. I don't know where she is. D'you want to come in; have a coffee?'

Why on *earth* did I say that, when I've so much to do already, she wondered.

'Oh, no thanks.' He backed away.

'I'll tell her you called.'

'It doesn't matter.'

'I should think,' said Lucy, hurrying back to the kitchen, 'that if Gabriel starts going out with Francis Ashwell, it really will be the end of Fashion-Aid.'

Elizabeth felt a stab of annoyance. Lucy hadn't taken

in a word of what she had been saying, but was slavishly following the general belief that a boyfriend had to come before everything else. Why should the male sex be so important?

'Poor Liz,' she knew people said behind her back. 'No boyfriends.' Well, she really didn't care. Loyalty between women was what counted most; hers for Amy, Amy's for her friends. If Lucy and Gabriel didn't see that, it was their bad luck.

⇉ 18 ⇇

Leaving Dorothy asleep, Gabriel set off for home.

Poor Dorothy, she thought; the last of her generation, solitary, stranded like driftwood in that awful flat. Something would have to be done. Gabriel went back to the idea she'd had in the kitchen. She could take Dorothy to London at the end of term, leave her with Sarah and come back to decorate the flat. Dark green walls, she thought; white paint. I'll scrap that carpet and choose something paler.

The prospect pleasantly filled the void left by her creative block. That was still too painful to think about. How could a mind sparkle for months with imaginative designs and suddenly go blank, hardly able to summon the simplest shape?

Oh, do shut up, she told herself; and forced her mind back to her family. She considered Dorothy, as she had described herself – young and anxious, dressing freakishly, desperately, to attract men. Who hadn't responded.

Sarah's friend Lyn held gatherings for women who had had bad experiences with men – rapes, assaults, betrayals – so that they could talk about what had happened and try to come to terms with it. She'd written articles about these discussions for *Boudicca*, the feminist magazine. 'Women and Men: a Problem of Relationships' was a title Gabriel remembered. Dorothy would have written: 'Women and Men: a Problem of No Relationships'.

Had Dorothy's clothes been as dire as she had said? Her trunk was still in Springfield's attic. It would have been fascinating to open it and examine the striped suits and cloche hats – but she couldn't go back to Springfield. She'd blown it with Francis Ashwell. Just another of those things that had gone wrong. Depression cringed close again.

She turned into Marlborough Street.

'Oh – Gabriel. Hi!'

He was standing beside his car, tall and thin, the streetlight picking out a lock of hair flopping on his forehead. She couldn't help noticing his hair, and his long, loose coat, though she was too surprised to speak.

'I just dropped round. Lucy said you were out, but I thought I'd hang on a bit.' And he smiled involuntarily because he'd expected her to come round the corner with a boyfriend, and here she was, miraculously alone. 'I wanted to say sorry for crashing in on you the other day – in the attic. Did it put you off? You've not been back since and if you want to – I'll keep out of your way.'

'I'm sorry too,' said Gabriel. 'I felt really bad afterwards. I'd like to go back some time.'

She paused, uncertain what the next move was. Fix a day? Invite him into her room? He took the initiative.

99

'D'you want to go out for a drink?'

And next moment they were in the dim, safe interior of the car; neither of them quite sure how it had happened; both nervous, but eager to make up for that clash in the attic.

Gabriel's going out with me, Francis told himself incredulously.

Francis! thought Gabriel, with a dizzying mixture of excitement and alarm, and a weird sense that Fate was taking a hand in things.

He led the conversation, rushingly, anxiously, at first; but they quickly established links. Both had divorced parents. Francis's mother was in California; Gabriel's father in Australia. She had no brothers or sisters; he only had distant half-siblings from earlier and later marriages of his father's. Both had lived at Springfield.

He parked and they went into an old pub, with a low-beamed ceiling and twinkling brasses, where they sat on velvet stools by a log fire. Its rosy reflections flickered over Gabriel's black and white skirt and glinted on her silver earrings and her blue-black hair.

The conversation drifted, wavered, and fixed on – 'What do you do?'

'Fashion,' said Gabriel guardedly.

But he suddenly, after weeks of loneliness, wanted to confide.

'I should be at Oxford,' he said; 'only – I've been rusticated.'

'What's that?'

'Suspended. I can't go back – except to take Finals. I'm supposed to be working at home, but it's just impossible.'

She knew the feeling.

'How come you got rusticated?'

He'd been at a party that was raided, he explained.

There was dope. They were sent to the college authorities.

'I hadn't touched the stuff,' said Francis, 'but I couldn't back out. Not at the time, anyway. And now it's too late.'

'So you said you'd had it?'

'I didn't say I hadn't.'

He stared gloomily at the fire.

'I'm really sorry,' said Gabriel. 'It sounds like bad luck.'

The delight of her sympathy completely changed his mood.

'We could get bar snacks,' he said. 'Shall we?'

And he went to order scampi at the bar.

Francis was really sweet, thought Gabriel, with his light hair and spidery hands. And how awful to be suspended – rusticated was the word – out of loyalty to your friends. He must feel terrible. She was quite surprised when he came back from the bar smiling.

It was cosy by the fire. They perched on their velvet stools, eating scampi, and he told her a bit about Oxford. She hadn't felt so relaxed for ages as she listened, enjoying the food, the warmth, the Cinzano.

'The summer term's the best,' he said; 'going punting with a bottle of wine, and seeing other people fall in. And there's the College Ball. It goes on all night . . .'

She didn't hear any more, for, at the word 'Ball', something extraordinary had happened. A picture of a balldress sprang into her mind, its every detail clear. It was white, scooped off the shoulder, with black and scarlet embroidery spiralling up from the hem. She saw exactly how tiny crescent darts would curve into the waist, how the sleeves would be ruched.

Joy surged through her. Family, boyfriends, were as insubstantial as ghosts. Her designing had come back and nothing else mattered. This was her life, for without it she was half dead. It must be seized and she snatched the notebook and pencil she always carried out of her bag to make a lightning sketch.

But what was happening? The dress was fading; its clarity blurring. What had the fabric been? What was the special shape? Agonizingly, she tried to force her brain to hold on. Her pencil touched the paper and dropped away. The dress had gone, like smoke in the wind. She could remember nothing.

'Gabriel!' Francis exclaimed. 'Are you all right?'

For despair had drained all the blood from her face.

⇒ *19* ⇐

The clock radio said 1.05, and still Gabriel lay rigid and unsleeping. It wasn't exactly that she'd spoiled the evening for herself and Francis, though she had. Far worse was the frustration of almost recovering her designing power, only to lose it again.

Francis had been kind. He'd bought her brandy and driven her home.

'What's wrong?' he kept asking, but she couldn't explain.

He would think she was cold – or mad. He wouldn't want to see her again. But it hardly mattered now. Nothing mattered but the heavy weight of loss, burying the world – burying Springfield, Dorothy, the trunks of clothes – under its smothering mass.

Yet inexplicably, maddeningly, the experience had galvanized her brain. Ever since she had got into bed, it had been cranking on, throwing up image after hopeless image. It offered her countless white ballgowns, each as stiff and lifeless as a shroud. It manufactured dresses, blouses, jackets, all shapeless and forlorn, like clothes on the last dusty rack of a charity shop. Unable to stop it, she lay and suffered.

Through it, like a flash of lightning, came the memory of the geometrical raspberry jacket she'd designed last autumn, inspired by a block of colour in one of her abstract prints. She switched on the light and gazed at her picture-crowded walls. Her abstract prints seemed as flat as bathroom tiles.

The picture which caught her attention was Millais's *Ophelia*. She liked it for its ominous brooding greens, its watery blues and greys, and for the broken garland of flowers trailing across the floating diaphanous skirt of the drowned girl. Now it chimed strangely with what Dorothy had said about the Floods. We're doomed, thought Gabriel; Iona, Lettice, Dorothy, Sarah and me. We're destined to tragedy. And at once her brain began tossing up ludicrous black garments, like nuns' robes, or eastern *chadors*.

She could bear it no longer. She crawled out of bed and went through to the kitchen. The doctor had said milky drinks – not that she really believed they'd help. How could milk cure a diseased imagination?

The door opened and Lucy, still dressed, looked in.

'I thought I'd heard you. Can't you sleep?'

Gabriel shook her head.

'Don't put that milk back. I'll join you. Or maybe coffee'd be better. I'm having an essay crisis.'

'Lucky you!' said Gabriel. An essay crisis was nothing.

Lucy looked at her.

'Same problem, or different?'

'Oh – the same.'

'It's bound to come right in the end.'

'You've got to be joking,' said Gabriel wearily; but she sipped her hot drink and felt fractionally better.

'You went out with Francis, didn't you?' said Lucy. 'I thought that'd be nice.'

'Yes, but – ' And Gabriel found herself telling the story of the disastrous evening. Lucy's sympathetic face somehow drew it out of her.

'D'you know what I think?' said Lucy, when Gabriel had finished. 'I think if you could just make yourself relax, you'd be OK again.'

'How'm I meant to relax when I've got this great black hole in my head?'

'Stop worrying.'

'Stop breathing,' Gabriel retorted drearily. 'I can't live if I can't create,' she said presently.

'Was it Fashion-Aid that messed things up for you?'

'Could be. I dunno.'

Lucy glanced at the photo.

'We could leave it all to the relief agencies, I suppose.'

'Resign myself to failure, you mean? Oh, God! You don't know how awful it is to fail. Just to be blank and empty and hopeless – '

Her voice trailed away.

'But you're not,' said Lucy. 'That's the point. You're really talented.'

'Am I?' Scepticism loaded Gabriel's words. 'D'you think Shakespeare ever had a writer's block?'

'Dozens, probably.'

'I dunno,' said Gabriel again. 'He was a man.'

'So what? We're all human beings.'

'There've been articles in *Boudicca*. 'The Problem of Women's Creativity'.

'About what, exactly?'

'Why 90 per cent of creative work comes from men.'

'Really?' Lucy considered the question. 'There are women writers – the Brontës, Jane Austen.'

'Everyone mentions those. And Agatha Christie and Enid Blyton. But can you name any well-known women painters or composers? Yes, I thought you'd look blank.'

'I'm so ignorant,' Lucy confessed. 'But what about actresses – Judi Dench or Penelope Keith?'

'They don't count, like musicians don't count. They're only interpreting not creating. You've got to explain why so few women have been properly creative.'

'Too busy creating babies.'

'I'm not,' said Gabriel. 'But I did once have a tiny creative spark. Maybe other women do too. And then they go out and life isn't worth living. Mine isn't, anyway.'

'Come off it,' begged Lucy. 'I'm getting depressed too.'

'The funny thing is,' Gabriel went on rather dreamily, not attending to Lucy, 'I've heard people say women lose their creative powers because of having to adapt themselves to a man's world. Strangling their souls to fit in. But that can't have happened to me.'

'How d'you mean?'

'Well – Sarah's friend, Josie Crewe, who's the editor of *Boudicca*, says that because women are trained from the cradle to please men, and men like them passive and amenable, they prune back the inconvenient parts of themselves. Men wouldn't like it if women were too busy writing or painting to get their dinner or go to bed with them. So women don't.'

'I'm not into theories,' said Lucy. 'They may make sense to some people but they sound like a load of rubbish to me. Why not concentrate on nice, proper things? Like seeing Francis again, or going back to Springfield?'

Francis? I've probably put him off for good, thought Gabriel. What a pain! But there were still Dorothy's clothes. A faint ray of light pierced her gloom.

'Why don't you get back to bed?' suggested Lucy. 'D'you want me to fill you a hotwater bottle? Oh – look at the time. I'd better leave my essay till tomorrow.'

⇒ *20* ⇐

Because of the rain, Gabriel took a bus up Wortley Hill and alighted near Springfield. It was afternoon. She'd slept late and then spent a long time screwing up her courage for the visit. Because what was she going to say if she bumped into Francis? Their acquaintance so far, lurching from one upset to another, was more than a bit nerve-racking. Maybe Sarah was right, after all, to warn her off men.

But she wanted to see Dorothy's clothes. She liked Dorothy despite her gruffness. She felt close to her. So it was worth going to Springfield and hoping that the housekeeper would open the door.

Wet branches tossed above the drive and rain billowed against her. Its grey scurries shaped themselves into Victorian ladies with wide skirts, blowing shawls, and bonnets – poke bonnets, whose brims were a protection from the weather and from the world as well; like horses' blinkers, shutting off a wider view. If Miss Cassia had removed her bonnet, she might have seen that it was possible to defy her family and marry a harp master.

There was the harp to look at as well as Dorothy's clothes.

Gabriel was suddenly aware of a tapping on one of the windows. Through its glass she saw, not Francis, but a grey-haired woman, beckoning. Alarmed, Gabriel stopped. Was she trespassing?

The window flew open.

'It's all right,' a voice called. 'Gabriel – it is Gabriel, isn't it? Come inside, dear. I want to meet you.'

There was no help for it. Gabriel opened the door and was met in the hall by an elegant woman in perfect, whisper-fine, blue-grey suede. And the woman's well made-up, rather hard face, relaxed into incredulity.

'You're so like your father!' she exclaimed. 'Your hair! And the way your eyebrows dip at the corners. Good Lord!'

It was no recommendation to be told she resembled Paul. Springfield hall was where she had last seen him, ten years ago. She'd been hovering, small and uncertain, aware of the looming crisis, and he'd rushed past without noticing her.

'How is he?' asked the lady.

'My father? Fine.' Gabriel shrugged, to hide her ignorance.

'I was responsible for your parents meeting. But I see you don't know me from Adam.' ('Eve,' Gabriel corrected silently. She'd not spent ten years in Warburton Street for nothing.) 'One forgets how time passes. Do hang up your coat and come and talk to me. I'm in the sitting-room.'

The hall's pinks and creams were complemented by

the pink and terracotta upholstery of the once shabby room where Gabriel had roasted chestnuts. She perched on a chair, feeling oddly uneasy. The woman's dominating personality filled the room.

'I'm Deirdre Russell,' she explained. 'Philip Ashwell's sister. Francis's aunt. My parents, George and Enid Ashwell, bought Springfield from the Floods. And I was the person who invited your father and grandfather to Springfield. Right?'

She smiled, confident of recognition, even of gratitude.

'I don't know anything about it,' said Gabriel, quite bewildered by so much information about a past which Sarah never mentioned.

'Really? I should have thought – but it must be some while since your parents separated.'

That was something Gabriel didn't like discussing. She remained silent.

Deirdre gestured with a sparkle of rings.

'I mustn't bore you. But if you're wondering where Francis is – '

'I'm not.'

Which wasn't true. She was longing for Francis to come in, rescue her from his aunt, say it was all right about last night – but she couldn't admit it.

'I've come to see about a few things for my sister-in-law, who's away; and I've persuaded Francis to go and do some work in Crosthwaite Library. I'm sure he's not done half he should, since this silly business of rustication. He mentioned that you might be coming, and as soon as I heard the name Klavir, I knew I must stop and see you. You're absurdly like Paul!'

Gabriel, tense on the edge of her chair, didn't answer.

'And what about your mother? You live with her, don't you? How's Sarah?'

'OK.'

'Is she still with – ? One never knows what to call these things. A women's commune?'

'She works on a feminist magazine. She's got her own flat.'

'It was so extraordinary, her leaving Paul. The last woman in the world to do it, one would have thought. Personally, I'm baffled by the Women's Movement. I like men. Which is why I lured your grandfather to Springfield, back in 1947. It had been a woman's house far too long. I remember that, during the last war, Anne Cropper had to answer the door to a woman inquiring if Springfield was a nunnery! That shows you what it was like!'

Gabriel stared down at the carpet. Deirdre's image of Springfield was nothing to do with her, though 'a woman's house' seemed rather apt for the home of the Hardcastles, of Iona and Lettice, Phyllis and Dorothy.

Deirdre considered Gabriel's pale face, framed by thick black hair; the dark circles of fatigue, or eyeshadow, round her lowered eyes; the slight body, rigid in its black shirt. She seemed as prickly as Paul. One had to be wary of Klavir sensitivities, Deirdre reminded herself. With little Sarah Orme – mousy, submissive as she had been – one never worried. Gabriel looked a real Klavir.

Deirdre remembered Paul still, breathtakingly handsome. It was hard to take one's eyes off him. He was difficult, of course. Sarah had doubtless had some good reason for leaving him, apart from going overboard about feminism. But, yes – eager to please – that had been Sarah. Unlike, clearly, her daughter.

'I mustn't keep you,' she said. 'I was just so – thunderstruck – when I heard Paul Klavir's daughter had been visiting Springfield. You've got some project, haven't you? Francis didn't really explain.'

She could smile charmingly when she chose, and she did so now. Gabriel thawed slightly.

'I'm studying the clothes in the attic,' she said, and she stood up. 'I won't disturb you.'

But Deirdre, looking interested, stood up too.

'Are you? Good gracious! I haven't thought about those trunks for years. There are some beautiful dresses of my mother's in one of them. I'd love to see them again! My dear, I think I'll come up to the attic with you.'

⇒ *21* ⇐

'Damnation!' Deirdre swore under her breath.

They had emerged into the attic, and there, prominent among the old trunks, was a hatbox, which she'd forgotten and didn't want to remember. Cautiously – but Gabriel had moved in another direction – she lifted the hatbox lid and saw again the black lace Edwardian hat with crimson satin roses heaped over the wired brim. At least her mother wasn't there to tell the tiresome story which had so often embarrassed Deirdre when she was young.

~

Before the First World War, Madam Logan's was the smartest hatshop in Crosthwaite. The showroom was luxuriously carpeted and furnished; the hats elegantly arranged on their stands – monstrous hats, flowered and feathered, needing to be skewered with large hatpins to Edwardian piles of hair. Above the shop was an uncarpeted flat where a roomful of women slaved over felt and straw and buckram, fashioning hats; and where

110

Mrs Logan, and her daughter Enid, ate and slept in cramped back parts.

Enid, who had left school at thirteen to help her mother, was a favourite with everyone. She was so lively and vivacious, dashing from the showroom to the workroom, flying out to buy ribbon and back to make tea.

She was on an errand, late one afternoon, when she saw a little crowd at a street corner. A dark-eyed girl, with a shawl over her waving hair, was standing on a soapbox, proclaiming her message.

'Votes for women! Come on now, ladies. Let's show the men we mean business. Let's take this country by the scruff of its neck and kick it into the paths of justice and commonsense. Oh – I can't rightly say what I mean; but I do mean it, I promise you!'

'Hooray!' called Enid, and gave a thumbs-up sign as she scurried past, with her packets of ribbons and pins. She admired the suffragettes. It was exhilarating to see what women could do. She flew back to the shop.

Mrs Flood of Springfield, one of her mother's best customers, was seated on a gilt chair. She had just bought a hat.

'Wrap this for Mrs Flood, Enid,' said Mrs Logan.

The wrapping was an expert job. Not one satin petal must be crushed. Enid set to work, with a pile of tissue paper.

'There was a girl suffragette outside on a soapbox,' remarked Mrs Flood. 'What a nuisance they make of themselves.'

'If they had their way,' agreed Mrs Logan, 'they'd have us all wearing red caps of liberty, and then I'd be out of business.'

An impulse of mischief made Enid seize a pencil, write 'Liberty' on a scrap of paper, and push it down into the heart of one of the satin roses.

'People won't be satisfied,' Mrs Flood went on, as Enid placed the hat carefully in a box decorated with pink stripes. 'It's all clamour for change.'

I wouldn't mind some change, thought Enid, pressing down the lid.

The change in her life came in 1918, when George Ashwell

111

bought her mother's shop. He was already middle-aged and, evading military service, had spent the war making a fortune in drapery. He was now buying a row of shops, including Mrs Logan's, which he planned to transform into a large department store. He offered a pension to Enid's mother; and to Enid herself, because she had lovely auburn hair and was full of vitality, he offered marriage. Enid, ready to try anything, accepted.

George bought Springfield from Phyllis Flood and took Enid to see her future home. For a moment she was uncharacteristically daunted. The rooms were so large, so beautifully panelled. It's not my world, she thought.

'Have a look round by yourself,' invited George, disappearing to inspect the drains.

Enid opened a few doors and, behind one on the landing, she found a staircase. She climbed up to a big, dim attic under the gables. Broken furniture, bundles and boxes were crammed untidily together. Boxes! There on a pile were the unmistakable pink stripes of a '*Madam Logan*' hatbox. Enid lifted the lid, and saw a black lace brim, heaped with crimson roses. She plunged her fingers into one, and pulled out a screw of paper.

'Liberty.'

Standing in the attic, she laughed and laughed.

~

How many times, Deirdre wondered, had she squirmed while her mother told that story. How many times had people tittered about it behind Enid's back?

'Poor Mrs Flood. She never knew she'd worn a cap of liberty,' Enid would exclaim. 'But there really had been a revolution. The hatshop assistant was mistress of the big house.'

Deirdre writhed whenever the hatshop was mentioned. It was bad enough to be connected with a department store – even the best in Crosthwaite; to see her name, Ashwell, vulgarly emblazoned above the plate-glass windows. She never understood the excesses of her

112

mother's nature, the shameless readiness to accept anything – or almost anything, Deirdre corrected herself, remembering things she hadn't liked to tell her mother. It was typical of Enid to have kept that hat. Luckily nobody would know about the screw of paper now.

No, Deirdre had never solved the mystery of her mother's personality; of why Enid could be so warm and open to others, and yet so careless of her daughter's sensitivities. Perhaps she should have spent more time with her children when they were small. She might have learned, then, to love them properly. Instead, adopting the ways of other well-off young mothers of her time, she handed them over to a nanny, exclaiming that she had simply no idea how to manage them. Deirdre wondered if she had ever secretly acknowledged her mistake and regretted it.

Gabriel had found the harp, abandoned in a corner. The strings drooped, broken and twisted. She fingered them gently, thinking of Miss Cassia; and they swung beneath her touch, as dusty and brittle as a long-ago love affair.

'Do look at these,' said Deirdre.

She had closed the hatbox and, from the trunk labelled 'Enid', she began to lift dress after elegant dress, each one ruler-straight and slender, with girdles round the hips, and Vs down the backs. They were dresses for dancing and flirting in the brave new world of the 1920s when Enid was just married, when hems were slashed and women's legs shown for the first time. Their silks and *crêpe de Chines* still shimmered and rustled after years of concealment.

Beneath the dresses were underclothes. Instead of the stays and flounced petticoats worn by the Floods, Enid had had wispy chemises and cobweb camiknickers.

113

'There was one advantage in Father's owning a department store,' observed Deirdre. 'Mother got the pick of the stock. She loved clothes.'

Gabriel carried one of Enid's chemises to the window to study it more closely. But it hardly needed examining. It was just a brief silk tunic, with inset bands of embroidered net and narrow shoulder-straps. Compared with Iona's and Lettice's things it seemed absurdly, frivolously scanty, as if it came from a different world.

'What did your mother do in the 1920s?' Gabriel asked.

'Enjoyed herself; went to parties; danced the Charleston – you know.' Feeling rather dashing for a woman in her sixties, Deirdre kicked her legs sideways. 'And she had Philip in 1919 and me in 1924. I believe I was a bit of a mistake. It was clever just to have one child, after those huge Victorian families. Friends told her that she'd let the side down. She should have read *Married Love*, which was a notorious book by Marie Stopes, the first guide to contraception – very revolutionary. One was supposed to cover it in brown paper, in case the maids saw it and got ideas.'

And Deirdre went on emptying the trunk, bringing out silk jerseys, still fragrant with Chanel perfume; and a jaunty striped swimsuit with a buckled belt.

Gabriel stood by the rain-spattered window, frowning at Enid's chemise. Previously the attic had seemed haunted by the romantic, tragic days of Iona and Lettice, when banners were sewn secretly and Miss Johnson hid treasonable papers under a mattress. Enid Ashwell's clothes signalled a startling change of mood; even, it seemed to Gabriel, a devaluation of ideals. Did emancipation merely mean short skirts and flimsy chemises? Had Ida Johnson gone to prison and Iona died so that Enid could dance the Charleston?

'Weren't women campaigning for things any longer?' she asked.

'Oh, God!' Deirdre exclaimed. 'I suppose that's the sort of thing your mother says nowadays.'

'It's nothing to do with Sarah,' Gabriel answered stiffly. 'I was thinking about the suffragettes, and how they didn't seem to connect with the 1920s. That's all.'

But they did, thought Deirdre, remembering her mother's connection with the ex-suffragette, Ruth Cropper. Oh, how she had disliked those Croppers, who had wormed their way into Springfield! Ruth, and her daughter Anne. She had dragged Anne's name into the conversation downstairs to show her up for the servant she should have been, answering doorbells for the Ashwells. Not that Gabriel would have got the point. She wouldn't know anything about the Croppers – or would she? Deirdre didn't want to ask.

The old bitterness was welling up.

~

In her early married days Enid threw herself into the pleasures of modern life. She could afford them; she loved them. She played jazz records loudly on a wind-up gramophone; she drank cocktails; she charged about in an open-topped car; she wore the short, straight dresses which, as if to disguise the loss of a generation of men, tried to turn girls into boys. She seemed a model mother to her snobbish, conventional little daughter.

But besides the pleasure-loving side of her nature there was the idealism which had responded to the suffragettes, waiting to be recovered.

One day, when she was driving Deirdre to a children's party, a car tyre punctured on Wortley Hill. She gave a passing boy threepence to fetch help from a garage; and she and Deirdre stood on the pavement, waiting.

A poor woman, in ragged clothes, tottered past. Through the barrier of her Chanel, Enid smelled poverty and remembered

115

the workroom at Madam Logan's. A little girl crept up silently, to stare. Her running nose and torn pinafore contrasted with Deirdre's shining curls and organdie party frock.

Enid felt as if she was waking from a long sleep. She looked round at the dark streets, the grim houses. Occasionally, when one of her mother's workers was ill, she had visited such homes. In her ignorance, she had imagined everyone's lives had been revolutionized, like hers. No – that wasn't true. She hadn't imagined. She had simply not noticed. And the lives of the poor hadn't changed. She felt overwhelmed with guilt.

From that day, with typical fervour, she threw herself into voluntary social work. There was a desperate need for it. Soon, Mrs George Ashwell's name appeared on half the Baby Clinic rotas and Childcare Committee lists for Wortley Hill. The most valuable source of information in this new work, she discovered, was a little greengrocer's shop, kept by a woman called Ruth Cropper.

Things had gone well for Ruth. Soon after she acquired her shop, Jack's sister Dora acquired a husband. He was a widower with a weak heart, who could be coddled by the Cropper family in Jack's absence. When Jack left the army, the creaking double bed was occupied by Dora and her Edwin. Jack had no option but to move in with Ruth.

He took over the marketing and deliveries while Ruth ran the shop. In 1921, Anne was born. Having a daughter filled Ruth with happiness – that, and the respect she'd earned on Wortley Hill. People turned to her for all sorts of help and advice.

In her new role as voluntary social worker, Enid began visiting the greengrocery. At first she just wanted to hear about the neighbourhood, but soon she and Ruth had become firm friends.

~

With some hesitation, Deirdre gave Gabriel this general outline. She said very little about the Croppers, preferring to concentrate on Enid.

'Child though I was, I was livid at the way Mother

altered,' she finished. 'I liked her buying pretty clothes and going to parties. Suddenly, she was disappearing nearly every day. "To help poor children," she said. I thought other people should look after them. I wanted her at home. I honestly believe it scarred my childhood.' She frowned. 'I felt – as I have done for most of my life – that a woman's place is in the home.'

'Some women had to work,' Gabriel protested. 'There was Dorothy Flood. I came to see her clothes.'

And she turned resolutely to Dorothy's trunk. She had, after all, come for the sake of Dorothy, not Enid Ashwell, about whom she had now heard quite enough. She couldn't warm to Francis's aunt, in spite of her elegant blue-grey suede.

She lifted the lid, and broad zebra stripes dazzled up from a folded suit. Gabriel took it out. The cloth felt shoddy. The jacket sagged apart between clumsily positioned buttons.

Deirdre looked up and laughed.

'Poor old Dorothy! She really was a bit of a joke.'

Those Klavir sensibilities! Deirdre had genuinely forgotten that, in Gabriel, they were mingled with Flood heredity – until she saw Gabriel's eyes flash.

'What was wrong with Dorothy?'

'Nothing. Don't be so touchy. She was very – ' Deirdre fumbled hopelessly for an adjective.

But Gabriel was stung to fury.

'You said she was a joke.'

'Her clothes were.' Deirdre seized the striped suit and flourished it. 'You must see that.'

'So you laughed at her.'

And Gabriel had a searing vision of Dorothy with her scraped-back hair and hen's legs, the butt of elegant Enid and Deirdre.

'Well, one was almost bound to.'

'Women shouldn't sneer at other women.'

The words came straight from Warburton Street, and for once they expressed exactly what Gabriel thought.

'Goodness!' cried Deirdre, exasperated by the whole train of events since she unwisely came up to the attic. 'I loathe that feminist cant.'

Gabriel shut the trunk and walked out of the room.

⇒ 22 ⇐

Seething with rage, Gabriel forgot about buses and rushed down Wortley Hill in the rain. How dared Deirdre Russell speak so slightingly of Dorothy? Who did she think she was, for God's sake? Poor Dorothy!

But it was just as she'd thought. A doom hung over the women of the Flood family. They were destined to suffer; to be despised and misunderstood. Maybe at this very moment she was passing the spot where Iona had been killed. So probable did it seem that Gabriel paused in her headlong flight and looked carefully at the wet road with its white markings and traffic bollards, almost expecting to see a lingering stain of blood.

The next minute she was ready to smile at her own fantasy. She felt calmer about Deirdre too. Some people were born snobs and you just had to put up with it.

I daresay I over-reacted. I usually do, thought Gabriel.

Gloom came hovering back, thickening as she imagined what Deirdre might say to Francis, when he got home.

'That Klavir girl. What a temper! She's really weird.'

'You're telling me,' Francis would agree.

No, he wouldn't.

But why did he let himself be shoved off to the library, if he knew I was coming, Gabriel wondered crossly. That's what's really bugging me, as well as the sneer about Dorothy. All the time I was at Springfield I was longing for him to come in – and he didn't.

She sighed. She was going to be disappointed; just like Miss Cassia, and Dorothy.

She remembered some of the conversations she'd heard in Warburton Street; her mother describing the stresses of marriage in her half laughing, half bewildered way; the other women listening sympathetically; a warm fire; coffee mugs, or perhaps a bottle of wine; and Gabriel herself in the background, torn in two, not knowing which side she was on.

'It was heartbreak with Paul,' Sarah lamented; and then smiled gratefully at Josie and the others for seeing her through.

But Gabriel had flung out of the room, twitching with irritation, wanting to defend her – probably indefensible – father, loving yet hating Sarah at the same time.

The rain sluiced down over her umbrella; and, on impulse, she turned into a little sandwich bar. She could have something to eat there and it would save her cooking when she got back to Marlborough Street.

She took a toasted sandwich to a table by the window and looked out at the raindrops slanting past the street-lights. Of course it was possible that his Aunt Deirdre got up Francis's nose too; that he'd been escaping her, not Gabriel. In which case . . . Gabriel relaxed and allowed herself to picture his soft fair hair and his grey eyes.

Suppose he stopped for a sandwich on the way home

as well? Suppose he came into this very sandwich bar and stood by the counter in his long, loose coat? And then turned and saw her? She glanced out of the window, almost expecting him; and a car that was disconcertingly like his wove past, through the traffic and out of sight.

Oh, well.

It was better to think about Dorothy. A lot of questions remained about her, and Gabriel longed for answers. How had she got on with Lettice when they settled down together, after Rufus died and Phyllis went to America? What was the story of Lettice's little girl, who must – presumably – have been Sarah's mother, and Gabriel's unknown grandmother? How had the three of them lived while Enid Ashwell was dancing the Charleston at Springfield and organizing babycare on Wortley Hill?

Shall I go to Dorothy's again next Sunday, Gabriel wondered. I don't want to be a nuisance to her, and she may just fall asleep. She's terribly old. But I liked her and it's nice to have something to think about, now that my work's so hopeless.

Which was a damaging reminder of other things she tried to forget. There was Fashion-Aid. She'd meant to do so much, and it was even more important now she knew that Amy Whittingham had been Iona's friend – but she felt helpless. There was the fact that she hadn't been to a single class at the Poly since the depression hit her. But she couldn't face them – not when she had that reputation for brilliance to live up to.

Doom, doom, doom! How awful everything was!

Number 1 Marlborough Street was in darkness. Neither Lucy nor Elizabeth was at home. Thankfully, Gabriel closed the door. She was in the mood for solitude – unless, of course, Francis came round.

The telephone rang. Gabriel shot across the hall and picked up the receiver.

'Is that Elizabeth Morley?' asked a voice – a woman's voice, quiet and precise.

'I'm afraid she's out. Can I take a message?'

'It's not vital. It's just that I sent her a letter about Amy Whittingham, and the Crosthwaite suffragettes. She said she wanted to do a magazine article about them. I wondered how she was getting on. You see, I'd like to buy the magazine, when it comes out – '

'Oh!' interrupted Gabriel. 'Excuse me, but are you Anne Cropper?'

For things were suddenly clicking together. Anne Cropper, who had written to Elizabeth and knew about Iona Flood; Anne Cropper, whom Deirdre Russell had mentioned – they were the same person and identical with the woman on the phone. Who might, quite possibly, be a source of information about the family.

'Yes, I'm Anne Cropper,' the voice was saying.

'Someone was speaking about you only this afternoon,' said Gabriel.

'Do you mean Elizabeth Morley?'

'No, it was Deirdre Russell. Mrs Russell,' Gabriel corrected, thinking the formal name sounded more polite.

There was dead silence at the other end of the line.

'Hello,' said Gabriel.

'Oh, I'm sorry.' The voice jerked back into life. 'Deirdre Russell, you said? Where was this?'

'I was at Springfield. I think she said you knew it – or you'd been there – or something.'

'Yes.'

'You see, my family lived at Springfield. Well, I did myself once, but that's not the point. I mean, some of

121

them were there before the Ashwells. I just wondered if you'd known any of them, by any chance? There was my great-grandmother, Lettice Orme, and my great-great-aunt, Dorothy Flood.'

'I knew Dorothy quite well at one time. Lettice, a little. And Geraldine, of course.'

'Geraldine?'

My grandmother, thought Gabriel. Her nerves tensed with excitement at the prospect of hearing more.

'Yes. We were friends.'

'If it wouldn't be too much trouble,' Gabriel said, 'I wish you'd tell me a bit about them.'

⇛ 23 ⇚

'I'll have to think about it,' Anne Cropper said. 'But I'll write – and very soon, I promise you.'

She put the telephone down and remained seated at her desk, pondering.

Since she had retired she had moved a little way out of Crosthwaite. She lived on the edge of a country village, in a small, modern house; neat, modestly furnished, inconspicuous. She knew herself to be neat and inconspicuous too. She had inherited Jack's slightness and pale sandy colouring, not Ruth's dark prettiness. In features she resembled her Aunt Lily, Jack's sister, though she hadn't Lily's beady eyes and shrill voice. Her face was calm and quiet, for self-control was a long established habit. She looked what she was – a kindly, retired doctor, ready to offer help when it was needed and fade into the background when it wasn't. She was unmarried with few close friends; not – most people thought – an especially interesting woman.

Yet, at the heart of her life was a secret; an old love, treasured still, though never talked about. That was why she had said she would write to the girl who answered the telephone; Gabriel Klavir, Geraldine Orme's granddaughter. The note of passionate enquiry in Gabriel's voice had warned her to be careful. If she had let Gabriel question her, then and there, her secret might inadvertently have slipped out; for, in describing Dorothy and Geraldine, she would have to mention Enid. She couldn't avoid it.

This, Anne reflected, was the result of writing down her recollections of her mother, Ruth Cropper, for the other girl. One thing led to another. Ruth was the starting point, too, in the story of Anne's relationship with Enid Ashwell.

She sat motionlessly at her desk, thinking back over sixty years to a little greengrocer's shop on Wortley Hill.

~

It was not always easy being the adored only daughter of a clever woman, oppressed by poverty. Ruth had a struggle to keep the shop going and support four sons as well as Anne. By the time Anne was seven, Jack had slipped into illness and early death. Ruth managed the shop, the household and half Wortley Hill.

Her punishing life fuelled her ambition for Anne. Anne must not live as she did, working from dawn till late at night. 'Things must be different for you,' she told Anne. She never used endearments, rarely kissed Anne: but love, half hopeful, half desperate, burned in her eyes when she spoke.

Underlying her ambition was her bitter disappointment over the Women's Movement. Women had achieved so little with their votes. Far from bringing about a social revolution, the first women MPs acquiesced in things as they were. The only movement was of hope, trickling away.

Ruth was a true feminist. She believed in freedom and equality for women. But there no longer seemed to be any group to share her aspirations. She stood alone, dispensing advice and medicine from behind her battered counter. In her suffragette days, the sharing of ideals and actions made life thrilling. Deprived of this outlet, everything seemed flat. Yet what cause was there now to unite women? She could see nothing.

There was still, of course, the help women gave each other. From the little houses in the dark streets they turned spontaneously to one another, or turned to Ruth as one of themselves; and Wortley Hill was favourite territory for amateur do-gooders, middle-class ladies mainly, who, in shapeless coats and unbecoming hats, ran church-hall clinics, weighed babies and proffered advice on vaccinations, spectacles and tonsils. Worthy though they were, they hardly brightened the cheerless streets where unemployed men clustered listlessly. They waved no rallying flag.

Into this, in the year 1930, came Enid Ashwell.

Returning from school with her satchel of books, nine-year-old Anne paused, amazed, to sniff a luxurious perfume floating over the cabbage and turnip smells of the shop.

'Lady talking to Ma,' explained Anne's eldest brother, Sidney, from behind the counter.

Anne went through to the living-room, and saw Enid – glossy-haired, beautifully dressed, with a rope of pearls and pink varnished fingernails. It was love at first sight.

Enid was looking in perplexity at Ruth.

'I'm sure I've seen you, long ago. I know! You were a suffragette. I heard you speaking from a soapbox.'

'Do you really remember?' Ruth was surprised and greatly touched.

'Of course. I was carried away.'

It was almost unfair, Anne thought afterwards. Enid floated

124

onto Wortley Hill like a creature from a fairy-tale. Where other voluntary workers were drab or bossy, she was charming and elegant. She soon became flatteringly dependent on Ruth.

'Goodness me, I know what you have to put up with,' she would exclaim. 'I worked in a shop myself – and lived above it. It was a hatshop.'

Her little, tilted, velvet hats seemed perfection to Anne.

Previously, everything had been serious. From before she started school, Anne had been told by Ruth that she could only win freedom by working hard; so, afraid of disappointing her mother, Anne worked feverishly. She read everything she could find, from Sunday School prize-books to the newspapers the potatoes were wrapped in. At eleven, she won a free place at Crosthwaite Girls' High School; and, in gratitude for all Ruth did, the neighbours had a whip-round, and provided the money for Anne's uniform and books. Anne worked even harder, topping every examination list.

'You must go to university, and then be a teacher,' the headmistress said.

Anne shook her head. She was going to be a doctor. That was the profession Ruth had longed for; that Amy Whittingham had practised. Anne knew she must achieve it. The headmistress looked doubtful.

'Medicine's a difficult career for a girl.'

Anne buried herself in science books. 'Swot!' the other girls taunted. She hardly noticed them. From the moment when she smelled the perfume in the shop, life had been shot through with ecstasy. The only person who mattered – apart from her mother – was Enid.

She worshipped at a distance, seeing little of Enid, just happy to know she existed. It was a time when everyone was crazy about the cinema, and other girls had similar feelings about film stars. But they talked of their idols. Anne was silent.

One summer afternoon in 1937 Anne flew home winged with happiness. She had scored 100 per cent in her chemistry exam! The chemistry mistress said nobody had ever done it before. If only Mrs Ashwell would call. Then perhaps her mother would tell her of the success and Mrs Ashwell would smile.

It suddenly occurred to Anne that she hadn't seen Mrs Ashwell for weeks.

The little shop felt stuffy. Sidney was behind the counter. Two other brothers, unemployed like many men on Wortley Hill, were lounging in the cramped living-room. Ruth sat by the window, adding up her accounts.

'Mother,' said Anne, 'has something happened to Mrs Ashwell?'

'Didn't I tell you?' Ruth looked up. 'Her husband's been killed in a motor accident.'

'Oh – poor Mrs Ashwell.'

Anne's eyes filled with tears.

'She came round – look, Anne, we'll talk about it this evening. I must straighten these figures.'

'I got full marks for my chemistry exam,' said Anne; and wished she hadn't when she saw the expressions on her brothers' faces. They were jealous of her. Bert stuck out a boot to trip her as she squeezed past to her tiny room under the stairs.

Because of her brothers, she and Ruth went outside to talk. They walked through the grimy streets and up the hill.

'Yes,' said Ruth. 'Mrs Ashwell came round. She'd a plan she wanted to talk over.'

'How was she?' asked Anne.

'Not bad. She was wearing black. She didn't weep, any more than I did when Jack died.'

George Ashwell, Ruth guessed, had been more a comfortable base for Enid than a lover. She'd never felt family life occupied much of Enid's attention. The children seemed to be left to nannies and then bundled off to boarding-school. Nice, of course, thought Ruth wryly, not to have them under your feet, as Bert and Len – poor jobless lads – were constantly under hers. That was why Mrs Ashwell's proposal was so tempting.

'Mrs Ashwell's wondering whether to take over running that big shop,' she said.

'Oh, no!' cried Anne; for if Enid did that, she would never see her again. She pictured the swinging glass doors of Ashwells, and knew she would never have the courage to go inside.

'Why shouldn't she take it on?' Ruth demanded. 'It may be unusual, but women ought to have the independence to do what they like. It's what I want for you.'

'Yes – but – ' Mrs Ashwell was different. She mustn't abandon Wortley Hill.

'I think she's fed up with visiting here,' said Ruth. 'She wants something a bit meatier than helping out on Wortley Hill. She was telling me the things she'd do with her shop, the beautiful clothes she'd buy. She seemed set on it.'

Despair clutched Anne. She couldn't speak.

'She made a suggestion,' Ruth went on. 'I've not said anything to the lads. I thought I'd tell you first.'

'What?' cried Anne. Something in Ruth's tone made her hopes soar.

'She'll be working long hours. She won't have time for running her home. She asked if I'd go to Springfield as her housekeeper – to live. I could take you.'

Anne couldn't speak. The pavement swung dizzily under her feet.

'I could give up my place at the shop to Bert and Len. They'll be off the dole then, and it'll take two of them to do what I do. And you'd have peace to study there, Anne. I suppose I could keep house. It would be a bit like living with Amy all those years ago.'

'Oh, Mother!'

Tears of joy, such as she'd never felt before, welled in Anne's eyes.

～

That was Anne's secret – her love for Enid Ashwell.

Had they met in the 1980s instead of the 1930s things might have been different. Nowadays, thought Anne, there was openness about women's love for each other, and support in women's groups for lovers. They wrote for magazines and appeared on television. 'The woman I love,' they said frankly.

Yet – would I have wanted it, Anne asked herself.

What she had felt for Enid was an adoring reverence which could never have been made public. To catch a trace of Enid's scent, to hear her voice, to touch the flowers she had picked, was bliss enough. I was passive, thought Anne; undemanding – things women aren't supposed to be. But I couldn't make demands on Enid.

More and more, in her retirement, her mind drifted back to the past. She had had other friendships since then, even other faint, wavering loves. But there had been no one like Enid.

'That letter to Gabriel Klavir,' she told herself; 'you'd better start it.'

But still she sat at her desk and dreamed of a woman long dead, with auburn hair and amber eyes, and scented dresses of rustling green silk.

≫ *24* ≪

Elizabeth came into the kitchen on Wednesday evening and found Lucy with her elbows on the table, staring at the diary in her Filofax.

'Crunch day on Saturday.'

'Crunch day?'

'When I've got to confirm my provisional booking on the hall.'

'Oh.' Here we go again, thought Elizabeth.

'I s'ppose Fashion-Aid's off. I wish it wasn't. It was such a good idea.'

'Blame Gabriel. She volunteered.'

'I know. But what's happened isn't her fault. She's got this creative block. That's why she's ducking out.'

'We'd better duck out too.'

'But that hospital, Liz!'

And Lucy raised anguished eyes to the photo on the cork board, half hidden now – symbolically? – by notices and invitations which had arrived more recently, but still hopefully presenting its shattered walls and frightened faces for assistance.

'I feel such a failure,' said Lucy. 'We got the letter ages ago and we've not done a thing except book a hall we probably won't need. Oh, I know there'll be relief agencies and all that; but we're supposed to be into women's causes and we might as well be completely callous and heartless, the amount we've done. They'll think we don't care; that we can't identify with problems when they're hundreds of miles away.'

'OK,' said Elizabeth. 'You don't have to shout. You'd better go and talk to Gabriel again. See if you can stir her up.'

'If I can't, could we got hold of some other fashion students?'

'Like how?'

'I dunno. Go and see them; talk to them.'

'Have you ever been in the poly?' asked Elizabeth.

'No, but – '

'Long glass passages, concrete staircases, totally impersonal, people dashing about like crazy. How'd you start?'

'Well, what do *you* suggest then?' cried Lucy, exasperated.

'Wait till my article comes out in *Cross-Questioning*.'

Elizabeth's voice was warm with anticipation. 'That'll be Friday. Then use the hall for a meeting. Tell people what happened to Amy Whittingham and how her hospital needs money.'

'Would they go to a meeting like that?'

The doubtful query needled Elizabeth.

'Would they go to a fashion show?' she countered.

'It's more likely.'

'Oh, thanks very much. That's really nice of you.'

'Sorry! Sorry! I didn't mean it, Liz. It's fifth week.' Which was the point in the term when people were traditionally edgy.

Elizabeth ran the sink tap and began scraping carrots.

'Go and talk to Gabriel, like I said. Twist *her* arm for a change.'

'Is she in? OK, I'll try.'

Gabriel was standing by her drawing-board, her black jersey stark against the coloured walls. Her black hair was fastened up with a silver comb. She looked remote, absorbed; but – she was drawing.

'Oh!' exclaimed Lucy in relief, seeing Fashion-Aid a reality once more. 'Are you designing?'

'No.'

Yet on the paper she had sketched a figure with bobbed hair and an odd, zebra-striped suit. She scored in pleats and erased them.

'Then what *are* you doing?' asked Lucy, mystified.

'Thinking about my great-great-aunt.'

Lucy's patience, fragile that evening, snapped again.

'Honestly, Gabriel, couldn't you be a bit more helpful? We're supposed to say by Saturday if we want the hall for Fashion-Aid. I thought it was something you cared about. I mean, if you can't do it yourself, you might find some other people at the poly.'

'I've stopped going.'

'What? Completely?'

'Yeah.'

Gabriel frowned, concentrating on striped sleeves.

'So Fashion-Aid's off.'

'I keep telling you, don't I?'

'Oh – !' Lucy vented her feelings with such a shriek of frustration that Gabriel was roused to make some response.

'Look, Lucy, I've got other things on my mind. It's no good trying to squeeze out some new designs right now. It just doesn't work. I'm sorry, but there it is. You're the one who feels so strongly. Can't you do something yourself?'

'Looks like I'll have to. Yes!'

The idea she'd had on Sunday, and subsequently forgotten, flashed back into her mind. Why hadn't she followed it through? Because the doorbell had rung. Because – Suddenly, a plan was forming, at lightning speed.

'Will you be seeing Francis in the next day or two?'

She realized immediately, from Gabriel's face, that that had been a mistake.

'Just a vague idea,' she went on quickly, 'but I might ring him –'

'Do you mind? I'm trying to work,' said Gabriel, in a stiff, tight voice.

'Sorry.'

Rebuffed, but with the plan bubbling in her mind, Lucy closed the door.

Gabriel put down the pencil, her hand shaking. Why had Lucy mentioned Francis? The thought of him made her tense with misery; because here it was, Wednesday evening, and she hadn't seen or heard from him since

Sunday's disastrous pub visit. She'd spent the last two days in Crosthwaite Library, unwilling to risk Springfield in case Deirdre Russell was there again, and hoping Francis would come in. Or, if not, call round at Marlborough Street. But he hadn't. As far as he was concerned, she might as well not exist. Which was why she'd reacted so badly to Lucy's harmless question.

So – forget him. Think about other things.

Could zebra stripes ever be flattering? That was the puzzle she'd set herself, after seeing Dorothy's suit in the attic. She had spent the last two days studying histories of fashion, trying to work out a way by which Dorothy could have made herself so attractive that the young men for whom she'd bought cigarettes would have turned from their official girlfriends, exclaiming, in proper twenties' language – 'Dorothy, you look stunning! How about a spot of dancing, or the flicks?'

Gabriel felt she needed to protect Dorothy. She'd lain awake at night trying to organize Dorothy's past life into happiness. She was family and the Floods had had more than their fair share of tragedy.

Abruptly, Gabriel tore her sketch of Dorothy off the drawing-block and began another. She outlined a slender young girl, ethereal, graceful; poor Geraldine – Lettice's daughter, Dorothy's niece, Gabriel's grandmother. That morning, Anne Cropper's letter had come, with Geraldine's story. Gabriel went over it to herself as she drew.

Lettice and Dorothy, waifs in an unfriendly world, set up house together in a quiet part of Crosthwaite. Dorothy taught in a second-rate girls' private school which limped along in the shadow of the Girls' High School. Lettice did nothing. She could have married again if she'd not had such a dislike of sex. Geoffrey Miles, a middle-aged solicitor, often visited the house but Lettice never encouraged him. Dorothy remembered how he liked his tea and laughed hopefully at his jokes – which weren't very funny – but he had eyes only for Lettice.

It was a restricted, joyless household for a girl to be brought up in, but Geraldine had her own way of escape. She lived in her imagination, acting out dramas which were far removed from her home or her school – the one where Dorothy toiled. Often her fantasies were based on legends of her two missing aunts. She engaged in secret adventures with Aunt Iona, and fled to new worlds with Aunt Phyllis. That Iona and Phyllis were disapproved of, added to their attraction.

'Will Geraldine follow in your sister Phyllis's footsteps?' Geoffrey Miles once asked.

Lettice laughed deprecatingly.

'Oh, Geraldine isn't clever. She's like me. And girls don't do themselves any good by being bluestockings.'

Lettice's views had become just the same as her mother's, and Geraldine questioned them to herself. Wasn't Phyllis's life preferable to Lettice's?

'Iona and Phyllis were always wilful,' Dorothy remarked another time. As a teacher, she liked good, obedient girls.

'They went their own way. So unfortunate!' sighed Lettice.

'So foolish,' corrected Dorothy.

They grieved over the sale of Springfield to the Ashwells. In their eyes, it demeaned the house to be connected with a shop – even the best shop in Crosthwaite.

'Ashwells' clothes are the height of fashion,' people sometimes said.

Lettice wrinkled her nose delicately.

'Modern fashions look hideous,' she murmured. Unlike Dorothy, she still pinned up her hair and wore ankle-length skirts.

'One thing's certain,' said Dorothy crossly. 'The Ashwells will have thrown out all the dear old things Phyllis so stupidly left in the attic.'

'Don't mention the attic,' Lettice begged, shuddering.

She couldn't bear Wortley Hill to be mentioned either, because of Iona; and she never went anywhere near Springfield.

One hot July day in 1938, Geraldine came downstairs to find a letter from Phyllis awaiting her. She read it, conscious of Lettice's and Dorothy's watching eyes.

'There!' she cried. 'Aunt Phyllis is on my side.' And she read from the letter. '"If you really want to be an actress, Geraldine, go ahead and try it. Find out about drama schools and how to audition for them. I wish you the best of luck."'

'Oh!' Lettice exclaimed. 'Phyllis would!'

'She always thought girls should have careers,' grunted Dorothy sourly.

'Not acting!'

'What else can I do?' Geraldine demanded. 'You sent me to Aunt Dorothy's idiotic school where the lessons are so bad I didn't get my School Certificate. If I don't act, I'll have to scrub floors.'

'You can't go away to drama school. There's going to be another war. I want you at home,' quavered Lettice.

'And I want to act.'

'It's no use thinking about what you want. You don't get it,' said Dorothy.

Geraldine flew angrily upstairs. It would serve them right if she ran off to America, like Phyllis, and got herself a film contract in Hollywood. She was sure she could.

She examined her reflection in the mirror. She had inherited Rufus's dark eyes with Lettice's pale hair – a fascinating combination, she considered. Her mouth was delicate, her skin flawless, her figure appealingly fragile. Wonderful parts must

134

be waiting for girls like her. She saw herself gliding across a cinema screen, hands outstretched to some handsome lover.

Instead, she was going out that evening with Bunny Tarrant.

Bunny! He had bulging eyes and protruding teeth – from which his nickname derived. His hands were clammy. He drove a small car with maddening caution. Still, he was a boyfriend. He would do till someone better came along; which, Geraldine hoped, wouldn't be too long.

And he was desperately in love with her!

'I say!' exclaimed Bunny, giggly with cider cup; 'see that chap over there? He's an actor.'

Bunny had, unexpectedly, taken Geraldine to a party. The hosts were his second cousins – she couldn't imagine any other reason for their inviting him. He had glued himself to her side, but this was the first interesting thing he'd said.

'Which chap?'

'Him.'

It was the tall, slim, golden-haired boy she'd been watching all evening. Instead of a tie, he wore a crimson silk cravat inside his shirt.

'Who is he?'

'Philip Ashwell. Connected with the shop – you know.'

Bunny hiccupped.

'Then he comes from Springfield, where my mother used to live. I'd like,' said Geraldine boldly, 'to meet him.'

'Right-oh! I'll tell Cousin Arnold.'

As easily as that, she found herself face to face with Philip.

It was as if her aunts, with their ideals of women's emancipation, had never existed. Geraldine succumbed utterly to Philip, as Lettice had to Rufus.

In his summer vacation from the Academy of Dramatic Art, Philip was at a loose end. Hoped-for parts in seaside repertory had fallen through. Fear of war was diminishing theatre audiences. Managers were cancelling productions, and Philip, his allowance overspent, sulked at home.

Meeting the pretty girl, with the fragile figure and adoring eyes, was the tonic he needed. She wanted to go on the stage, she told him, breathless for his approval. Could he give her any help? It occurred to him that coaching her could be a pleasant way of getting through the summer. He discovered she had some talent. He enjoyed himself.

Dorothy fumed enviously as Geoffrey Miles and Bunny Tarrant rang the doorbell constantly, enquiring for Lettice and Geraldine. There was some hope for Geoffrey. He had devised a plan for emigrating to Canada if war broke out, taking Lettice with him. Lettice, petrified of bombs, was considering it. There was no hope for Bunny.

Philip invited Geraldine to Springfield, which was where Anne Cropper first met her. It appeared that Anne's mother had known Aunt Iona. Geraldine wasn't interested in Mrs Cropper, or her reminiscences. Philip, his hand through her arm, had told her she would be perfect as Ophelia.

~

'My earliest memory of Geraldine,' Anne Cropper wrote in her letter to Gabriel, 'is of her listening, spellbound, as Philip said she should play Ophelia.'

Gabriel looked at the picture on her wall, of the drowned girl with the garland of flowers; and wondered if an aura of doom was already hanging over Geraldine.

⇛ 26 ⇚

Anne hardly noticed Geraldine coming and going with Philip that summer. She had completed the first year of her medical course and was spending the vacation studying in a white-walled bedroom at Springfield which was unbelievably comfortable and peaceful after her old cranny under the stairs. The only sound to draw her from her books was Enid returning from Crosthwaite. When she heard the car, Anne would rush to the window and peep out as Enid emerged, pulling off her hat so that the wind ruffled her bright hair. Chanel drifted upwards. Jaunty footsteps rang on the staircase. Anne hugged herself in anticipation of dinner with Enid.

'Do Mrs Cropper and Anne *have* to dine with us?' Deirdre grumbled. 'Aren't they servants?'

'Don't be such a snob,' Enid retorted. 'Mrs Cropper's my friend.'

'From that poky shop!'

'I run a shop too.'

'I wish you didn't. But Ashwells is different.'

And, when Enid refused to acknowledge the difference, Deirdre began going to visit friends as often as possible. She avoided dinner at Springfield and counted the days till she went back to boarding-school.

Geraldine didn't count the days; and the discovery that Philip was about to return to the Academy in London was like a dagger in her heart.

'You can't go!'

He laughed, flattered. But of course he was going; and suddenly the enchanted summer was at an end. For six timeless weeks they had been inseparable. They had rehearsed *Romeo and Juliet* in the attic – Philip seriously, Geraldine in a passion of love. He had sung and recited poetry to her. He had driven her over the moors in Enid's car; and, when he wasn't talking, he sometimes pulled up and kissed her. But she was no more than a passing distraction. He had proper girlfriends in London.

Until, one day before Christmas 1938, Anne rang Lettice's doorbell, she had had no idea that Geraldine might have suffered over Philip's departure. She scarcely thought of Geraldine at all. She had come, rather shyly, on an errand from her mother.

A maid showed her into a little sitting-room, crowded with Edwardian *bric-a-brac*. On either side of the fire sat Dorothy

137

Flood, plain and bespectacled; and Lettice Orme, languid and fadingly pretty, with a gauze scarf round her shoulders. It was Geraldine who leaped up to meet her, crying 'Anne!' with hopeful surprise; but for a moment Anne didn't recognize her, she looked so thin and wan.

'I've brought something,' Anne began awkwardly. 'Mother found it in the attic at Springfield. She thought you might like it.'

She unfolded a banner, with 'VOTES FOR WOMEN' embroidered in purple and green.

'Iona Flood made it,' she explained. 'It's not finished. There should be an edging of braid. Mother thought that you should have it, since you're her sisters.'

'Poor Iona,' said Lettice. 'But we don't really care to be reminded – '

'It was romantic nonsense,' said Dorothy.

'I've never understood. Iona liked dances, pretty clothes. Why worry about votes?' Lettice murmured.

'Self-indulgence!' snorted Dorothy.

It wasn't, Anne wanted to argue. The banner stood for hope and idealism. Too shy to express her thoughts, she began refolding it, along its worn creases.

'Shall I take it back to Springfield?'

Lettice shrugged.

'Throw it in the dustbin,' advised Dorothy.

Geraldine laid a fragile hand on Anne's sleeve.

'Will you come up to my room?' she whispered.

The bedroom was as charming as muslin frilling and pink ribbon could make it; but Anne could only stare at Geraldine.

'Are you ill?' she asked. 'You look – awful.'

'Don't say that.' Geraldine sprang to the mirror, curling her hair round her fingers. 'I haven't eaten much lately, but – is Philip back?'

'He's not coming home this Christmas.'

If Anne had understood, she wouldn't have spoken so bluntly. Geraldine gazed at her, aghast. Tears filled her eyes.

'Why not?'

'He's got a part in a London Christmas show. Oh – don't cry.'

For Geraldine was sobbing desperately.

'He never answers my letters. I was living for his holiday. Won't he be home at all?'

'I don't think so.'

Deirdre was going to Switzerland with some friends. There would only be Ruth, Anne and Enid at Springfield for Christmas. Suddenly, for Anne, the expected bliss was smudged with guilt. Her beloved would be there; Geraldine's wouldn't.

'I must see him, Anne. I must!'

She raised a ravaged face. Anne took her thin hands.

'His life's in London. Hadn't you better forget him?'

'I can't.'

Anne felt helpless. She put her arm round the quivering body. She spoke, unavailingly, of Geraldine's finding other boyfriends, other interests.

'I've got another boyfriend; Bunny Tarrant. He's an absolute chump. I can't stand him. And I've got a sort of job. I answer the telephone every morning at the Royal Hotel. They say I've got a nice voice. That's Philip's coaching.'

Weeping overcame her as she pronounced his name.

'Then you've got more than a lot of girls,' said Anne gently.

'All except the one thing I want!'

Anne befriended Geraldine through her Christmas holidays. It was the more necessary because Lettice had finally decided to marry Geoffrey and go to Canada with him. Since war seemed inevitable, a husband offered protection; and, at fifty-four, Geoffrey should be less demanding than Rufus.

Dorothy was obstructive over the wedding plans. Geraldine tearfully refused to accompany her mother abroad. Her visits to Springfield gave both relief from the stresses at home, and useful information.

'Bunny,' she said, telephoning him, 'there's a show in London I'd like to see. Would you take me?'

It would be all right, she told Lettice afterwards. An elderly aunt of Bunny's would be able to put them up for the night. Lettice, busy with her own plans, did not demur.

Bunny didn't understand Geraldine's motives until the final curtain fell. He had clapped and chortled through the review, delighted to be with Geraldine, and unaware of the identity of the fair young actor, playing an occasional minor scene. Only when Geraldine said – 'Let's go and meet Philip at the stage door' – did he realize what had been happening. Then it was too late to protest. Seething with jealousy, he followed Geraldine down to a dingy back-street.

She started forward every time the stage door opened. At last the unmistakable gold hair glimmered under the lamp.

'Philip!'

He looked surprised.

'Sylvia?'

'I'm Geraldine – from Crosthwaite.'

'Oh, yes. Enjoy the show?'

His voice was slurred. Bunny, with satisfaction, guessed he'd been drinking in his dressing-room. Geraldine didn't notice. She clung to Philip's arm, and somehow they were in a taxi, with two or three others, heading for a party.

'You on the stage, Sylvia?'

'Geraldine,' she repeated lovingly. 'No. I was too late to audition for drama schools. I'll try next autumn .'

'Bloody places'll be closed down. We'll be fighting.'

He turned his head and kissed the pillarbox lips of a girl who was snuggling beside him. Bunny clutched Geraldine's arm protectively and a shade triumphantly. She shook him off.

'Do you remember doing *Romeo and Juliet* in the attic?'

'Thought it was on a balcony. Hope Wilmington's laid in plenty of drink.'

The party was in a basement. There was loud music on a gramophone and huge nudes on the walls. Someone handed Geraldine a glass.

'Have some jungle juice.'

She gulped. Her head spun but she gulped again. Bunny stuck grimly to her side.

140

'Where's Philip?'

'There.'

He was lolling on a black divan with the girl of the pillarbox lips.

'I must talk to him. Philip!'

Philip poured a drink down his throat, raising his eyebrows above the glass.

'I've come specially to see you. You haven't answered my letters.'

'Never got 'em.'

'You must have done. I wrote dozens.'

'Stop rabbiting on, Sylvia.' He took a glass from his girl-friend's hand, drank, dropped it, and let his own hand settle comfortably under her thigh. 'You're too thin,' he told Geraldine.

Bunny's aunt's maid let them into the house. Mrs Tarrant apologized for having gone to bed with a toothache, they were told. She hoped they had everything they needed.

Bunny led Geraldine to her room, weeping and ill with gin; and she hadn't the will-power to resist him.

'The bounder!' Bunny was muttering as he undid her dress.

Was Bunny being kind? She hardly knew. She let him pull her towards the cold, narrow bed.

≫ 27 ≪

For her second wedding, Lettice wore grey silk and a small hat with a veil. It was a very quiet occasion.

'Once we're settled, you must come and join us,' she said as she kissed Geraldine goodbye. 'Forget this nonsense about going to drama school.'

'You'll like Canada,' promised Geoffrey.

Geraldine didn't believe she'd ever like anything again. She was utterly desolate. In the mornings she could hardly drag herself to the Royal Hotel, and often she let the phone ring without attempting to answer it. The image of Bunny's excited, bulging eyes haunted her; the feel of his hot damp hands fumbling over her breasts and legs; the sensation of being crushed, bruised and humiliated in every inch of her body. She had told him, on the train back to Crosthwaite, that she would never see him again.

Presently, appalling bouts of nausea added to her misery. She had never felt so ill. When, after retching uncontrollably for the fourth morning running, she tottered out of the bathroom, Dorothy was waiting on the landing.

'How long has this been going on?'

'A few days. I must have caught a chill.' And Geraldine wiped her sweating forehead.

'I'll call the doctor,' said Dorothy grimly.

Never for a moment had Geraldine suspected what his diagnosis would be. When he said 'pregnant', she was horrified.

'I can't be.'

'I'm afraid there's very little doubt,' said the doctor, as he departed.

'Well, miss.' Dorothy stood with folded arms, glaring down at Geraldine. 'This is a pretty kettle of fish. What, in heaven's name, have you been doing?'

'I don't know,' Geraldine wept.

'Don't play the innocent. There must have been a man. Was it young Ashwell?'

Geraldine shook her head.

'Bunny Tarrant?'

'I don't know.'

'Really, Geraldine.' Baffled, shattered, more sorry for herself

142

than Geraldine, Dorothy plumped down on the bedside chair. 'Hasn't Lettice spoken to you?'

'What about?'

'Facts of life. Men and women.'

'No. Never.'

'Typical!' snorted Dorothy. 'She fails in her duty and I'm left to pick up the pieces. Stop crying, Geraldine, for pity's sake. I'll do my best to decide what's right, but it won't be easy. And I warn you, I'll not have you trying to get rid of it the way some foolish girls do, wrecking their health in the process.'

'Get rid of what?'

'The baby, of course. Really, Geraldine; are you simple?'

'Can you get rid of babies?'

'There are back-street quacks,' said Dorothy cryptically. 'Funny medicines. It's a crime,' she added, jerking the curtains together and stumping out of the room.

But that was the idea which lingered as Geraldine lay, shivering and distraught, under her muslin coverlet. You could get rid of babies. She couldn't bear to have one, and certainly not Bunny's. Disgusting, wicked Bunny, doing that to her, when she was so upset about Philip. She'd never forgive him. She'd have to get that medicine Dorothy spoke of. Medicine. She remembered Anne Cropper.

She staggered out of bed and found paper and pen.

'Dear Anne,' she wrote. 'I need your help urgently. Please come and see me.'

She addressed the letter to Springfield.

While she waited for Anne's reply, the days crawled. She slept, woke, and was sick. Dorothy, who had told the maid Geraldine had gastric flu, fretted in case her figure betrayed her, before she could be despatched to some suitable home for unmarried mothers. She would bear the child at a distance from Crosthwaite, and surrender it for adoption; and then, Dorothy hoped, they could both forget about it.

'Or you could go to your mother,' Dorothy suggested.

'Not with Geoffrey there.'

143

She woke suddenly, one Saturday afternoon, with a cool hand on her forehead. Anne was bending over her.

'Anne!' Geraldine clutched the coolness with sticky fingers. 'At last!'

'I had to wait till the weekend.' Anne sat down and gently studied Geraldine's face. 'Are you expecting a baby?'

Tears poured over Geraldine's cheeks.

'How did you know?'

'Something about you. Your eyes; your face – '

'Do you think I'm awful?' sobbed Geraldine. 'Aunt Dorothy does. Everyone will.'

'Don't worry about everyone,' said Anne. 'Let's consider you.'

Geraldine's fingers tightened on Anne's hand.

'I don't want the baby. I must get rid of it. Can you help?'

'I'll help, but not with an abortion. That would be wrong,' said Anne.

'Why? It's my body. Can't I do what I like with my body?'

'Not really. The law gives your child the right to be born. And think – it'll be a person. It'll love you.'

'Never! I shan't keep it.'

'You won't marry the father?'

'No.' Geraldine shuddered.

'He's not – Philip?'

'No. Why do you look like that? Are *you* in love with Philip?'

'I was thinking of Mrs Ashwell. She'd mind if Philip was responsible.'

'It's strange,' said Geraldine. 'Not long ago I was obsessed with Philip. Now I can only think of me.'

'Don't worry,' said Anne when she got up to go. 'I'll find a way of helping you. Trust me.'

Her parting smile lulled Geraldine into sleep.

Much later she heard voices downstairs. Cautiously, she sat up. The overpowering nausea had gone. Had Anne's visit chased it away?

Somebody tapped on her door.

'Come in,' she called, expecting Dorothy.

Enid Ashwell, scented, elegant, came over to the bed and kissed her.

'My dear, with your aunt's permission, I'm going to whisk you away to Springfield for a long holiday. Miss Flood's busy with her schoolwork, but we're a household of women, dying to take care of you. I'm going to pack your things and carry you straight off in my car.'

'But,' Geraldine stammered, not understanding, 'I'm expecting a baby. I've got to go to an unmarried mothers' home.'

'We're not going to worry about that. We're going to keep you at Springfield until it's born.'

⇒ 28 ⇐

From the moment when, rescued by Enid, Geraldine stepped down into the Springfield hall and felt the sheltering embrace of its old walls close round her, she began to relax. When she had been with Philip, she had hardly noticed the house. Now she was vividly aware of the warmth and safety it offered.

She loved the sitting-room, with its great arched fireplace for burning logs and roasting chestnuts; the pretty, long-windowed dining-room where ghostly memories of old dinner parties lingered – flowers, laughter and candle-flames gleaming upwards from looking-glass stands; the staircase, bending like a hairpin between panelled walls, climbing to the creaking, sloping landing; the attic stairs, mounting still further, hidden behind one of the many deep-cased landing doors. It was a house of phantoms and secrets, but a happy house too, thought Geraldine; pulling its gables down like a hood and drawing the trees round to protect its inhabitants.

'We're safe here,' said Geraldine to Anne; and Anne, less responsive to beams and panelled walls, but thinking of Enid, replied enthusiastically, 'Yes!'

Nevertheless, Geraldine couldn't forget her worries.

'I can't possibly keep the baby,' she said, gazing at Enid with frightened eyes.

'No, dear; but there are *months* to think about it yet. You can change your mind a hundred times, if you want to.'

There were depths of calm in her voice.

'People will be horribly shocked if I've got a baby, but no wedding ring.'

'The war's going to shake everything up,' Enid answered. 'By the end, there'll be so many widows and fatherless children and heaven knows what, you'll be just one of the throng – an insignificant pebble on the beach.' She laughed, and lit a cigarette. 'And don't tell me men won't be clustering round a pretty girl like you, even if you do have a dear little brat in tow. But of course you can choose adoption. It's your right, and we'll support whatever you do.'

'I'm terrified of the actual birth.'

'Most people survive. Still,' added Enid, 'I'll ask the nurse to soak your hanky in chloroform, so that you can knock yourself out; and if she objects, I'll scrag her!'

'Dear Geraldine, I was simply aghast . . .' wrote Lettice.

'Oh, goodness; it wasn't your fault!' cried Enid. 'Of course, your mother can't judge, from so far away. I'll write and explain, if you like.'

'Look what Mrs Ashwell's given me,' said Geraldine to Ruth Cropper, whom she knew well now, as Enid's housekeeper besides Anne's mother. She displayed a tiny petticoat, inches deep in lace.

'You're lucky,' said Ruth. 'Anne was bundled up in rags. Your baby'll look like a princess.'

146

A baby like a princess. The idea was attractive. Perhaps, perhaps –

'If I keep the baby, I'm afraid nobody'll want to be friends with me,' she confessed to Anne.

'What about us?'

'Yes – but can I stay on here?'

'You can't come back to me with a child,' snapped Dorothy, when Geraldine went to visit her. 'Schoolmistresses need to have a good reputation. They can't be seen pandering to immorality. Besides, babies yell, and I like a good night's sleep.'

'Well of course you can stay at Springfield, you and the baby, as long as you like,' said Enid. 'Ruth and I have been discussing it, and we're agreed that we couldn't bear to lose you. And babies are gorgeous.'

So when, in October 1939, a six-pound daughter with blue eyes and downy hair made an easy entrance into the world, Geraldine knew that she wouldn't have to abandon her.

'Thank heaven for something to celebrate in wartime,' rejoiced Enid, popping a champagne cork.

~

Anne Cropper, writing to Gabriel, had paused at that point in her long letter, and looked at the photograph of Enid which stood on her desk. Though she knew it so well, her gaze still lingered on the thick shingled hair, the lively eyes, the amused mouth, the rope of pearls.

Enid's impromptu rescue of Geraldine always struck her as remarkable. Illegitimacy carried such a stigma in the 1930s. To be known as an unmarried mother often blighted a woman's life. Enid soared above all prejudice with practical kindness, sympathy and common sense.

In the modern world, Anne reflected, Geraldine would have had an abortion. There probably would have been no question about it. And certainly abortions saved a lot of misery. Yet Anne wasn't altogether happy about them. She was glad Geraldine had had her little girl, Sarah.

147

Enid's support had made all the difference; indeed the support of everyone at Springfield. In the words of Deirdre's favourite gibe, it had been, during the war, 'a house of women'. But what, thought Anne, could have been better for Geraldine? Deirdre didn't understand.

Besides Enid, Ruth, Anne in her vacations, Geraldine and Sarah, there was Ethel Pearson, a housemaid from Wortley Hill, who was lame with a bad foot. It was typical of Enid to employ a maid like that, instead of a smart girl who'd impress callers – though it made a bone of contention between Enid and Deirdre, who, for a mother and daughter, never seemed at all close; not like Ruth and Anne were. Fortunately, Deirdre was seldom at Springfield. When she finished at boarding-school, she joined the Services.

Philip never came home. Anne didn't know if this was his own choice. She suspected Enid might have asked him to stay away for a while, for Geraldine's sake. He left the theatre, when war was declared, and joined the Navy.

Looking back, Anne wondered how Enid had coped with everything. Only her tremendous vitality had carried her through. She ran a big department store at a time when few women had business careers; and the stock she kept had to be first class. She came home quite late in the evening – those car wheels on the drive! – but she wanted to hear about, and discuss, all that had been happening at Springfield. She was endlessly supportive to Ruth – still only forty-seven when the war started, but, from her hard life, seeming much older. There was the occasion when she'd forgotten to order the meat, and Enid, just back from work, swept into the kitchen and beat up a superb cheese soufflé. 'A special treat!' she said, laughing. Anne could see her still.

Without any fuss, she soothed and cherished Geraldine. She seemed to know, without being told, that both Geraldine and Anne had missed out on things in childhood. She got them playing games with her round the table after dinner – just simple card games, but it was surprising how much excitement they generated. Fun was something new to the girls. At eighteen, they enjoyed themselves as much as if they'd been eight.

She brought lovely maternity dresses back from Ashwells for Geraldine, and gorgeous baby clothes. Ruth dug out others from the attic; old but still beautiful. The sight of her drawers filling up with such exquisite things reconciled Geraldine to the baby, as much as anything.

In the late stages of Geraldine's pregnancy, they had evacuees from London to accommodate as well. They had been sent north to escape the threatened bombing. Anne could still remember a forlorn straggle of mothers, with frightened toddlers and howling babies, drooping in the hall. Then Enid had sailed in, bringing a rustle of silk and a cloud of perfume, which made the women stare. She'd smiled round, hugged the grubbiest children and ushered them into the dining-room, where a huge teapot steamed and delicious food was laid out. Most of the evacuees hadn't stayed long; but a couple of mothers and toddlers had settled down at Springfield for years.

Enid found a good nurse to look after Geraldine when Sarah was born. Geraldine had the baby at home; most women did in those days. Enid produced champagne and there was quite a party round Geraldine's bed. Even the nurse, who might have disapproved, joined in happily. The baby was passed from hand to hand, snuggled in a shawl Enid had managed to knit in secret; she was a dear little child, Anne remembered.

All Geraldine's old prettiness returned. She'd come to

Springfield painfully thin; anorexic, probably. She hadn't eaten properly for months. Feeling at peace, she soon put on weight, and looked better.

Yes; for all Deirdre's sneers, the 'house of women' had been a wonderful place. There'd never been anywhere like it afterwards. Anne yielded herself again to its spell.

~

It was a bad winter. They were snowed in at Springfield. The hilltop wind blew harshly; snowflakes fell; pipes froze; but Sarah thrived, and Geraldine had never been so happy. Motherhood delighted her.

By early summer, as the Germans overran Europe, Sarah was laughing and kicking in Deirdre's old pram.

'I've never known such a sweet baby,' declared Enid.

She came to Geraldine one day, looking grave. The newspapers listed Bunny Tarrant among the troops killed at Dunkirk. Geraldine felt only relief. Sarah seemed to have nothing to do with Bunny, just as she had nothing to do with far away Lettice, or Dorothy, who occasionally stumped up to Springfield, but never admired the baby. Besides Geraldine, Enid, Ruth and Anne seemed to be Sarah's family.

Not Deirdre. When she was at home Deirdre wasn't unfriendly, but she wasn't exactly friendly either.

'Good deeds boost Mother's ego,' she remarked once. The words sounded light but there was an undercurrent of jealousy.

Luckily, she was seldom there. When Enid, saying – 'Let's discuss holidays' – proposed renting a country cottage, Deirdre said she was holidaying with friends.

The holiday was perfect. The sun shone, everyone lazed, and Sarah turned into a brown-skinned, crawling cherub.

'I've had a nice letter from Philip,' said Enid, basking in a deckchair. 'I told him that you got prettier every day, Geraldine. He says he's looking forward to meeting you again.'

Geraldine gazed at the sapphire sky and let herself anticipate ecstasy. Philip knew about Sarah but he couldn't mind too much.

'Doesn't Mrs Ashwell make holidays lovely?' said Anne, walking beside Geraldine, as she pushed the pram along a bumpy farm-track.

Something in her tone made Geraldine glance round. Anne's face confirmed a truth Geraldine had suspected for a long time.

'You – love Mrs Ashwell, don't you?' she hazarded.

'I think I'd die for her,' said Anne.

Geraldine pondered. She thought of Lettice's tepid affection, which could easily sour into disapproval; of Dorothy's grudging kinship; of Philip's meaningless flirtation, and the terrible night with Bunny. Against them shone the steady beam of Enid's loving-kindness.

'I think I feel the same,' she said.

In late summer the war worsened dramatically. There were widespread German bombing raids. Crosthwaite was suddenly full of sandbags, water-buckets and hoses. Enid instituted a fire-watching rota at Ashwells.

'It would be frightful if the shop was bombed now,' she remarked over supper one evening in October 1940. 'I've had such a stroke of luck! My suppliers have got me a consignment of French silk dresses. Don't ask me how, but they'll cheer my customers wonderfully.'

And then the phone rang.

'Bother!' said Enid, coming back from it. 'My fire-watcher for Ashwells can't manage tonight. His wife's ill. I suppose I'll have to – '

'No,' Anne interrupted. She was temporarily at Springfield, since her London medical school had been blitzed. 'You look tired, Mrs Ashwell.'

'I'm done in. It's murder running a shop in wartime. But how can I get a replacement at such short notice?'

'I'll do it,' Anne volunteered.

Why Geraldine offered to go with her, Anne never knew. Perhaps she just felt like an adventure. Sarah slept angelically and, if she woke, Enid and Ruth could cope. Anne and

Geraldine caught a bus down Wortley Hill, and unlocked a back door of the shop.

It was eerie inside. Blackout shrouded the windows. Anne's torch picked out buckets of water and sand on the red-carpeted stairs.

'Can you work a stirrup pump?' asked Geraldine, pointing to one.

'You do it with your foot.' And Anne demonstrated the action.

'Let's hope we don't need to,' said Geraldine. 'Shall we go upstairs and see the new dresses?'

She sighed with pleasure as she saw the faintly gleaming silks on their rail.

'Luxury,' she murmured.

'Not my style,' said Anne.

'Oh, but mine! – What's that?'

The siren's harsh wail screeched out.

'A raid!'

Anne snatched the stirrup pump.

'We can't stay here!' cried Geraldine. 'Where's the air-raid shelter?'

'In the basement.'

They scuttled downstairs as a battle broke out above them. Bombs whined and crashed; guns pounded; the shop rattled and swayed. The girls darted into the reinforced shelter and huddled together, frightened and excited.

'I wish Mrs Ashwell was with us,' gasped Geraldine.

'I'm glad she isn't,' said Anne.

'Oh, those dresses! If they're ruined – '

In the torch light, Geraldine's eyes were bright with dismay.

'We should have brought them down,' said Anne, furious with her own stupidity. 'They'd be safe in here.'

After a while the uproar quietened. Fire engines roared clanging past, but there were no more explosions. Cautiously the girls crept back to the ground floor. The torch showed mahogany counters and shelves powdered with dust but apparently undamaged.

'Let's fetch the dresses,' said Geraldine.

They hurried towards the staircase.

There was another violent crash. Blood-red light flashed round the shop.

'Stop!' cried Anne. 'We'd better go back.'

'The stairs are all right,' called Geraldine, beginning, instead, to run forward. 'We needn't take long.'

Anne stood petrified. Yet – for Enid's sake, she thought. She dashed after Geraldine.

Crash! Bang! She was almost thrown off her feet. Black smoke, starred with sparks, engulfed the shop. Through it, she just glimpsed the staircase, and Geraldine running up.

'Don't!' Anne tried to call, but the acrid fumes filled her throat. Gasping and choking, she clung to a counter.

With a roar and a whoosh, the roof blew apart. In the glare, Anne saw the staircase shudder and topple sideways. Bricks, buckets and bannisters flew; and amongst them flew pale hair and outstretched hands.

Then Anne lost consciousness.

⇒ 29 ⇐

Gabriel stood in Crosthwaite churchyard, staring at the family graves.

Rain was pattering down on her umbrella and splashing over the flat stones on which well-known names were carved. They were gathered inside a low iron railing, the Floods, exclusive in death as they had been in life; unloved now and forgotten, with neither grass nor flowers to soften the bleakness of their resting place.

There were Lionel and Mary Flood, from Edwardian Springfield; Iona, their daughter; Rufus Orme, their son-in-law; Lettice, his wife (later the wife of Geoffrey Miles, buried elsewhere); and Geraldine Orme, daughter of Rufus and Lettice. Mary Flood had died at fifty, and Lionel at fifty-eight; Rufus had been thirty-one, Iona twenty-one, and Geraldine only twenty. Lettice, dying at the age of seventy, had outlived them all. Except, of course, for Dorothy, Sarah and Gabriel herself.

We're a doomed family, thought Gabriel. The gloomy skies, the rain slanting over grey acres of stone, under-lined her conviction. Almost, she could feel the chill of funerals around her; see black gloves, crêpe armbands, umbrellas raised against similar wintry showers. Black boots edged carefully round puddles on the path; long black skirts were lifted above them. Gabriel sensed hopelessness, anger, waste, self-pity – dark emotions suiting the dark clothes. The gentlest, most loving tears fell, she imagined, for Geraldine, shed by mourners who weren't her relations.

There, beside the graves, she realized again why friends were so important to her mother. As the wartime group at Springfield had supported Geraldine far better than Lettice or Dorothy; so Josie, Lyn and the rest had offered Sarah a warmth which Paul, her husband, had been incapable of giving. And, after all those deaths, Sarah had been chronically short of relations.

Standing beneath the tiny black-and-white checks of her umbrella, Gabriel felt solitary too. And depression hung over her, heavy as the rain-clouds, because her designing flair had still not returned; and though, in the last couple of days, she had found some interest in sketching variations on a striped suit for Dorothy, and copying dresses of 1938 to fit an imagined portrait of

154

Geraldine, real inspiration was as dead as the bones railed in under their churchyard slabs.

The gravestones seemed the end of a story, begun in the Springfield attic, and continuing through Dorothy's conversation and Anne Cropper's letter. She had enjoyed it while it lasted, but now it was finished. There, in the rain, she couldn't even summon up the enthusiasm to visit Dorothy next Sunday. Everything's finished, thought Gabriel – and knew that she also meant that it was now Thursday, and Francis hadn't contacted her again.

Why should I agonize over someone who's only a potential boyfriend, she wondered; who, precisely once, took me out because he felt guilty about disturbing me in the attic, but who was then put off by the way I behaved in the pub? I'm over-reacting, as usual. Why should I expect him to come back into my life? 'Those lovesick girls who mope beside the telephone!' she had heard Fleur of *Boudicca* exclaim; Fleur, secure in her relationship with Nina.

And I'm alone, thought Gabriel – except for Sarah, of course.

Her mind went back to the most disquieting point in Anne Cropper's long letter. Francis was the son of Philip Ashwell, who had played so casually with Geraldine's feelings. Was Francis like his father? She remembered how he had said that Philip had married several times. Were the Ashwells incapable of proper relationships?

It might be best to forget him. It might be best to leave Crosthwaite altogether; find a new place, and a new career. What was there to keep her in Crosthwaite? Certainly not her course; just her great-great-aunt, who didn't need her at all. There were still clothes to see in the Springfield attic. But if she returned there, Francis might ignore her, or his aunt, Deirdre Russell, might be there. It was all so depressing.

The rain stopped while she was waiting for a bus back to Marlborough Street; so, when she boarded it, she saw from the top deck something which might otherwise have been hidden by kindly umbrellas.

Almost before she noticed the long loose coat, she felt her heart thumping, as if it had reacted while her eyes were still wiring their message to her brain. Francis, with his soft, fair hair stirred by the wind, was standing below her on the pavement. His collar was turned up, like a screen against which she could discern the hollowed line of his cheek. And, talking to him was Lucy, her curls on end, her face aglow. She was on tiptoe with eagerness. She laid her hand on the fine tweed of his sleeve. They began to walk away, side by side – and the bus rattled off and left them.

Lucy had said yesterday that she was thinking of ringing him. Did she fancy him, in spite of her throngs of male friends? Did he – terrible thought – fancy her?

I can't bear it, Gabriel moaned to herself.

Unsteadily she descended the bus stairs, and climbed off at the corner of Marlborough Street. A letter had come for her by the second post. She stared at the stiff white envelope, stamped DEPARTMENT OF FASHION AND DESIGN at the top, and guessed its contents before she tore it open.

Dear Miss Klavir, wrote her director of studies, *It appears that you have not attended any classes for several weeks. I must ask you to come and explain your reasons at 10 a.m. on Friday morning, without fail . . .*

Friday was tomorrow. Dropping the letter into her waste-paper basket, Gabriel seized a suitcase and began to pack.

There were two good reasons now for leaving Crosthwaite. She could catch the early evening train to London,
and Sarah.

⇒ *30* ⇐

Dorothy Flood drowsed in an armchair, her shins as close
as was bearable to the gas-fire. The stuffy brown sitting-
room faded away. She was back at Springfield; not the
Springfield of her childhood but of October 1940, when
her niece, Geraldine, was killed by the bomb that hit
Ashwells.

Talking to Geraldine had revived old memories. No,
not Geraldine; Gabriel. She gave herself a shake. Gabriel
was the girl with the black hair. Where had that come
from? The Floods didn't have black hair. Geraldine's was
fair, a pale drifting gold, like Letty's.

The funeral had been terrible. Lettice and Geoffrey
were unable to return for it, so Dorothy was the chief
mourner, standing by those gaunt gravestones and the
hole into which the coffin was lowered. The earth was
piled in heaps, ready to be shovelled back, burying
pretty, delicate Geraldine for ever. Even the flowers –
and there had been masses – couldn't disguise such
appalling finality. Geraldine had been twenty. And I'm
eighty-eight, thought Dorothy, snorting with amazement,
yet those days are as clear to me as if they only happened
last week.

~

Mrs Ashwell invited her back to Springfield for tea, after the funeral. She stood beside the polished table, fiercely trying to concentrate on the changes to the dining-room since her childhood. Cream paint covered the walls above the panelling, where her parents had had thick, dark wallpaper. The curtains were chintz, not tasselled velvet. Chrysanthemums stood on the sideboard, instead of her father's decanters. Yet all she could think of was Geraldine, whom she had blamed – naturally, naughty child – but who had been her only living relation in England, apart from the baby in the pram, Sarah; whom Mrs Ashwell – to Dorothy's relief – had promised to care for till Letty came home at the end of the war. Letty was far away. Geraldine was dead. Sobs swelled painfully in her throat.

Mrs Ashwell came up and spoke so kindly. When they had met before, Dorothy had only envied her poise, her elegance, her wedding ring. Now she saw that, under their tweezered brows, Mrs Ashwell's eyes too were full of tears. She treated Geraldine a lot better than I did, thought Dorothy uncomfortably. She must be missing her; and she was worried too about the other girl, Anne Cropper, dug from the wreckage with concussion and a broken shoulder, who was still in hospital. Yet she wanted to comfort Dorothy. That was when she began talking about the things, still in the attic, which had belonged to the Floods; the clothes, the boxes of school stories –

'My Angela Brazils!' exclaimed Dorothy.

'Would you like to have a good look through them?' asked Enid.

After that, visiting Springfield became a Saturday habit. Dorothy began by falling eagerly on the books, but their old sparkle had gone.

'Oh, isn't it piggy and nasty,' said Annie.

'Poor martyr. Here, squattez-ici on the hearthrug, and I'll toast you a triscuit. Don't you twig? It's a biscuit toasted three times.'

Dorothy closed the book. Girls she taught never talked like that; and, instead of frolicking, they were preoccupied with the war, bombs and which armed service they might join.

Dorothy turned to the trunks in which Phyllis had once

158

stored piles of family possessions. Each one revived a lost memory – the hats her mother had worn for afternoon calls; Iona's and Lettice's evening dresses – 'I never had one,' lamented Dorothy; baby-clothes, miracles of frilling and tucking, in which she herself had been carried up and down between the drawing-room and the old nursery with its high fireguard and dappled rocking-horse.

How much happier those days had been, when she used to play at being married with her own nursery of children; when war had not spoiled life, as much for women as men.

She started to divide things into individual heaps – her mother's, Iona's, Lettice's. By contrast, her father's suits were dull. She bundled them into a dustsheet, to be passed on to bombed-out families.

Withdrawn in the attic, she was nevertheless aware of the life around her. Springfield hummed with talk and small activities. There were no longer calls and formal dinner parties; but there were knots of women, drinking tea in the kitchen or sewing to the accompaniment of dance music on the wireless. And chatting; always chatting.

'What do you think I should do about Ashwells, Miss Flood?' asked Enid, offering cigarettes and regarding Dorothy with genuine inquiry. 'It's badly damaged. Should I aim to open again or sell the site?'

She was interested in everyone's opinions – Dorothy's, Mrs Cropper's, those of Anne, the pale student with her arm in a sling; of Ethel, the lame housemaid; of the evacuee mothers. She probed; she threw light into dark corners. Dorothy, bred to reticence, had never known conversation like it.

When Enid had decided to sell Ashwells, there were still things to discuss. What vegetables should be planted? How could a puny evacuee child be helped through his nightmares? What should the English war strategy be? Dorothy felt her mind, atrophied by years of monotonously repeated lessons, awakening again. She began asking questions herself.

Why had women's clothes been so restricting, she wondered, as she moved round the attic. In a far corner, near the broken harp, she found an ancient domed trunk, which had belonged to the Miss Hardcastles. Dorothy hauled out a few dresses and was shocked by the sheer volume of merino, alpaca and velvet. Some dresses were nearly twenty feet round the hem. They were looped over underskirts and piled above horsehair bustles.

'Monstrosities!' ejaculated Dorothy, holding up something in moss green and mauve, overtrimmed with beading and braiding and dusty crumpled ribbon.

That women should have consented to wear them revealed an amazing attitude to life. How submissive they must have been! The enslavement to bustles and crinolines reflected the way girls were enslaved by their parents, and wives by their husbands. There was no freedom; only the shackles of clothes and conventions.

And passive too! Well, no one could be very active, dragging twenty feet of velvet around with them. A gentle walk would be all the exercise the Miss Hardcastles ever achieved. With a passive body probably went a passive mind. Initiative would be frowned on. If it hadn't been, Miss Cassia might have decamped with her harp master.

Dorothy burrowed down into the domed trunk. It's not just submissiveness and passivity, she thought. All those rich materials, the muffs, parasols, shawls and jewels, were designed to proclaim the wealth and prestige of fathers and husbands. They were status symbols. The Hardcastles were well-off – hence the array of mouldering accessories, in which their daughters would have been decked like so many Christmas trees.

And hence the suffragettes, thought Dorothy, with sudden enlightenment.

She had hated the suffragettes for what they had done to her family. Happiness had fled when Iona was thrown from her bicycle with a pocketful of subversive leaflets. But the Hardcastle dresses showed how much women had needed liberating. They had had to be turned from dolls into people; and because men had been unwilling to help, they had had to do it for themselves.

160

Had Iona been sensible, after all?

~

That, Dorothy remembered, edging back as the gas-fire scorched her shins, was how she became friends with Ruth Cropper; discussing the suffragettes over those endless wartime cups of tea. She had enjoyed telling Ruth about the cramping life against which Iona had rebelled.

~

'You should write it down,' suggested Enid, who enjoyed listening too.

'I couldn't. I'd need all those relics on hand to remind me – '

'Look,' said Enid, 'why don't you come and live here for a while? We've enough room, and it must be awful for you to be alone in an air-raid.'

It was the kindness of Enid's voice that Dorothy noticed; and the understanding that, after Geraldine, raids were terrifying. Nobody had spoken to her like that for years. Why should they, she sometimes asked herself. Who could love a disgruntled spinster? Yet Enid and Ruth did.

She left her home and moved to Springfield. She pottered about the attic in the evening after school; and then went down to the room where she'd slept as a girl, and wrote her account of the family.

It was a strange experience. They seemed so near, in the old surroundings, that she felt with a queer sharpness the wounds of their deaths. But, at the same time, she had miraculously regained a family.

'I've altered this blouse for you,' said Enid. 'There are far too many in my drawers, and the colour will suit you better than me.'

'Aunty Doffy!' squeaked little Sarah, who was learning to talk.

'Here's a book about Mrs Pankhurst, from the library. Would you like to read it first?' offered Ruth.

Oh, I am lucky, thought Dorothy.

161

'I thought we could do a play,' Lucy said to Francis. 'You must know about plays, with your father being an actor. Could you help?'

And, from the bus station where she'd asked him to meet her, she steered him to a small café, for a proper talk.

'There are those costumes in your attic, that Gabriel goes on about. D'you think we could use them?' she asked. 'I'm thinking I'll try and get hold of a proper suffragette play, as it's a sort of feminist cause, so we'll probably need mostly girls in the cast; but it would be great if you'd do something on the producing side.'

She looked so eager, that it was hard to rebuff her. But the result of being brought up in an actor's family had been to make Francis determined never, under any circumstances, to have anything to do with the theatre. Theatre people were inconstant – his father had married four times. They were terrible egotists – as he'd often experienced. Reason told him that he needn't project his resentments onto mere student productions, but he couldn't help it. He loathed anything to do with plays.

Lucy, who had been bubbling with enthusiasm ever since she rang him, felt badly let down.

'Won't you really? Oh, well; I s'ppose I'll find someone else. We're a bit stuck over money-raising, since Gabriel's backed out of Fashion-Aid.'

'Will Gabriel be in the play?' he couldn't prevent himself asking.

'I shouldn't think so.' Lucy sighed. 'She's being incredibly negative about everything at the moment. It's because her designing's gone wrong.'

He'd heard enough. He stood up.

'I'll have to go. See you around.'

Incredibly negative. That fitted with what his aunt, Deirdre Russell, had said on Monday. Crazily, he'd let himself be driven to the library, because Deirdre seemed to have planted herself at Springfield that day; and he couldn't bear to see her – hard and dominating as she was – with fragile, exquisite Gabriel. He wasn't even sure if Gabriel would be going to Springfield. But she had.

'Oh, yes; she's been,' Deirdre said. 'Weird child. I can't say she seemed at all interested in you. In fact, she positively denied that she was.'

For three days he'd felt wounded and rejected. But if she was only negative because her designing was going wrong – ? Later that evening, he called round at Marlborough Street.

'She's rushed off to London,' said Lucy, when he asked for Gabriel. 'I don't know what's got into her. She's just left a note saying she's gone.'

'Where does she live?'

Lucy hadn't an address; but, being resourceful, discovered in Gabriel's room a copy of *Boudicca*, which Sarah had sent.

'I'm sure it's this magazine her mother works for. I've a feeling they live next door, or up above, or something. Take it, anyway. You could always try the office phone.'

And ask at the switchboard for Gabriel? At half past nine in the evening? He took the copy of *Boudicca* back to Springfield, because Lucy seemed to expect it; and sank down in the panelled, pink and terracotta sitting-room, thoroughly depressed.

The problem of girlfriends!

Because his childhood had been, after his parents split up, divided into mutually hostile compartments – and lonely as well, sometimes at school, sometimes at Springfield, sometimes travelling the world, as one or other of his parents pursued their careers or their lovers – he'd gone up to Oxford looking for love. At first, Helen had seemed the answer. There was a comfortable roundness and placidity about Helen which was pleasantly unlike his thin, predatory mother, or his latest, modish stepmother. But he had grown dissatisfied. Things were too cosy with Helen. He kept plodding round to her room for tea and toasted sandwiches, and appalling vistas opened of them married, snugly watching television every evening ('We must see *Dallas*' 'Have you put the kettle on?'), losing out on life's richness and romance.

'I thought we were a settled couple,' Helen had wept when he broke with her. She hadn't understood that, to him, being a 'settled couple' sounded sickeningly middle-aged; that he wanted the freedom to explore relationships with lots of girls. He'd let Helen down. He realized that and felt bad about it. But why did girls want to shackle you? Why did they stretch out fingers so pleadingly for rings that could stunt their development too?

In his second year at Oxford, there had been a procession of girlfriends; Tessa, Rachel, Jane, Louise . . . Tessa repeated everything he said to her, to half a dozen other girls. Rachel only wanted to take off her clothes and scramble into bed with him. Jane talked obsessively about a previous boyfriend. Louise – well, he couldn't now recall what was so awful about Louise. Maybe she bit her nails.

Gradually, as he discarded them – feeling guiltily like his parents whose love affairs he'd always destested – an image grew in his mind of the perfect girl. She didn't snatch at him. She was remote, melancholy, beautiful; a princess locked in a tower. She wasn't at Oxford. He

164

decided, in his third year, to abandon girls and concentrate on his work.

Then came the fatal party, the rustication and the spell of lonely frustration at Springfield. And out of that came Gabriel.

When he had seen her for the first time, black and white against her coloured walls, with her silver earrings swinging between the blue-black of her hair and the white of her neck, he'd known she was the princess in the tower. But he'd made a mess of approaching her and now he'd lost touch.

He sprawled over the sofa, thinking of Gabriel. Would he ever see her again?

The clothes in the attic! They could still be the link. He could contact Lucy and say that, although he wanted nothing to do with her play, he would willingly lend some costumes.

'But don't come and look at them till Gabriel's back,' he would say casually. 'It'd be pointless choosing without an expert. You need the right things. D'you think you could get her to come back?'

He smiled with relief at the idea.

≫ *32* ≪

It was the second time Gabriel had run away from Crosthwaite; but the time before it hadn't been her decision.

She had been eight, old enough to know what was

happening, although for a long time she had closed her mind to memories. Now, as the train gathered speed out of Crosthwaite, she suddenly saw her mother slamming down a final note for her father on the hall table at Springfield; and a little puff of dust rising, because Sarah hadn't cleaned the house properly for weeks. She remembered vividly too how she had stood beside the suitcases while her mother watched from the window for the taxi she'd ordered; and how she had clenched her teeth and twisted her fingers to stop herself crying, because she couldn't bear to leave her lovely home.

Beyond the window, above Sarah's outlined head, branches tossed against the grey sky. Flagstones, worn with the tread of generations, transmitted their familiar chill through the soles of her shoes; and she'd known that it was for the last time.

'I'll be glad to leave all this wind and cold,' Sarah had said; but cheerfully, not bitterly.

Gabriel hadn't answered.

Then the taxi had come, and they'd driven away. Gabriel didn't look back at the gables, the trees and the garden wall.

'I've got an idea,' said Sarah. Her slightly protruberant blue eyes, inherited from Bunny Tarrant, were beaming with excitement. 'You can stop calling me Mummy, and just call me Sarah instead. It sounds more grown-up, and it'll fit better into this new life we're going to have. I'm going to be my old self, Sarah Orme, not Mrs Klavir any longer.'

She hugged Gabriel, as if to make up for any betrayal; but Gabriel felt her body stiff and unyielding inside her school coat.

'It's not that I don't love Daddy,' Sarah began again; and Gabriel interrupted.

166

'Shouldn't you say that it's not that you don't love Paul?'

'Oh, darling, you're ridiculously like him!' exclaimed Sarah. 'Yes, you're right. Well, I still love Paul, but he's not letting me lead the life I want. You understand that, don't you?'

'Yes,' said Gabriel.

It had seemed true, but, looking back, she realized she hadn't really understood that story of her parents. How could she have done, at eight?

Sarah ran away for positive reasons, thought Gabriel. I'm running away for negative ones – because Francis doesn't seem interested in me; because I can't face my director of studies; because my creativity has gone. It was comforting, against all this, to think of Sarah.

From habit she looked round the carriage, studying the clothes. There were none to strike a spark of interest; just dull skirts and trousers, woolly scarves and chainstore jerseys. There would be none to admire at Warburton Street either, she thought wryly.

From the mainline station she made her way home by underground, and on foot. Darkness had fallen. There were no lights in the downstairs windows, which belonged to the offices of *Boudicca*; or from the flat above, which belonged to Josie Crewe. The top windows luckily shone. Sarah was at home.

'Darling!'

Jumping up from her chair, with the warmth that had made her so popular in the *Boudicca* circle, Sarah hugged her daughter. She was round-faced, with Bunny's teeth as well as his eyes, and light brown hair; and she wore a checked shirt and trousers that did nothing for her figure. But her expression was one of purest love.

167

'How marvellous to see you, but why've you come? Nothing's wrong, is it?'

'I just felt like a break.'

'Sit by the fire, darling. You're cold. How beautiful you look – but pale too.'

If only, thought Gabriel, Sarah could have given some of her lines to Francis. 'How beautiful you look,' would have come much better from him. Then immediately she was annoyed with herself. Her mother could say what she liked. Gabriel had never met anyone else as loving as Sarah and probably never would. That was part of the trouble. It seemed to illustrate something about Sarah's life. For if living amongst women promoted such spontaneous warmth, why take the risk of settling down with a man?

'What happens if I fall in love with a boy?' she had asked Sarah once.

'Oh, be very careful about giving your heart away, darling. It's so chancy,' Sarah replied.

'Marriage is such a legal thing,' Fleur remarked another time. They had been in Sarah's flat as usual, Fleur draped gracefully over a chair, her bare feet in Nina's lap. 'I mean, if you're contracted to someone, you've no freedom. That cramps a relationship.'

Nina nodded agreement.

'We don't have any formal arrangements here, but we all support each other,' said Josie. 'Women helping women – that's how it should be.'

Gabriel couldn't pretend these high-sounding claims didn't work out in practice. Sarah had lived in Warburton Street for ten years and she was still happy. The flat – there was no denying it – felt very peaceful.

Gabriel yawned uncontrollably.

168

'Are you sleeping badly? Just wait, and I'll put some sheets on your bed.'

Sarah's words were about the last thing Gabriel remembered that evening.

⊱ 33 ⊰

Love between women, mused Anne Cropper.

She had come downstairs in the early hours of Friday morning, relit her fire and made some tea. Her recent contact with those two girls seeking information – Elizabeth Morley and Gabriel Klavir – had stirred up a host of memories, which clamoured in her brain, so that she couldn't sleep.

Outside the curtained window lay night's profoundest silence. No traffic; no winds, as there were at Springfield. She felt alone but not desolate. The photograph on the writing-desk smiled at her, and she surrendered herself to the past.

~

Anne lay in a big women's ward at Crosthwaite Hospital, in a line of twenty beds. Gradually, groggily, consciousness had returned. Her mother had visited her and told her that she'd been injured when Ashwells was bombed, and that Geraldine had died. Geraldine! With her swimming head and bruised body, nothing seemed quite real to Anne.

The scent of Chanel roused her. Nurses were bustling round.

'A private room, *immediately*,' said Enid's voice.

Someone was wheeling her on a trolley. The Chanel faded,

169

revived. She opened her eyes in a small side-room. Enid was arranging roses and carnations in a tall china vase she had brought from Springfield. Dimly Anne heard her say – 'I thought they might only have jamjars here,' but she couldn't make sense of the remark. Enid had come; that was enough. She closed her eyes again.

Her mother came to see her daily, but it was Enid's visits she lived for. Ruth brought her medical books and the newspaper. Enid brought grapes and Eau de Cologne. Ruth greeted her with a quick peck on the cheek. Enid sat at her bedside, holding her hand.

How can I let her know my love, Anne wondered. There seemed no answer.

Presently she went home to Springfield. It was sad without Geraldine, and she found herself no closer to Enid who was immersed in the problem of Ashwells' future and devoting time to a difficult evacuee child, to Geraldine's Aunt Dorothy and to the little orphan, Sarah. I'm just one of a crowd, thought Anne, trying to be humble, trying to forget those evenings of cards with Enid and Geraldine, which now seemed so far away.

'You must miss Geraldine dreadfully,' said Enid; and Anne's tears overflowed because of Enid's sympathy. Not well enough to return to her medical school that term, she moped in her room.

When Deirdre came home for the Christmas holidays, she sulked because the house was so crowded with miscellaneous inhabitants.

'And Anne Cropper's such a wet blanket!' she exclaimed.

She was standing at the foot of the staircase. Anne, coming down, hadn't made the turn between the panelled walls, so she heard Enid's reply.

'She's a sweet girl, with a loving nature. It's a pity you're not more like her.'

Anne disregarded the second sentence, unaware that it had fuelled smouldering fires of jealousy. But 'sweet', 'loving'. That was what Enid thought of her! If only she could say such things back!

Somebody gave Enid a book called *Lyrics from the Chinese* as a Christmas present. Because Enid had been reading it, Anne picked it up, and came across a poem which expressed exactly her own inhibited emotions; for the place in it, Sung, could stand for Enid, while the river, Ho, was like the gulf between them.

> *How say they that the Ho is wide,*
> *When I could ford it if I tried?*
> *How say they Sung is far away,*
> *When I can see it every day?*
>
> *Yet must indeed the Ho be deep,*
> *When I have never dared the leap;*
> *And since I am content to stay,*
> *Sung must indeed be far away.*

Anne wrote out the poem and laid it on Enid's dressing-table, among her silver-backed brushes and cut-glass scent-bottles.

That night Enid came into her room. She wore a white woollen dress, simple and beautiful, against which her copper hair glowed.

'Did you copy this for me, Anne?'

'Yes.'

Anne could say no more. Her heart thumped. Enid regarded her with a kind of amused sweetness.

'It's lovely. I wonder – might you equally well have written *My love is like a red, red rose?*'

'But you aren't,' said Anne. 'You're like a tawny chrysanthemum.'

'I see,' said Enid. She sat down on the bed and took Anne's hand. 'This will pass,' she said. 'You'll fall in love with a boy your own age.'

'Never,' said Anne.

'Ye gods, all these women!' groaned Deirdre. In the kitchen Ruth was washing sprouts, and an evacuee mother was soaking

171

nappies. In the dining-room small Sarah was 'helping' Ethel Pearson to dust. Upstairs in the attic Dorothy Flood was grubbing through trunks of old clothes. In the drawing-room Enid and Anne had their heads together over a medical book, since Enid, with no shop to run, was taking a First Aid course so that she could help at the Ambulance Station.

'Springfield might as well be a nunnery!' said Deirdre disgustedly.

She repeated this remark to a friend on the Wortley Hill bus; and it must have been overheard, if misunderstood, for next day an unknown Irishwoman hobbled up the drive, to ask hopefully if Springfield was a convent.

Home from boarding-school next summer, Deirdre was still dissatisfied. 'You've changed so much, Mummy,' she complained, finding Enid gardening under Anne's window. 'You were lovely when I was little, with your tennis parties and your dancing; then you went through that awful do-gooding phase; then you ran Ashwells, so that I never saw you; now you're trying to win the war single-handedly.'

'People must be able to change; that's freedom,' said Enid. 'As for winning the war, I'm only sowing spring cabbage. We must grow as much food as we can.'

'It's not just the growing. It's your minding snivelling kids and practising bandaging and living on matey terms with Dorothy Flood and the Croppers, because we're all in the war together.'

'It's fun,' said Enid.

'Not for me.'

Enid didn't deserve a daughter like that, thought Anne. She redoubled her efforts to please Enid and make up for Deirdre's churlishness. During her vacations she tried to keep her clothes nice and her hair well washed and brushed; to have a fire blazing when Enid came in on cold evenings; and to put posies on her dressing-table in summer.

Things went on changing. Deirdre became an officer cadet. There was a bombing lull and the evacuees went home. Sarah grew. Most surprisingly, Dorothy acquired a new role.

She began seriously studying the history of costume. She had taught History at school as a dead subject, all dates and wars and Acts of Parliament. Now it suddenly came alive as she looked at clothes and considered the attitudes they represented.

She became known as an authority and was asked to speak to local groups. Because she was interested, she spoke well. Soon she was much in demand as a lecturer and a writer of magazine articles. She talked about costume and sociey, explaining how the tall pointed hats ladies wore in the Middle Ages symbolized – like church steeples and lancet windows – the medieval aspiration towards heaven; while the jewel-encrusted dresses of Tudor courts illustrated the change of emphasis from the glory of God to the splendour of man. She often went out lecturing in the evenings with a box of lantern slides.

Anne completed her medical studies and took a post at Crosthwaite Hospital. She and Enid grew closer. They discussed their work, the war, their lives. Ruth got tired easily now and went to bed early, leaving Enid and Anne by the drawing-room fire. Sometimes they held hands. Occasionally they kissed lightly.

'There's a nice young doctor,' said Enid once. 'Tom Willis – do you know him? He was wounded; that's why he was invalided home. I think he'd take an interest in you, if you gave him some encouragement.'

'Enid!' Anne was horrified.

'Dearest.' Enid stroked her hand. 'You must marry one day.'

'Why?'

'It's the right thing for a woman.'

'You're the right thing for me.'

'But if people knew your feelings – ? Seriously, Anne.' Enid drew away a little. 'You'd find yourself facing scorn, ridicule, incomprehension, a total lack of sympathy. People are so conventional. They expect women to love men. It's home life. It's the stuff of novels and agony columns. People don't acknowledge – yet – that women can love other women.'

'What people?' asked Anne sharply.

'Deirdre, for instance.'

There was silence for a moment.

'She's very conventional,' said Enid. 'You know how she dislikes my "house of women". On her last leave, she made some extremely barbed remarks – as if she might have guessed your feelings.'

'Would it matter?'

'It could matter. She could make trouble. So, be careful. And try to fall in love with Tom Willis.'

Anne never even looked at him. She didn't want anything except life in Enid's house of women.

≫ *34* ≪

Gabriel woke late the morning after she arrived at Sarah's. Ten o'clock – the time when she should have been seeing her director of studies. She closed her eyes, meaning to drift back into sleep, but she couldn't; so presently she opened them again. It was strange to see her old familiar bedroom with its cream furniture and Laura Ashley wallpaper, which she had loved two or three years ago, and which now looked frivolously pretty.

If I stay here I shall change it, she thought.

Stay here? Was that what she was going to do?

Instantly, her body was recharged with tension. The problems of her designing, and her relationship with

Francis, buzzed round her head. Once again her imagination wildly threw up all kinds of hideous, stereotyped clothes, interspersed with pictures of Lucy gazing up at Francis. Why could the mind never be controlled? Why did it have to race, like a freewheeling bicycle?

She sprang out of bed, wrapped the sickeningly charming quilt round her shoulders and hurried into the kitchen to shock her system with black coffee. The kitchen was just about bearable. The walls were scarlet, the shelves white, the cannisters a very dark green. Great leafy things burgeoned in corners and along the windowsill. Even Sarah's plants seemed happy.

Interior decoration? Could that be her career? Might she cut her ties with Crosthwaite and study for a new profession in London?

She dragged one of her big old portfolios out of a cupboard, untied the tapes and began to turn over the loose sheets. Hadn't she once done some wallpaper patterns? But immediately her attention was caught by all the clothes she had drawn and copied. That Elizabethan ruff of pleated gossamer lace, sketched with her hardest, sharpest pencil point! She could feel its stiffness, like a frozen cobweb, under her fingers. And there was a dress, designed in her Laura Ashley phase, with a frilled camisole top, and bands of inset lace. How funny, she thought. It's a sort of unconscious reflection of the baby-clothes at Springfield, or even Iona's petticoat, which I might have seen and forgotten. But she didn't want to think of them now. She closed the portfolio and retied the tapes.

For a moment her mind seemed numb. She sat at the table with her hands round her mug, staring at the oddly iridescent surface of the coffee. Far below she could sense the activity in the *Boudicca* offices, though not even the

175

click of a typewriter rattled up through Josie's intervening flat. All the same, she was aware of the women downstairs, purposefully busy while she was idle; knowing where they were going, while she was lost. No wonder Sarah was happy.

Last month's *Boudicca* lay on the fridge. She picked it up and examined the cover critically. It was a mess – just as she'd thought when Sarah sent an identical copy to Crosthwaite. Fleur's artwork was getting sloppier, reflecting that droopiness of personality which needed Nina's support. I could be art editor, thought Gabriel. I'd do it better than Fleur. Why go on being a student, if I could earn some money?

Forgetting that Fleur might object to being ousted, Gabriel developed the fantasy. It was definitely appealing. She could blot out the design course, Springfield, Francis . . . She suddenly realized that she had been thinking about Springfield and Francis for at least ten minutes, while her feet grew as cold as the coffee. Sighing, she took a shower and dressed herself in black.

'Darling!' Sarah flew into the flat. 'How are you this morning?'

And she wished Gabriel wasn't so like Paul, who had also affected black sweaters in his youth, worn with tight jeans which showed off his long slim legs marvellously – but depressingly when hers tended to shortness and plumpness.

'I'm OK,' said Gabriel, because it was the easiest answer. She wasn't sure yet what she was going to tell Sarah.

'Will just a sandwich do for lunch? I've been seeing to next month's letters' page.' That her jobs on *Boudicca* were humble didn't trouble Sarah. 'I never know which to choose, so I just squeeze in all the subjects I can –

dress sizes, Child Benefit, sexist ads. It's a struggle, half the time, to read the writing. And the spelling – ! You've no idea how many versions there are of 'cervical smear'; s's and y's and k's all over the place.'

'Sarah,' said Gabriel, 'I've been visiting Springfield.'

Sarah was astonished.

'Really? What's it like now?'

'Beautiful.'

'It would be,' said Sarah. 'Paul spent so much on books, we could never afford to have it looking as it should; as I remembered it when the Ashwells and the Russells lived there. Does Philip Ashwell still own it?'

'Yes.'

'So you've met him?'

'No; I went to look at the clothes,' Gabriel answered hastily, eager to avoid mentioning Francis.

'The clothes?'

'In the attic.'

'Oh – those old things. Aunty Doffy was mad about them.'

'Dorothy Flood, you mean? Was she?'

'Yes. She was a real expert on clothes.'

'How funny!' said Gabriel. 'I'd never have guessed. I wish I'd known. I went to her flat, you see. I rather liked her.'

'You never told me!' exclaimed Sarah.

'I was finding out about the family history. Don't you think it's absolutely fascinating? Except that we're all doomed.'

'What *are* you talking about? I'm certainly not doomed. Pass the mustard, darling.'

'You and Paul – ?' Gabriel let the sentence hang in the air. 'And your mother, Geraldine. Anne Cropper wrote to me about her.'

'Anne Cropper! Goodness! Names from the past.'

'Do you remember her? And Dorothy?'

'Yes, Dorothy quite well. We still send cards at Christmas, and I think I let her know you'd be in Crosthwaite. Anne Cropper, though – she's a bit of a blur. I think we must have lost touch when Granny came home from Canada to look after me, poor thing. I sort of remember Anne, at Springfield during the war, when Enid Ashwell had that house full of women.'

'Sounds like Warburton Street,' Gabriel remarked.

'M'm.' Sarah pondered a moment. 'But it wasn't.'

Like Warburton Street, Springfield had been a hive of activity, but what was all the activity about? Certainly not running a feminist magazine, counselling women, raising their consciousness. No, it must have been the sheer business of wartime life which took all the time and effort.

Ruth Cropper was always busy in the kitchen, making jam, bottling fruit, boiling mash for the hens, and pickling their eggs in waterglass. Ethel Pearson wielded carpet-sweeper, mop and dusters. There was a continual fight against dirt, when smoky coal fires provided the only heating and the vacuum cleaner was heavy and cumbersome for a lame woman to manage. The washing was done by hand; everything scrubbed and boiled and mangled in the stone-floored wash-house. There was no time for women to debate their rights. They didn't even think of them.

They must, thought Sarah, in a moment of illumination, have been the natural successors of the women who first lived at Springfield, in the seventeenth and eighteenth centuries, before it became fashionable for ladies to do nothing. Those early women of the house would have been profitably at work from dawn to dusk, cooking and baking, spinning and weaving, growing things and preserving them. Women earned their own status then. It wasn't conferred on them by husbands and fathers. In their own way, they were the equals of men. They must have been more fulfilled than those Victorian and Edwardian drawing-room paragons, who left everything to their servants. Yes, Springfield in wartime had been like an eighteenth-century household – lively, busy, truly communal.

And, amongst the busyness, everyone had been kind to the little orphan, Sarah. Enid Ashwell read to her, and bought her a tiny trowel to 'help' in the vegetable garden. Ethel lavished her sweet-ration on the child. Ruth bathed her and told her the country folk-tales she'd never had time to tell Anne.

No, busyness hadn't prevented kindness; and it hadn't at Warburton Street. There was a parallel surely between Enid Ashwell and Josie Crewe . . .

'D'you know,' said Sarah, 'you've started an interesting train of thought. Have I told you we're beginning to work on the tenth anniversary edition of *Boudicca*? Josie wants to feature a big reappraisal of the Women's Movement, and I'm just wondering if I could hack out something on the contrast between Springfield and Warburton Street.'

'There wasn't any women's movement in the war though, was there?' asked Gabriel.

'No, very little during the war, and only isolated campaigns for things like equal pay and birth control in the twenties and thirties. It's sad, really. I can imagine someone like Enid would have loved a Feminist Movement. But Josie thinks women weren't really conscious of themselves as women. After the suffragettes, they went back to seeing themselves only in relation to men – or lack of men.'

179

'Dorothy did,' agreed Gabriel. 'Poor Dorothy.'

She remembered her idea of bringing Dorothy to Warburton Street, and going back to decorate her flat. She still meant to do it – but not yet. She couldn't face Crosthwaite again for a while. So she said nothing about it, and Sarah went on talking about the Women's Movement. It had been her lifeline.

'People can say what they like – and, my goodness, they do,' added Sarah, remembering the *Boudicca* postbag; 'but on the whole we're very lucky nowadays.'

⇌ *35* ⇌

I loathe this house, thought Deirdre Russell.

She had gone unwillingly to Springfield on Friday afternoon, to check once again her sister-in-law's cherished, but delicate, plants, which couldn't be entrusted to the housekeeper. Now she replaced a creamy cyclamen she'd been feeding on the staircase windowsill, regarded it critically, and shifted it an inch to the right.

I've always loathed it. Edward and I were reasonably happy here after we married, and I had my babies in the big bedroom at the corner. But Springfield always felt wrong, though I never said so to Edward. Thank God Philip wanted to take it over from us.

Bleakness, she thought, gazing through the staircase window, refusing to see that, in the sunshine, the leafless trees glimmered a silvery green; that the wall, which she believed to be a monochrome grey, was actually yellow-brown, tinged with black; and that snowdrops sprinkled the grass. It was easier to blame her dislike of Springfield on its hilly position than on memories of unpleasant scenes which had taken place in its rooms. To admit that, was to open the dangerous doors of memory.

~

'How can you stand it?' she raged at Enid once in her teens. 'A household of lame dogs.'

'Don't be rude about Ethel, please.'

'It's not just Ethel. It's those whining evacuee kids, and Dorothy Flood peering through her spectacles.'

She didn't trust herself to mention Anne Cropper.

'You're going to have a surprise.' Enid sounded pleased.

'Well?'

'Far from being a lame dog, Dorothy has just been appointed headmistress of Crosthwaite Girls' High School.'

'Ye gods!' cried Deirdre. 'Whoever chose her must be off their heads.'

'The governors chose her, and they're perfectly sane. Dorothy's made a name for herself. Most people know her lectures and her articles on historical costume. The school will be proud to have someone so distinguished.'

'You put her up to it,' said Deirdre accusingly.

'Possibly; but why not? She deserves some success and happiness.'

'You care about everyone's happiness but mine!' shouted Deirdre.

She stormed out of the room, banging the door.

Why were she and her mother at daggers drawn? Perhaps because they both had that coppery hair – Deirdre refused ever to concede that it was red. But mainly it was disappointment that Enid had failed to be the mother Deirdre wanted. That 'house of women'! It was oppressive. Certainly it was funny when people mistook Springfield for a nunnery, but Deirdre often thought it was more like a den of witches – black-eyed Ruth; limping Ethel; Dorothy with her idiotic clothes – historical costume clearly inspired no chic; intense, peaky Anne. The atmosphere – so cliquey and claustrophobic! That Enid loved her unlovely brood seemed treason to Deirdre.

She herself loved men. She couldn't remember when she hadn't preferred boys to girls. She attracted men too. Even as a schoolgirl, she had had sexual encounters and adventures which would have horrified Enid, if she'd known. That fact added spice to the glorious moment when, aged sixteen, she had rolled, flushed and naked, on a boyfriend's bed, rejoicing that her virginity had gone for ever.

She had power over girls as well; a share of the power by which her brother, Philip, dominated theatre audiences. As a school prefect, and a junior officer, she had been obeyed. In those Army days, she had been for a time a mess orderly officer. She had walked down the room, between the crowded tables, and the girls – many older than herself – had dropped their knives and forks, swallowed and sat to attention.

'Any complaints?'

'No, ma'am.'

They dared not complain to her, though she knew how disgusting the boiled cod, and prunes and semolina were.

But she hated the female barracks. It was as bad as Springfield. She was thrilled when she wangled a transfer to a regimental headquarters full of men.

~

How odd, thought Deirdre, that this modern 'women's lib' seemed to be about separating oneself from men. For her, in her youth, liberation had meant something quite different – smoochy music, perilously high-heeled shoes, the bite of an iced martini, and always a man beside her, waiting, hot-eyed and passionate, till she chose to say 'yes'.

Deirdre suddenly realized that she was still staring through the staircase window. She went on, up to the

182

landing, and shied away, as she invariably did, from a door on the left. 'Such a nasty little room. It'll do for your *au pair*,' she had said to Francis's mother – a brittle, racehorse type of woman – when she had moved into Springfield with Philip. To abuse the room was part of her revenge on Anne Cropper, who had slept there. Alone? Deirdre wished she knew.

~

She had been summoned to Springfield in February 1946, to discover that her mother was dying of cancer. Deirdre had known that she was ill but, engrossed in her own life, she had shelved the thought. Edward Russell, with whom she was sleeping, was badgering her to marry him. He was attractive, a good lover, and definitely upper class, which appealed. Deirdre never mentioned Ashwells to him. Unfortunately he had very little money, and was about to leave the Army with no notion of any job he might like. At twenty-one, Deirdre felt it was time she married; yet the penniless Edward might be risky. Other men hovered.

There was no time to worry about Enid until she reached Springfield and saw the state of her mother. The glowing, vibrant woman was a mere husk, voiceless, since the cancer had attacked her throat. And Anne, of course, was doing everything for her.

But why remember the wounds of that time, when snow lay round Springfield in ghostly lumps and an icy wind lanced through every window-frame? The bleakness outside only mirrored the bleakness inside Deirdre as she realized it was now too late – far too late – to regain the loving relationship of her childhood with Enid; that Anne, ghostly pale herself and seeming years younger than the sophisticated Deirdre, though she was actually twenty-four, had taken her place.

On the very last evening, she looked into the bedroom where Enid lay. Anne sat beside her, holding her hand.

'Go away. I'll stay with her,' said Deirdre roughly.

The dying woman feebly shook her head. Anne, her hand

clasped round Enid's, didn't move. Deirdre retreated, furious and miserable.

Was it an hour, two hours later, that she crept back? She opened the door soundlessly. Anne was bending over Enid, kissing her. A tiny sigh rose from the bed, and then silence. Anne dropped her head into her hands.

Deirdre dashed across the room, but it was too late. She could never say goodbye now to her mother; never. She rounded wildly on Anne.

'You devil! Why didn't you call me? Get out!' she shrieked.

⇒ *36* ⇐

'Springfield's mine, and I want it to myself. You must all go – at once.'

It was the morning after Enid's death. Deirdre stood in the dining-room, dynamic and dominating, and stared across the table at the little mourning group of Ruth and Anne Cropper, and Ethel Pearson. Dorothy, with unexpected independence, had swept off to school, taking little Sarah with her.

Deirdre had chosen the dining-room deliberately. Anne had sat with Enid in the drawing-room, so Anne must never enter it again.

'How can we go, just like that?' protested Ruth, recalling, sickeningly, how Amy Whittingham had once abandoned her.

'I've no idea,' said Deirdre. 'You can make your own arrangements.'

'You must realize,' said Ruth bitterly, 'that with the post-war housing shortage, there's no accommodation to be had.'

'I'm afraid that's your problem. You should have known that you were only living here on sufferance. Besides, I'm going to

184

be married, and my husband and I will need the house to ourselves.'

'At least keep Ethel.'

Deirdre turned her eyes to the quivering face of the lame housemaid. Her appearance had always let Springfield down.

'Certainly not. You must all be out before the funeral.'

The terrible thing was that she was enjoying her power over these shattered, much older women. Her fierce pleasure helped to burn up the grief for her mother.

'You may go now, Ethel and Mrs Cropper. I should advise you to write by the next post to some relatives and ask them to take you in. I want to speak to Anne.'

Anne looked as limp and white as a rag-doll that had been left outside in the rain; but Deirdre thought only of her revenge.

'I wonder,' she began easily, 'if you know how often my mother laughed about you, behind your back? Or if you can guess the amusement your grand, ridiculous passion caused us and our friends?'

'You're lying,' said Anne.

The blood raced, pounding, through Deirdre's head; not least because she often found truthfulness unaccountably difficult.

'How dare you speak to me like that, you little lesbian tart? You came here like a thief, with your wiles, to steal my mother's love.'

'I didn't need to steal it. She had enough, and to spare, for everyone.'

'Not you.'

'I think,' said Anne, 'that I knew her a good deal better than you did.'

Deirdre snatched a bronze ashtray off the sideboard and hurled it at Anne. Missing, it cut a lump out of the doorframe.

But it didn't do to remember these things; to recollect how, when Philip flew in, on compassionate leave from his ship, she told him that the Croppers and Ethel had preferred to leave at once. Yes, truthfulness was difficult; but Dorothy, presumably, kept silent. She was the only old inhabitant of Springfield to

185

appear prominently at the funeral, though no doubt the others were lurking at the back of the church. Philip asked no questions, readily accepting that Dorothy would share a flat with another teacher, and keep Sarah until her grandmother returned from Canada; that Ethel and Mrs Cropper had found homes somewhere, and Anne a room at the hospital.

'Anyway,' said Deirdre, 'I'm going to marry Edward Russell, and we'll be glad to make a fresh start.'

Philip was willing to let Deirdre have Springfield. He planned to live in London himself, and resume his theatre career. With a house at their disposal, Edward was very happy to slide a large diamond ring onto Deirdre's fourth finger; and she found that when she mentioned to old friends of her parents that he was one of '*the* Russells,' several offers of jobs in family firms were forthcoming. They were married in the summer, with as decent a show of splendour as post-war restrictions allowed.

But somehow shadows lingered at Springfield. It was a haunted house. There were ghostly people in the hall, on the stairs. She didn't know who they were. She feared they were Anne Cropper and her mother. She seemed to hear them whispering – she, who had never been superstitious or timid in her life. She hated it.

'I think,' she said to Edward one day, 'that it would be rather nice if I had a job. Mrs Brooks keeps the house clean, and I've nothing to do.'

Edward, who had an elongated face with regular features, and sleeked down hair, frowned.

'Nonsense, dear. What are you thinking of?'

'Just that I'm the tiniest bit bored.'

She couldn't mention the ghosts to Edward.

He laughed, quite kindly.

'Take up golf, bridge – But seriously – '

And he explained, at some length, that it would be disastrous for the national economy if women expected to get jobs now. Finding work for all the returning servicemen was hard enough. Women's duty, to their husbands and their country, was to stay at home.

'You all had your little fling in the war,' he said. 'I know you enjoyed it, but you'll have just as much fun staying here. And perhaps,' he added coyly, 'there'll be a pram to push one day.'

He didn't know, of course, how the ghosts of Ruth Cropper and Ethel Pearson chattered behind the kitchen door, falling silent when she opened it. He wasn't aware of the dark, threatening cloud, spreading outwards from the bedroom where Anne had slept. A house of women! The very cups they had handled, the carpets they had trodden, rasped her nerves. When she closed her eyes in the drawing-room, she knew that, if she opened them, Enid and Anne would be sitting on the sofa.

'Wouldn't it be fun to move house?' she suggested to Edward, with desperate gaiety.

'Now you're being silly, dear. With the housing shortage we'd never get one. Besides, Springfield is one of the most attractive places in Crosthwaite.'

And then Deirdre had her brilliant idea.

'I feel rather guilty about having so many spare rooms. Could we offer hospitality to some of these poor refugees who are coming to Britain? Perhaps a man . . .'

'It's funny you should say that,' responded Edward. 'When I was lunching at the Club, I was introduced to a fellow, displaced from somewhere in eastern Europe. Brilliant chap, apparently, with just one son. His wife was killed when the Russians overran – wherever it was. He's got a lab job in one of the chemical firms, but nowhere satisfactory to live. He seemed a decent enough bloke. I'd be prepared to rent him two or three rooms.'

A man and a boy! They'd scotch the women. Deirdre's heart leaped.

'What are their names?'

'The man's a Dr Klavir. I believe the boy's called Paul.'

~

187

37

Elizabeth sat hunched in her chair. It was cold but she'd neither switched on her heater nor drawn the curtains. Friday evening . . . The copy of *Cross-Questioning* lay on her desk like a pile of dead ashes.

The front-door slammed. She heard voices – Lucy and a boy. Robin Cole, she thought, without any interest.

'If you could look at it,' said Lucy on the stairs. 'I mean, I wouldn't expect you to repair it if it was something major – '

Lucy's cassette-player, thought Elizabeth. She remembered hearing it had gone wrong. Things did. She hugged herself, as if her disappointment was a wound in her heart.

'Tea or coffee?' Lucy had whisked out of her room onto the landing, still talking to Robin. 'I saw Liz's light on, so I'll ask her too.' There was a tap; the door opened. 'Liz, I'm making Robin some – are you all right?'

'Yes,' said Elizabeth tonelessly.

'No, you're not. Is it a headache? Your period? Oh, there's *Cross-Questioning*, and I forgot to buy one. Is your thing in?'

'No.'

'No? How awful! You poor thing! No wonder you look so fed up.'

Elizabeth didn't answer. She'd rushed to buy her copy when it came out at midday, and flicked excitedly through the pages. Travelling round Turkey at discount prices; a would-be witty guide to local pizza parlours; a cluster of reviews – but 'Heroines and Martyrs' wasn't there.

'Why ever haven't they put it in?'

Seizing the magazine, Lucy too flipped through, as if she might discover something Elizabeth had missed.

'They're mad! When they had something really original, to stick in all this garbage about pizzas. It's a carbon copy of the one they did last term on kebab houses. Honestly, Liz!'

'Nick Hillary doesn't like me.'

'What on earth's that got to do with it? He should be able to spot talent when it's there under his nose. Did you go round and ask why?'

'I tried, but there was only some wimpy little first-year in the office. He didn't know a thing. He just gave me back my script. It's there on the desk.'

Lucy picked it up, and looked at it again. She'd read it before.

'It was going to raise Amy Whittingham's profile for us. And it's so good, Liz.'

'It's not. It's rubbish. Nick thinks so, anyway.'

'You should write and complain.'

'Oh, what's the use? If you look through it – through most copies, in fact – you'll find they hardly print anything by girls, or on feminist subjects. I was stupid to send it in, now I come to think of it.'

'Deliberate discrimination?'

'Probably. You know, they say editors don't usually let women take on the big assignments. They're just relegated to a women's page, or a cookery column, or something. You've got to be twice as brilliant and pushy as a man to make a proper career. It's the same everywhere. I keep thinking about the Sex Discrimination Act, and then I look at our lecturers, and there are far more men –'

'Sorry,' said Robin, peering through the door. 'I did

knock, but you didn't seem to hear. I think I've got your cassette-player working, Lucy.'

'Already? That's brilliant! Perhaps men can be useful after all.'

'What's that?' asked Robin. He was lanky, with spectacles, and a kind, earnest face. Elizabeth knew him a bit, because he was reading English too.

'Just a moan about men, after the way Nick Hillary's treated Liz.'

'What's he done?'

'Turned down a particularly interesting article about the suffragettes in Crosthwaite, that she's been writing. This, in fact,' finished Lucy, waving the script.

'Let's have a look.' And he took it from Lucy's hand. '"Heroines and Martyrs" – sounds original.'

'I don't really know if it is,' sighed Elizabeth, although the sympathy was helping her to feel a little better.

'You probably sent it to the wrong person. Wait a minute!' Lucy suddenly looked excited. 'What about that feminist magazine – *Boudicca*? Doesn't Gabriel's mum work for it?'

'Oh! I think she does,' said Elizabeth.

'Why don't you send them "Heroines and Martyrs"?'

'I couldn't possibly.'

'Why not?'

'Well, I mean, it's an important magazine. It's nationwide.'

'So? Isn't it the kind of thing you'd like to write for? And the kind of thing that'd take an interest in Amy Whittingham?'

'It might be.' Elizabeth felt both hopeful and alarmed.

'You could give them a call tomorrow; ask if they'd be interested. Give Gabriel's name as a reference. She might back you up.'

190

'You reckon?'

'It's worth a try.'

Elizabeth's heart pounded. She gazed at Lucy in excited anticipation. Robin broke the silence.

'This is really dramatic stuff,' he said. 'Plots, and bombs and sudden death. Have you ever thought of turning it into a play?'

'*I* thought of suffragette plays,' said Lucy; 'but then I thought they'd be too difficult to cope with.'

'Hang on. I'm not following,' said Robin.

'Sorry. I mean I had a mad idea that we might do a play to raise money for the Amy Whittingham Hospital – she comes into "Heroines and Martyrs". She founded this hospital in the Sudan, that's been wrecked; you know, there's a photo of it in the kitchen. I thought, only a day or two ago, that we might put on a proper suffragette play, if we could find one; but a real play about Amy herself would be tons better.'

'I've done some writing and producing,' said Robin. 'I'd help you with it, if you wanted.'

And Elizabeth found herself laughing helplessly, and even half hysterically, at the ideas which had been generated by the article Nick turned down.

38

A late Saturday afternoon peacefulness had fallen over
Sarah's flat. Sarah herself was reading, with her legs
tucked under her, and lamplight falling on her soft brown
hair. Gabriel was sitting at the table. Spread in front of
her were the materials for a patchwork quilt she had once
almost started making.

She had collected the pieces for over a year, from
jumble sales and old-clothes stalls in street-markets,
searching out the exact shades she needed; for the quilt
was to be no ordinary, multicoloured one, but a quiet
symphony of cream, beige and palest coffee, lightly
touched with grey and black, which, when completed,
would resemble the old lace coverlets which people used
to soak in milk. A faint sprigging on the chosen pieces
gave to the whole the netted effect of lace.

But before she began making it, Gabriel had been
sidetracked into dress designing, which quickly grew to
be such a passion that the patchwork was put away and
forgotten. Now she had found the pieces again and was
shifting them about on the table, pondering the best
arrangement. She loved pattern and structure. They
satisfied something very deep in her nature.

When I'm an old lady, I expect I shall love crosswords
and jigsaw puzzles and playing patience, she reflected.
And being an old lady reminded her of Dorothy.

There she was, stuck in her flat, the last of the family
left in Crosthwaite. If Sarah's marriage hadn't broken up,
if they'd still lived at Springfield, she and her mother
could have looked after Dorothy a bit, visited her, taken
her out, talked to her. If only –

She suddenly wondered what exactly had gone wrong,

and why Sarah had broken up her family life. Of course there were aspects of it which Sarah often spoke about, and Gabriel had her own memories too. But Sarah and Paul had once loved each other. What really had happened?

'Sarah,' she said, 'when did you fall in love with Paul?'

Sarah looked up from her book, startled by the question.

'Goodness, darling! Why do you ask? I was about eight.'

'As young as that? I know you saw a lot of each other as children, but were you actually in love?'

'I was; madly.' Sarah closed her book, gazing down the dark past. 'Haven't I ever told you about it?'

'Well – not properly.'

~

The beginning of Sarah's passion for Paul was bound up with her disappointment in her grandmother.

Lettice had been a figure of romance in her early childhood.

'Look!' said Dorothy. 'Your grandmother's ballgown.'

She had taken Sarah into the Springfield attic; and now she lifted, from one of the trunks, an armful of softest, grey-green chiffon. Only a princess could wear such a dress, thought Sarah, sturdily clad herself in a Fair Isle jersey and navy kilt, with sensible fawn kneesocks on her plump little legs.

'Was Granny pretty?'

'Very. I remember her putting up her lovely fair curls for a dance. She needed twenty-five hairpins.'

'Crikey!' sighed little Sarah, deeply impressed.

So when, inexplicably, she and Dorothy were banished from Springfield, her dismay was eased by knowing that her grandmother was coming back from Canada to look after her. Then a fairy-tale life would begin. Balls! Fair curls!

Lettice climbed stiffly out of a taxi. Her slenderness had thinned into brittle emaciation. Her hair was white. Pale eyes peered querulously through spectacles.

193

'We shall have to get a nanny,' she told Geoffrey, staring discontentedly at her small granddaughter.

'Nonsense. We'll manage very well,' Geoffrey responded.

He hadn't told Lettice exactly what the war had done to his capital.

Sarah wasn't a difficult child. The loving security of her earliest years had made her loving, obedient and eager to please. Unfortunately, Lettice had never liked children, and she saw her duty to this grandchild of disreputable origin as a martyrdom. She would begin reading to her, and then break off, remarking plaintively – 'Granny's very tired.'

'You mustn't be tired for your balls,' said Sarah.

'Balls? What do you mean?'

Sarah saw that she had blundered – and indeed her grandmother was far too stiff to dance.

'Oh, nothing,' she said. 'Sorry. Shall I read to myself?'

The pattern was often repeated. Sarah liked books, and Geoffrey kept her shelves well stocked. But sometimes she wished she didn't have to spend every Saturday and Sunday reading.

She loved Lettice; it was her nature to love. Nevertheless she was disconcerted when she accidentally overheard Lettice on the telephone. 'My grandchild? Oh, no; not like me. Dreadfully plain, I'm afraid.'

Sarah crept to her bedroom mirror, examined her round eyes and protruding teeth, and felt a great weight of sorrow on her heart.

When she left Springfield, she was only six. She soon forgot the details of life there. But, like the fragrance of a rose, the memory of care and kindness lingered on. People had loved her then; made her feel wanted and important. Granny didn't.

Lettice and Geoffrey, having heard nothing of Deirdre's behaviour – for Dorothy kept her own counsel – called on the Russells at Springfield; and one day Sarah was taken there to tea. The odd, painful joy of going down the steps into the hall and seeing again the familiar rooms and furnishings was quickly eclipsed.

194

'Meet our European visitors,' said Deirdre, with conscious cordiality.

Sarah didn't notice the man. Her eyes were riveted on the boy. He was about her age, but unlike any boy she had ever seen. He was slim, with an ivory skin, against which his hair gleamed with a blue-black lustre. His eyes were blue-black too, extraordinary, under brows which ran like level bars towards his temples, and then angled sharply down. The English blazer and shorts he was wearing only emphasized his exoticism. He was holding a book and, almost before politeness allowed, he had buried himself in it again. Sarah was filled with awe.

She thought a lot about the strange, wonderful boy, repeating his name – 'Paul Klavir' – to herself in bed; but she hardly expected to see him again. As soon expect to re-encounter a unicorn! Then, one wintry Sunday afternoon, Geoffrey, unable to play golf, took her for a walk near Springfield.

Running ahead, Sarah found herself at the edge of a frozen pond. She was staring out at its white, steely expanse, furred with rime, when something dark blue whisked past her and onto the ice. Immediately, she saw Paul Klavir running, bareheaded, towards the pond, and knew that the dark object was his school cap, which had blown off. Without a second's thought, she launched herself after it.

'Don't! Come back!'

Though she caught his words, she paid no heed. She slid carefully forward, hearing strange cracks, seeing air bubbles spread below her feet, but intent only on helping him. She snatched up the cap, turned back and, just as she reached the bank again, the ice broke, so that one leg went, boot deep, into the freezing water.

'Here,' she said, clambering out with all the dignity she could muster. 'Your cap.'

'How brave you are,' he said. She could see that he was impressed.

'Not really,' she answered, wondering if she was brave enough to draw attention to the penalty she had paid, by taking off her boot and tipping the water out.

195

'My grandfather,' said Paul, 'was chased onto a frozen river by a pack of wolves. The ice broke and he was drowned.'

Sarah knew this was his excuse for not venturing onto the ice but she didn't care.

'He'd be a lot heavier than me,' she said. 'Were there really wolves? How awful!'

By now Geoffrey had joined them. There were explanations, but Sarah didn't mention the icy water in her boot.

'I thought I knew your face,' said Paul to Sarah, and she was ecstastic. His face, his eyes, seemed more marvellous then ever; but it was amazing that he remembered hers.

They walked back towards Geoffrey's car. Some rather serious conversation passed over Sarah's head. She didn't listen to the words – just Paul's voice, its pitch and intonation. She wouldn't have minded if he hadn't spoken to her again. What he had said already was enough to treasure for months. But he did speak, while Geoffrey was rather fussily removing the newspaper which had protected his windscreen from ice.

'Who is Pooh?'

'Winnie-the-Pooh?'

He frowned.

'Possibly.'

'A teddy bear, in a story. Haven't you read it?'

'Not yet.'

'But you heard someone mention Pooh?' she guessed.

'Yes.'

She could see he hated not understanding.

'Grandpa,' she said to Geoffrey, 'can I lend *Pooh* to Paul?'

After that, Paul seemed to trust her. He began ringing up for information.

'What is ken?'

'A boy's name.'

'It goes with John Peel.'

'Oh! "Do you ken John Peel". It means – do you know him.'

'Who is he?'

Paul's questions were very direct.

'A foxhunter.'

196

'What is that?'

'Gosh!' Sarah, who was addicted to pony stories, launched into an explanation so long that Lettice emerged from the drawing-room, looking cross, to say that Sarah might be preventing important calls coming through.

The Russells left Springfield. Deirdre had two babies and blamed their frequent colds on Springfield's exposed position. They bought a modern house in a smart part of Crosthwaite. Philip Ashwell, thinking a time might come when he would like to use Springfield himself, didn't sell it, but rented it to Dr Klavir.

And so, with freedom to go to Springfield whenever she wanted, the intense friendship between Paul and Sarah, which lasted all their schooldays, flourished. Paul was determined to be completely anglicized; and, with this purpose, he devoured books of English history and geography, novels and children's stories. At first he often needed an interpreter, and who better than Sarah, who responded eagerly to his every demand and read herself to exhaustion-point for his sake; counting herself privileged to have a focus for her life and to be needed. Together they listened to 'Children's Hour', deciphered cricket scores, played Monopoly and pored over fairy-tales.

'You are like Beauty who serves the Beast,' Paul said once.

'You aren't a beast!' cried Sarah, quite discounting the beauty; but her heart fluttered, as it always did when he looked at her with his strange burning intensity.

'No, but you serve me. Oh, go away!' he called crossly as Dr Klavir hovered in the doorway, murmuring that supper was ready.

A General Knowledge competition, to be held at his school, kept them busy for hours, but Paul won easily. Sarah sometimes looked pityingly at his school-fellows, shouting and thumping each other. Paul was so much cleverer and more handsome than they.

At seventeen his ambition turned to reading English at a university. He plunged into Shakespeare and Dickens, with Sarah toiling gamely after him.

'I need to know the double epithets of Keats,' he would say; and Sarah combed Keats's poems, to present him with a complete list.

'I think I should study English myself,' she remarked.

He laughed indulgently.

'What use is that to a girl? You can stay at home, and take care of me.'

Her heart thudded. She looked at him questioningly.

'Oh, yes. You won't need a university degree when you are my wife.'

⇒ *39* ⇐

'You were engaged for *eight years*!' exclaimed Gabriel disbelievingly.

Sarah nodded.

'Why?'

'Paul wanted to finish all his courses before we married. After English he read Philosophy, and then did his doctorate. It took a long time.'

'Didn't you mind?'

'I just accepted Paul's decisions. You see – ' Sarah paused, considering – 'I was besotted with him. I thought he was frightfully attractive, and he loved me. If he'd said black was white, I'd have agreed with him. I didn't think for myself. Besides, there was no one to advise me. First Geoffrey died, then Granny, and Aunty Dorothy was always a bit funny about engagements. I clung to Paul.'

~

She was quite friendly with Deirdre Russell in the early days of her marriage. Deirdre came up to Springfield occasionally, to keep an eye on the property. Dr Klavir had moved away and Paul had taken over the tenancy. There was a row once about leaves blocking gutters. Paul lost his temper and shouted, but Deirdre seemed quite amused by the incident.

'He's a bit thin-skinned and prickly, isn't he, if he can't get his own way,' she said to Sarah. 'But when he's so good-looking, you forgive him.'

Which Sarah, looking back, supposed must have been her own feelings.

In the early stages of their engagement she was dizzy with happiness. He bought her a ring the day after they both left school. Scorning ordinary jewels, he chose a single pearl in a chased gold band. Sarah gazed at it for hours when she should have been practising her typing and shorthand.

He went to university; she took a secretarial course and then an office job. Other girls, who worked with her, had common-place boyfriends and listened admiringly – or so it seemed – to her accounts of Paul. But gradually they married, and she was left with her single ring, wondering when her time would come.

Looking at herself in the mirror, she was often humbled. How could Paul love someone as small and plump as she? Yet love her he did. He wrote to her almost daily, long letters of high-flown rhetoric, which impressed her enormously, and he frequently brought her presents.

'You don't mind waiting, pussycat?' he asked, with his arms round her; and, nestling close, she assured him she didn't. Once or twice she shocked herself by wishing that he would suggest they went off and slept together. Nice girls in the early 1960s shouldn't have such thoughts, and Paul certainly didn't seem to. So she waited, in a void, promising herself that once they were married, real life would begin.

Only, somehow, it didn't.

They married when Paul got a lectureship in Crosthwaite. Sarah was twenty-six, and thankful to abandon her dull job. She enjoyed taking care of Springfield – her own old home.

Since Paul spent so much on books, their furniture was sparse and many of the old sloping floors went uncarpeted; but Sarah dusted and polished diligently, and cherished pots of plants on every windowsill. At the back of her mind she wondered why she wasn't completely happy. Partly, she was lonely. She ran to embrace Paul when he came home. Partly, she was bored.

'Would you like to join my Thursday afternoon Bridge Club?' asked Deirdre.

Sarah consulted Paul, who was horrified.

'You don't know what it means to me, pussycat, to think of you safely in our home while I'm working. I'd hate to imagine you among silly, gossiping women.'

'I don't think I'll come,' said Sarah to Deirdre, who smiled and replied that she wouldn't want Paul upsetting. She knew how sensitive he was.

The thought strayed across Sarah's mind that he might also be insensitive, in failing to understand her needs, in caging her. But she stifled it. She stayed at home, dusting, gardening, reading; and, when she'd almost given up hope, she became pregnant.

With the birth of her beautiful child, so like Paul, Sarah no longer felt bored and lonely – or not very. 'Now that you have Gabriel, I can work until later,' said Paul. Was a baby always marvellous company, Sarah allowed herself, sometimes, to wonder. When Paul was at home she followed him round, rather like the pussycat he called her. He was busy writing a book, but he graciously let her type out his scribbled pages.

Sarah longed for another baby, a big family, but it didn't happen. There was only Gabriel, and presently she went to school. Then there was solitude again in the bare house, under the wind-lashed trees.

She hadn't realized how deeply depression was gathering, until a minor incident which – she knew afterwards – was the turning point of her life. She was wandering round Crosthwaite Library, looking for a novel – an escape – and, in pulling one out, dislodged another, which crashed onto her toe. She was hardly hurt, yet, unaccountably, she burst into tears. She knelt

200

by the bookshelves with her head in her hands, sobbing and shaking.

An arm came round her shoulders and, looking up, she saw a woman's face – strong, quite young and very concerned, with piled-up hair and glasses.

'What's the matter?' the woman asked.

It seemed silly to say she was crying because a book had fallen on her toe. Besides, Sarah knew that wasn't the real cause of her tears.

'I'm – miserable.'

The word startled her. She gazed at the stranger, with tears running down her cheeks.

'Another one,' said the woman unexpectedly. 'Let me buy you a coffee. Come on.'

And she piloted Sarah out of the library.

That was Sarah's introduction to the Women's Movement; for the stranger was Josie Crewe, an investigative journalist on a local paper, who had persuaded a sceptical editor to let her study the plight of housebound women.

'Are others unhappy, as well as me?' gasped Sarah, when she heard this.

'Hundreds; thousands,' answered Josie.

It was a revelation. If she had thought about it at all, Sarah would have assumed that most other women in Crosthwaite were happy. But Josie began inviting her to a small group of women who met in her flat and seemed to share very much the same problem as Sarah. They called themselves the Women's Movement.

A movement of women! Sarah had never dreamed of such a thing – not in modern life. There had been the suffragettes, of course; long, long ago. She mentioned them to Josie, and Josie looked pleased.

'Yes. They're heroines of mine. They showed what women could do if they banded together. But of course they had a clearcut aim – getting the vote. We're different in that.'

'What is our aim?' Sarah asked humbly, feeling ignorant.

'It's not so much an aim, as an ideal,' said Josie. 'We want to free women from the shackles men have been imposing on them, all through time. What those shackles are differs, from woman to woman, and society to society. Here in Britain some are trapped in unfulfilling marriages; some are kept down in low-paid jobs. Many are so enslaved by this apparent obligation to please and attract men, that they've no time or freedom to be themselves. Freedom to be ourselves – that's the key, and the ideal.'

'Yes!' breathed Sarah, gazing into a vague, wonderful future, with round, dreamy eyes.

She said nothing of all this to Paul. She felt that she had stumbled on something – a promise, a treasure, a time-bomb – which she must examine and consider in private. The group met in the morning and could legitimately be combined with a shopping trip. The women sat in a ring, sharing their experiences and articulating troubles they had never faced before.

Together they voiced the feeling that marriage was set up for men's convenience, so that husbands could have a cheap housekeeper and an easy way of satisfying their sexuality; while women got only restraints and obligations, and an occasional caress to keep them quiet. They pointed out how impossible were the role-models set up for women. They agreed that, though they slaved over their appearance and their housework, advertisements, television programmes and magazines made them feel dowdy and inadequate. But though the topics they discussed might have seemed depressing, the effect was very different. It was exhilarating; liberating.

'Women's Lib,' thought Sarah, amazed. She had heard the phrase without understanding it; scorning, indeed, what it seemed to imply. How mistaken she had been! Women's liberation meant freeing the real Sarah from the Sarah who had been forced upon her, from right back in the days when she lived with Lettice.

Josie lent her books; books that were no longer an escape but things she could get her teeth into. The ideas they taught seemed new and exciting to Sarah, although they had been

202

moulding Josie's thinking for several years. From Betty Friedan's *The Feminine Mystique* she learned that she must forget the conditioning of years and establish her own identity. In Germaine Greer's *The Female Eunuch* she discovered the deadening effect of conforming to a female stereotype. Women needn't just be passive, the books told her. They could take hold of life and shape it in their own best interests.

Sarah felt both wildly happy and wretchedly unhappy; happy because new ideas were flowing like adrenalin through her system, and unhappy because they seemed antagonistic to Paul. He loved her; he was handsome and brilliant. The easiest thing in the world was to continue as his adoring slave. The easiest and the most foolish.

She made feeble attempts to rebel. When he said – 'I'll be late home, pussycat,' she murmured that she'd be lonely.

'Nonsense,' said Paul indulgently. 'Busy yourself with making a nice meal.'

Fool, thought Sarah – of him, not herself. The thought shocked her but pleased her too. She was beginning to learn the right priorities. Josie would understand, even if Paul didn't, that cooking was no substitute for company.

'Paul treats me like a pet,' she said at the next women's meeting. 'And he's so complacent about it. He doesn't realize I'm a separate person.'

Other women, with similar experiences, shared her indignation; but there was one in the group who seldom spoke. She was a little, ancient, dried-up creature, blinking through thick spectacles. Sarah only knew her name – Jane Hawkins. They had never exchanged a word, until one day they found themselves side by side in a post-office queue.

Paul had asked Sarah to wrap up and return some books he'd borrowed. He was incapable of packing and posting his own parcels; and Sarah, who had done it for years, was beginning to be irritated by his feebleness. She recognized Jane Hawkins, smiled, and exclaimed – 'How can I make my husband grow up?'

'You want to put a bomb under him,' said Miss Hawkins.

203

'A bomb! That's a bit drastic.'

'Metaphorically, I suppose. Actually, I planted a real bomb myself once.'

She dropped her voice conspiratorially and gave Sarah a little secretive nod.

'Goodness! Where?'

'In a derelict farmhouse on the moor. It was part of the suffragette campaign. We blew things up!'

'How awful!'

'Not at all! There's a great deal to be said for administering shocks. The suffragettes shocked the country and made people think. No one had expected women to be brave enough, or clever enough, to take action in their own interests – but we were. It's beginning to happen again now.'

'What else did you do?' asked Sarah.

'Blew up a railway signal-box; spilled acid on a putting-green; broke countless windows. I was gaoled three times.'

'You must have been very brave.'

'Women have to be brave,' said Jane Hawkins. 'Men will keep us down if they can. Remember what I said. Shock your husband into taking notice of you. What do you most want to do?'

Sarah thought, and remembered Josie's books.

'I'd like to study; find out the history of women's rights, maybe.'

'Well, then – '

And the movement of the queue separated them.

'Paul,' Sarah began that evening. 'I might try an Open University course.'

He smiled patronizingly.

'University! You, pussycat?'

'Yes. I'd like to use my brain; work out ideas.'

'Really, Sarah; don't make me laugh.'

'That's not kind. I used to help you a lot.'

'With *Winnie-the-Pooh*.'

'And other things.'

'Darling, you'd be going off on courses and leaving me. And who'd look after Gabriel while you tried to write essays.'

The 'tried' was wounding.

'I want to do it,' said Sarah.

Suddenly angry, he slammed his fist on the supper-table.

'I won't allow it. You're my wife. You look after my house and my child.'

Courage welled up from somewhere.

'You're denying me my rights. You're like an oriental despot!' she cried.

Paul threw back his chair and stalked out of the room.

⇒ *40* ⇐

A knocking at the front door of her flat roused Dorothy from an evening doze.

'Coming!' she grunted; and, taking her stick, she shuffled through to the tiny hall. She opened the door a crack on the chain, peered out, and saw a teenage boy.

'Your school magazine, Miss Flood,' he said, offering it.

She took it, through the crack, staring at him in perplexity.

'Why are you delivering it?'

'My job.'

'You aren't a girl.'

'No.'

She looked down at the magazine. Instead of 'Crosthwaite Girls' High School', it was headed simply 'Crosthwaite Grammar School'. Then she remembered. The

Girls' High School no longer existed. It had been merged with other schools into a single comprehensive. They pretended, by bringing her the magazine, that it was still her school, but it wasn't.

'Thank you,' she mumbled. She wouldn't ask him in. If a girl had brought it – but you couldn't trust boys. She shut the door and shuffled back to her chair.

It was a shame!

She'd enjoyed being headmistress. Closing her eyes, she imagined herself back on the platform for Prayers, distinguished in her black gown. Below her spread neat rows of docile girls. She never had any discipline problems with them – partly because an invisible aura of power surrounded her; partly because her costume lectures had given her confidence; and partly because the girls she had ruled, from 1946 to 1964, were so good.

Nowadays, she understood, girls rarely sat in tidy, obedient rows.

She owed her appointment to Enid Ashwell. Enid lent her a smart hat for the interview and advised her to stress her public achievements. She was successful. Suddenly, she was a person with status. She was even, occasionally, taken out to dinner by the chairman of her governors, a bachelor surgeon. There was no romance; but it was pleasant entering a hotel dining-room with a man.

She'd enjoyed ruling her docile girls. Jane Hawkins was critical – tiresome woman! Dorothy was interested when Ruth Cropper introduced her to another former suffragette; but Miss Hawkins – they were never on Christian-name terms – seemed to despise the High School pupils. Invited once to lecture by Dorothy, to the school, she had made sharp comments afterwards.

'Such apathetic girls! They don't care a rap what women did for them in the past, and they've no idea of their responsibilities for the future. Talk about stuffed dummies!'

'Their exam results are good,' Dorothy protested.

'I daresay they can take notes and regurgitate facts; but what's the use of that? I'd like to put a bomb under some of them, with their blank, boring faces. They should be planning to shake the world, and they look as if the summit of their ambition is a semi-detached and two babies.'

Well, the world had been shaken since then! Was the Women's Movement – so ardently espoused by Jane Hawkins, though she must have been well into her eighties – partly responsible? Certainly it was one of the forces which stirred up discontent, and changed girls' education beyond belief.

With slow, arthritic fingers, Dorothy opened the magazine. She fumbled through, ignoring the boys, seeking news of the girls. It was incredible what they did. They studied computers and electronics. They took engineering degrees. They tried abseiling and even parachuting. They had 'work experience'. They involved themselves in pollution control and sponsored fasts for Oxfam. There had been nothing remotely like any of that, when she retired. '*Après nous, le déluge,*' Madame de Pompadour had said. After Dorothy, too, there had been revolution. There seemed to be nothing a boy could do which a girl couldn't do as well. They even dressed alike, she thought, studying the jeans, the cagoules, the thick socks and climbing boots, in photographs of school expeditions.

'I don't know,' said Dorothy aloud, shaking her head. 'I suppose it's right that girls should have all these experiences.' Jane Hawkins – dead more than ten years ago – would, no doubt, have rejoiced. So would Ruth Cropper, who had died years before that new Women's

Movement started. And the Women's Movement could, she supposed, take credit. But –

She was back in her elder sisters' room at Springfield. Iona smoothed her flounces of cream and apricot silk. Letty stuck her twenty-five hairpins into her pretty curls.

I'm antediluvian, thought Dorothy, but they were the girls I should most like to have been.

❧ 41 ❦

'What's this book doing here?' Paul's angry voice roared up the panelled stairs.

Sarah, reading Gabriel's bedtime story, broke off.

'This book!' Paul roared again.

'Wait, darling,' said Sarah to Gabriel. She ran downstairs, her heart thudding. She'd not expected Paul home so early. That was why *The Female Eunuch* was lying on the sitting-room table.

'It's mine,' she said, seeing he had picked it up.

His blue-black eyes flashed at her.

'I forbid you to read such rubbish.'

'It's not rubbish. Listen.'

Meaning to read the striking passage about women being groomed into glossy, vacant dolls, soothed with soap powder and *bouillon* cubes, she tried to take it; but he snatched it away and flung it onto the fire. It crashed against the logs, and sparks flew.

'So they've been getting at you,' he said; 'those so-called liberated women; those bra-burners.'

'Better to burn a bra than a book!' cried Sarah. 'Anyway,

bras weren't burned. That's a myth. A male photographer caught some women stuffing some bras into a dustbin and added phoney flames to his picture to dramatize it.'

He was hardly listening.

'Your book,' he said, 'just tries to dramatize a new-fangled set of ideas which will pass.'

'You haven't read it.'

'I have.'

She was astounded.

'Then – didn't you believe it?'

'Believe the twitterings of a neurotic female? Sarah, you of all people, who've loved me so much, can't swallow this anti-male stance.'

There was a silence, in which she screwed her courage higher.

'I can. Paul, let me explain – just give me a chance. You see, I'm beginning to understand that women have been genuinely oppressed for centuries. They've simply not had the freedom that's due to them – '

But already Paul had slammed the door. Sarah stood shaking, gazing at the burning pages.

Presently she returned to Gabriel's bedroom. It was empty. Sarah opened the door of the attic stairs.

'Are you up there, darling?'

'Yes. I'm looking at the clothes.'

Sarah hardly noticed the unchildish detachment of the little voice. She locked herself into the bathroom to cry.

Fear chilled them both. Paul clearly feared the new independence of Sarah's mind. Sarah feared he might drive her to some irrevocable step for which she wasn't ready. She, at least, had Josie's women's group and her new convictions behind her. He had nothing; and if he hadn't been so prickly, she could have felt sorry for him. She couldn't mention their mutual fears – he wouldn't acknowledge his. Truth was, for him, a matter of convenience. She had long ago discovered that the wolves, chasing his grandfather, were a fabrication, to cover his fear of the icy pond.

209

He wasn't very brave. That was another discovery. He escaped from quarrels when she was nerved to speak her mind. It would have been better if he had heard her out, rather than taking flight, and patronizing her afterwards, as if he expected her to apologize for unwifely behaviour. He took to checking on her as well, which was horrible – arriving home at odd times as if to catch her out; even opening her infrequent letters.

'You're a real tyrant!' became one of her cries.

'Shut up, you silly little pussycat. I'm your husband.'

'The institution of marriage is oppressive,' said Josie, at one of her meetings. 'When you become a wife, all sorts of basic rights go. You don't even keep your own name. You become *his* person.'

But the marriage was crumbling away. With injured dignity, Paul moved into a single bedroom. Sarah wasn't surprised. Their sex life had never been exciting. Perhaps the eight years' engagement should have given warning of Paul's fundamental coldness.

She let him go. She bought paint and, abandoning the cleaning she had done so faithfully for years, she devoted herself to decorating her room a bright blue, which she knew he would dislike. (So did Gabriel.)

'You deceitful, rebellious woman!' he rasped, when he saw it.

'It's my bedroom now. I want freedom to do my own thing.'

'I thought "your own thing" was pleasing me. It has been for most of your life.'

But it was so no longer. She began to consider jobs she might take to win herself some independence – and then Josie made her offer.

'I'm planning a magazine,' she said; 'a feminist magazine. I shall call it after that splendid queen, Boadicea – except that Boudicca's supposedly more authentic. I've got financial backing, but I shall have to operate from London.'

'You're not moving!' cried Sarah, horrified.

'I must. Would you like to come too? I need someone to share the work, and we've always got on well.'

210

Sarah quaked.

'I couldn't.'

'Tell your husband about the offer,' Jane Hawkins suggested. 'It'll put that bomb under him.'

The rest of the women's group shared her opinion.

'Paul,' Sarah ventured. 'I've been offered a job – in London.' And, as gently as she could, she began to explain.

He was aghast, furious. For once, he didn't run away. He clasped her in his arms.

'You can't leave me. You're my wife, Sarah. My wife!'

He even swept her off to bed; but next morning she discovered he'd purloined her car keys. That meanness was the final straw, for it proved conclusively that, in his vocabulary, wife meant slave.

I shan't need a car in London, Sarah told herself. She threw clothes, books and toys into a couple of suitcases and ordered a taxi to the station.

~

'I wanted freedom,' said Sarah. 'It boiled down to that. I'd spent most of my life doing what Paul wanted, and I only seemed to have got distrust and opposition in return. He didn't even try to understand me. Of course I felt sorry for him. In an odd sort of way I still loved him. But I couldn't stand the way he treated me any longer. *Pussycat*! Do you blame me?'

She looked pleadingly across the room at Gabriel.

Gabriel had been working on her patchwork as she listened. There were some squares of black velvet which could be edged with grey ribbed silk, to make a dark border for the creamy, lacy quilt. It would be a pattern; a whole. In her mind's eye, she saw Sarah's life as a delicate, woven fabric, jagged into holes, and then rewoven to a different design. As, maybe, her own life would have to be, if she could gather something of Sarah's purposeful courage.

211

'No, I don't blame you,' she said. 'As a matter of fact, I think you were rather brave.'

'Oh, darling!' Sarah was delighed. 'How sweet of you. Especially when I've always felt a bit guilty about dragging you here.'

Gabriel didn't answer that. She pushed aside the grey ribbed silk and laid fragments of creamy glazed cotton and ivory cheesecloth against the black velvet, lightening its darkness.

'Well,' she said, 'you escaped your doom.'

'You were talking about doom the other day!' Sarah exclaimed. 'What exactly did you mean? I didn't follow.'

'Just that the Flood girls seemed fated to be unhappy. I mean, Iona was killed, and Lettice turned against Rufus, and poor Dorothy felt slighted and despised, and Geraldine made a real mess of things. And then there was you.'

'I broke the mould,' said Sarah. 'Except that, really, Josie broke it for me. I was so lucky!' she paused a moment, marvelling at her own good fortune. 'Yes – coming to Warburton Street was the best thing I ever did. Women need women.'

'I s'ppose,' said Gabriel, not totally sure.

'What can you remember about our arrival here?' asked Sarah.

'Chaos,' said Gabriel.

Bewildered and homesick as she had been, the confusion at Warburton Street had driven her further back into herself. Sarah's flight had landed them in a building that was far from ready. Furnishings, suitcases, office equipment and numerous boxes were piled everywhere; and only gradually were the *Boudicca* offices and the two flats made habitable.

One memory still sickened her.

'You shared your clothes,' she said.

Nina and Fleur had been there, as well as Josie, and a few others, in high excitement about the new magazine. They had all tipped their clothes into a big pile, from which everyone helped themselves. There had been long skirts and minis, frayed jeans, dresses, sweaters – not all clean.

'Poor love – does it rankle?' said Sarah, but lightly. 'That's your clothes thing, I suppose. It was different for me.' She sighed happily. 'It was wonderful, after years of loneliness, to find people willing to share things – personal things. I just felt incredibly moved and privileged. I put on Fleur's kaftan – do you remember? It was red and white. We felt closer than sisters, starting our new life together.'

'I couldn't have shared,' said Gabriel.

'No. Well – clothes mean different things at different times. You see, when I was young, I was really fenced in by my clothes. I didn't realize it then; it's only now, if I look back. I was wearing tight girdles with suspenders at the time I got engaged to Paul; and skirts with tight belts over stiff, starched petticoats; and little white gloves to go out in. No wonder I was inhibited! And even after we were married, Paul liked things formal – pleated skirts, which never suited me, and good quality cardigans well buttoned up. Mini-skirts really shocked him – I never had one, needless to say. So, you see, that kaftan, all loose and colourful, represented everything I hadn't had with Paul. Yes; in all sorts of ways that pile of clothes meant freedom.'

213

With two sharp pings on the doorbell, Josie Crewe blew into Sarah's flat.

She tried to put down a bottle of red wine on the table, saw the patchwork, and transferred it to the mantelpiece instead.

'I'm interrupting,' she said, 'and you'll curse me; but I've been flogging my brain over this article reappraising the Women's Movement, until my head feels as if it's full of scrambled egg – all clogged and squashy. So I thought I'd give myself a break. I've switched the *Boudicca* phone through to you, Sarah – not that anyone'll ring on Saturday evening. Have some Beaujolais, Gabriel. You look pale. Are you two having a cosy chat?'

'Actually,' said Sarah, getting up to fetch glasses, 'I was telling Gabriel my life story.'

'Bring tumblers!' Josie called after her. 'I need restoring. You knew the story before, didn't you?' she said to Gabriel.

'Not every detail.'

'Ah, well; it's a tract for the times. Or rather,' she added, uncorking the bottle, 'it's a tract for ten or a dozen years ago. Things have changed. Do you realize, Sarah my love, that when I rescued you from your impossible husband, like Queen Boadicea herself in shining armour, we were still part of a pure, unadulterated Women's Movement which has since splintered into God knows how many factions. That's what's driving me spare now. Cheers!

'Yes,' she went on as she sipped her Beaujolais appreciatively, 'we were still reeling from the discovery of our identity – a united band of women in an uncomprehending world, self-aware for the first time. Wasn't it great? I look back and marvel at my own good luck.' She stretched out her long legs, hooked her elbow over the chair-back, and sighed. 'We've lost that single unitedness somehow. You aren't just a feminist now. You're a radical feminist, or a socialist feminist, or a black feminist, or a militant feminist, or a feminist historian researching the past, or a feminist writer describing the present, or God knows what. Unfortunately.'

'I don't think it matters if we go different ways,' said Sarah.

'But we were so *pure*! It makes you weep. We were a crusade. Do you remember how we used to picket porno bookshops, and write "This insults women" on the adverts in the tube? Wasn't it fun? There was just one priority – reasserting the true value of women. Now every group seems to have a separate aim. Oh, for the old simplicity! Which reminds me, Gabriel, I was talking to a friend of yours on the phone this morning.'

'A friend of *mine*?'

'Yes. Elizabeth Morley. Doesn't she share a house with you in Crosthwaite? She's written an article she wants us to consider for *Boudicca*.'

'That's great,' said Sarah. 'What's it about?'

'Some local suffragettes, with an ancestor of yours thrown in among them, apparently. But chiefly about a woman doctor called Amy Whittingham. You must know about her, Gabriel.'

'I know a bit. Only,' added Gabriel puzzled, 'I thought Liz had sent her article to a university magazine.'

'They turned it down,' said Josie; 'but I've an idea it might fit rather well into our anniversary issue. It's real, historical, Women's Movement stuff, or so she tells me;

complete with quotes from unpublished letters. It's genuine raw material. It really grabbed me, when she was talking about it. And she sounded so keen! Imagine being nineteen again, Sarah; the world at your feet – '

'No, thanks,' said Sarah firmly. 'I'm not going back.'

'She wants to go in for journalism,' Josie continued. 'She seems to have loads of ambition. If the article's any good, we might ask her up for a chat. We could use one or two younger feature writers. Anyway, just fill me in with a few details about Amy Whittingham, Gabriel, will you? I've not heard of her before.'

Gabriel stared down at her patchwork, thinking. She only really knew Amy in relation to Iona. While Elizabeth might be an expert on Amy's beliefs and activities in a general way, Gabriel saw her simply as the woman whose magnetism had drawn an Edwardian girl out from the muffling walls of her home and inspired her with a new ideal of independence.

For, it suddenly struck Gabriel, doom wasn't the whole story of the Flood girls. Awful things had happened to them but good things had too. They might seem victims, yet, when they came into contact with women who fired their imaginations and their sympathies, they were charged with surprising boldness. Iona had dared to shelter Ida Johnson, and foil a police search; Geraldine had found the courage to keep her illegitimate baby; Sarah had left her husband for a new and fulfilling lifestyle; even Dorothy had managed to become a headmistress.

Compared with them, thought Gabriel – and her heart sank with horror at the realization – I've been really pathetic. Running away!

'Come on, Gabriel,' prompted Josie. 'Don't go into a trance. I'm panting to hear about Amy Whittingham.'

'She was driven out of Crosthwaite because she was a suffragette,' said Gabriel. 'You see, her beliefs annoyed some important people. So she went to the Sudan, and after a bit she started a hospital there. It's been wrecked in the civil war. Some people sent us this photo of it.' She saw, in her mind's eye, the hot blues and browns, the white shattered buildings; and revulsion at her own feebleness in doing nothing about it made her blurt out the truth. 'We wanted to help with raising money for it – that's the three of us at Marlborough Street; Elizabeth and Lucy and me. I said I'd put on a fashion show. I began designing clothes for it. My head was full of ideas – loads of them. I gave up going to classes so's I could work . . . And then, suddenly, it all went. I just couldn't design another thing. My mind was an absolute blank. So – I left Crosthwaite.'

She gazed down at the velvet and cheesecloth, quivering with the effort of the confession.

'Gabriel, darling!' Sarah was all sympathy. 'What a shame! I *am* sorry. I thought something was wrong. You should have told me.'

Josie was more robust.

'Don't get too worked up. These things happen. We all hit a bad patch now and again, but we mostly come out on the other side. The times I've torn my hair over *Boudicca*, thought we'd never meet our deadline – and we've always managed to put something together in the end.'

'That's different, though,' protested Gabriel. 'I mean, it's my creativity – it's just gone. I used to see things – clothes – so vividly, every detail. I can't any longer. I know it happens to other people; you've printed articles about it –'

'Well, yes,' Josie cut in. 'We've certainly aired the

subject from time to time. It's rather a fascinating one. Personally, I tend to think that creativity is 90 per cent hard work; just battling on till things come right. My guess is that women often don't allow themselves time to be mentally and artistically fertile. They think spending time on art's a luxury; it's self-indulgent; it makes them feel guilty – '

'I'm not like that,' Gabriel interrupted, in her turn.

'No? Then it's back to hard work, my love.'

There was frequently a sarcastic intonation when Josie said 'my love'.

'I *did* work hard. I stayed up night after night. It was no use.'

'As a matter of fact,' said Josie, 'I think your fashion show's been superseded. Your friend Elizabeth, not content with merely doing an article on Amy Whittingham, seems to be planning a play about her as well – or so she said on the phone. She, and the friend Lucy you mentioned, and some boy. I told you she was keen, Sarah. She was talking about it being a money-spinner, and about this wrecked hospital. Now where's Gabriel going?'

'Oh, dear. I think we've upset her,' said Sarah.

'I have, you mean. But, you know, I can't just be cushy with her all the time. She's brilliant, that girl. She mustn't be allowed to give up. I mean, clothes sense is just a great big void, as far as I'm concerned, and I can't pretend it bothers me. Look at us with our eternal trousers and sweaters! But some of those things I've seen of Gabriel's have really had my mouth watering. She could be sensational. I'm afraid that's what makes me prod.'

'Like you prodded me,' said Sarah, 'in those good old days. Well, I'll leave Gabriel for the moment. It's just like her to go rushing off; I know it only too well. I'll try and talk to her later, poor darling. I should have realized about this creative block.'

So Elizabeth and Lucy were planning a play; and with Francis – or so she guessed – helping them. Shaking all over, Gabriel stared down through her uncurtained window at the gathering darkness, painted with the flares of street lights. For once, the effects of light and colour meant nothing. Despair and frustration gripped her, and a piercing sense of failure.

Elizabeth and Lucy were successful. Elizabeth was 'keen' – to use Josie's word. Lucy bubbled with energy – all those racings in and out of the house, and rushings up and downstairs as callers rang the bell. But she, Gabriel, could do nothing. She was paralysed, dense, hopeless, uncreative. And Francis . . .

The well-rehearsed image of him, coming into the attic with the Crown Derby cups, flashed through her mind, for – it seemed – the hundredth time. But she'd rebuffed him. And so Lucy had taken over. Maybe he would move on to Elizabeth next.

She clenched her fingers. Forget him, she told herself. Concentrate on other things. Clothes – not Klavir designs; others. They were safe. Remember Iona's trunk. Picture its contents. Think of that long slim skirt in fine, olive-green wool; that high-collared blouse in rough, creamy, tussore silk. You could wear it still; show it off –

'Oh!' Gabriel exclaimed aloud. 'Fashion-Aid!'

That was what she could do. An idea was unveiling itself in her mind, with all the swift clarity she experienced when she was designing.

She could arrange a fashion show which told the story of women's clothes; for items to illustrate all the last hundred years were ready and waiting. Quite possibly,

Victorian dresses belonging to the Miss Hardcastles still lay in the dome-lidded cabin trunk she hadn't yet opened. She could start with them. Or, if none were there, what about her great-great-grandmother, Mary Flood? Certainly there was a trunk full of her things; and Deirdre Russell had half lifted a black lace hat piled with crimson satin roses, which must have been Edwardian, out of a striped hatbox. Lettice's evening dresses could be used; the underclothes bundled away when Iona died; Enid's cocktail frocks, and Dorothy's zebra-striped suit. Dorothy! Sarah had said she was once an expert on clothes. Why not involve her as an adviser? It would be good to make Dorothy feel wanted.

Right, thought Gabriel – and the sense of relief was enormous. I'll go back to Crosthwaite tomorrow, and tell Lucy and Liz that I'm going to do Fashion-Aid after all; but that I'll use the clothes in the attic, not ones I've designed. They won't mind. Then I'll –

Oh, no! Reality ripped through the vivid fabric of her new hopes. For a few exciting moments she had forgotten. The clothes were at Springfield; Springfield, which meant Francis. And Francis was now attached to Lucy.

Or at least, she thought – suddenly more rational, for the brief spell of planning had calmed her nerves – he might be. Though really, the evidence was pretty flimsy. She'd seen them together at the bus station, but that could have been chance; and Josie had linked the Amy Whittingham play with an unnamed boy, who wasn't necessarily Francis, as she had imagined when she fled from the living-room. Over-reacting, as usual. Lucy knew dozens of boys.

So – could she contact Francis, tell him her idea, ask to visit the attic again? Well, why not? And now she found herself remembering that strange premonition she had had as she lay on her bed in Marlborough Street with the elegant patterns of the *Water Music* weaving their familiar enchantment, and thought about families. Herself and Francis – living at Springfield –

She almost seemed to hear words in her head. 'This is it. This is your fate.' But not fate in the sense of doom; rather, fate in the sense of promised happiness. She tensed with excitement.

I'll ring him now, she thought. I'll get the number from Directory Enquiries. I only need say that I want to visit the attic again.

And then, forestalling her, the phone in Sarah's tiny hall began to ring.

⇒ *43* ⇐

'How's it going?' asked Lucy.

She had come running down into the dim basement flat that Robin Cole rented with his friend Alec, her arms full of bags of rolls and cheese and apples.

Robin and Elizabeth were side by side at the table in Robin's room. They'd been sitting there all Friday evening and all Saturday morning. Lucy had been to a Greenpeace debate, and a Christian Union breakfast; she had taken clothes to the launderette and books to the library. And, all that time, Robin and Elizabeth had stayed in the basement, working on their Amy Whittingham play – except for the ten exciting minutes when Elizabeth had phoned *Boudicca*.

Liz, Lucy reflected, had hardly spoken to a boy before except in the most casual way. Yet there they were, totally engrossed, tossing ideas to each other, arguing, falling out and agreeing again, as if they'd been friends for months. Elizabeth was looking unusually alive too, with her fair hair a bit ruffled and her eyes alight with enthusiasm.

'It's going OK,' said Elizabeth, turning back at once to the drift of scribbled papers on the table.

'Well, lunch coming up in a few moments. Where's the marge, Robin?'

'What? Oh – er – fridge.'

'Dairylea okay?'

They didn't answer.

'We've got to get across the awfulness of those prison conditions,' Robin was saying. 'What did they give the suffragettes to eat?'

Elizabeth flicked through her notes.

'Gruel for breakfast – that's oatmeal and water; like porridge, I s'ppose, but no sugar, of course. One slice of bread, dry – '

Lucy went through to the kitchen.

'Talk about concentration,' she remarked to Alec, who was hanging about, waiting for her to provide lunch.

'Right. I'm cheesed off with them.'

And he opened the Dairylea, grinning.

'Here's your gruel,' said Lucy, taking sandwiches back to Robin and Elizabeth. There was barely a flicker of response.

'But we can't really have a prison scene,' Elizabeth was objecting. 'The play's long enough already.'

'How long d'you reckon it'll be?' asked Lucy.

'Ten scenes approx,' answered Robin. 'We start with Amy coming to Crosthwaite, and meeting Ruth; then there's the forming of the suffrage group; then Black Friday; then a dramatic arson scene; then maybe prison – '

'Hang on,' interrupted Lucy. 'You won't have all this ready before the end of term.'

'No. So we'll do it next term.'

'But the hall's booked.'

'What?'

'The hall. For the play. For the last week of term.'

'We'll have to unbook it, then,' said Robin amiably, getting cheese all over his papers.

'It's too late. I should have done it this morning. Oh, honestly!' Lucy's patience snapped. 'I didn't know you were planning some great long drama. Can't you make it a bit simpler?'

'And spoil the story? Certainly not. We must do it properly, mustn't we, Liz?' said Robin.

'Oh, yes,' Elizabeth agreed. 'It would be awful to shorten it.'

'Specially when the whole country'll be reading about it in *Boudicca*,' Robin finished; and he and Elizabeth smiled at each other, revelling in their collaboration.

'But who's going to pay for the hall?' cried Lucy. 'I mean, I had to put down a deposit. I'll have lost it now.'

'Couldn't Gabriel come back and do Fashion-Aid?' said Elizabeth vaguely.

'Oh – ha-ha!'

'We'll share the cost of the hall,' said Robin, 'pay ourselves back out of the proceeds of the play, maybe. Do you think we should put in a scene at Amy's surgery, Liz?'

'Don't forget to say on the tickets that the audience'll have to bring sleeping bags,' said Lucy. 'They're going to be there all night.'

And she retreated towards the kitchen with her roll and apple.

'We'll need loads of costumes,' Elizabeth called after her. 'You are going to ring Francis Ashwell, aren't you? Sorry to put so much on you, but you do mind about the hospital, don't you? And we're terribly busy.'

'Oh, it's OK,' said Lucy, over her shoulder.

But Francis was out when Lucy tried him after lunch; so she went to see Dave instead, and persuaded him to go skating with her. And since any outing with Dave invariably ended at the Old White Horse, she didn't phone Francis again until around half past seven. He sounded a bit aggrieved.

'Oh, Lucy; I've been trying to get hold of you.'

'Really? Sorry. I've been out. Liz was too.'

'You don't have to tell me. I've been down to your place three times in the last twenty-four hours – yesterday evening, this morning, and about five-ish this afternoon.'

'What on earth for?'

'Well – ' For a moment he hesitated. 'I was going to say that it was all right for you to borrow those clothes in the attic, if you still needed them; but Gabriel ought to be there when you choose them.'

'How funny!' exclaimed Lucy. 'I was ringing about the clothes. Not Gabriel, though.'

'Is she still in London?'

'I s'ppose so. We've not heard anything from her.'

There was silence.

'So we're going ahead without her,' Lucy went on. 'Liz and Robin Cole've got together to write a play of their own about the suffragettes, and they seem to think they'll need loads of costumes. So they wanted to have a look at the stuff in your attic, if you don't mind.'

'Without Gabriel?'

'Well, she's not here, is she?'

Silence again.

'Liz talked about maybe looking at the clothes tomorrow,' said Lucy, rather desperately.

'There's not much point without Gabriel.'

Why was he so stubborn?

'Look,' said Lucy, 'if you're that keen to have her, why don't you ring her yourself? Try the number in the magazine I gave you.'

'On Saturday night? I won't get an answer.'

'You might. Liz rang there this morning, and got straight through to the editor, as if she lived on the premises. She said she knows Gabriel very well, so I'm sure she could tell you where to call. She's – Francis? Hey – Francis?'

He'd put down the receiver.

'Damn! That's the *Boudicca* line,' said Josie, as the telephone rang in Sarah's hall. She sighed, and remained sprawling in her chair.

'I'll get it,' said Sarah, hurrying away.

'It'll be someone wanting a shoulder to cry on,' predicted Josie; 'someone who's read our editorials, and thinks we'll be sympathetic. Rightly,' she added.

'It's for Gabriel,' said Sarah, putting her head round the door. She looked oddly flustered. 'I'll just get her. Gabriel! Phone for you.'

'On the *Boudicca* line?' protested Josie. 'Oh – is it that friend from Marlborough Street; the writing one?'

'I don't think so,' said Sarah.

Gabriel closed the living-room door, and picked up the receiver. She heard – 'Hello! It's Francis Ashwell' – and

225

her knees nearly gave way. She sat down carefully on the carpet.

'Francis! How did you know where to find me?'

'Lucy told me – at least, she gave me a copy of your mother's magazine.'

Lucy? Gabriel's heart sank like a stone.

'Oh,' she said, in her coolest, most offputting voice.

'Are you going to be in London long?'

Already she had rearranged her plan for returning.

'I might be.'

'Oh, Gabriel – I want you to come back.'

She couldn't believe it. She stared incredulously at the telephone.

'Gabriel? Are you there?'

'Yes. Yes, of course I'm here.'

'Those friends of yours, Lucy and Elizabeth,' (so they were her friends, not his!) 'they're putting on this play. They want to look at the clothes in our attic, but I can't bear to have them rummaging about without you. I sort of think of those clothes as belonging to you anyway. So won't you come back?'

'Who was it, darling?' asked Sarah, when, after a long time, Gabriel went back into the living-room. Sarah's eyes were round with curiosity.

'Francis.'

'Another of the girls from Marlborough Street?' said Josie.

'Francis with an "i". A boy.'

She couldn't help smiling at their questioning faces.

'Is he from Crosthwaite?'

'Yes. Springfield.'

'*Springfield*!' echoed Sarah; and a thousand anxieties

connected with Paul, and thus all boys who might happen to live at Springfield, flew across her face.

'He's Francis Ashwell. You knew the Ashwells yourself didn't you?' said Gabriel. 'Don't you remember?'

'Oh – yes – '

'Anyway,' said Gabriel, 'I think I'll go back to Crosthwaite tomorrow. I'll have to face my director of studies some time,' she added, for Josie's benefit, though really she hardly knew what she was saying for the great flame of happiness that was burning inside her. She was longing to get Sarah on her own, tell her all about Francis and assure her that he was *quite* different from Paul.

⇛ *44* ⇚

As the Sunday train for Crosthwaite pulled out of King's Cross, Gabriel glanced at the clothes of her fellow-travellers with a new interest. She admired a jaunty beret and a silky fringed shawl, and then she looked down to enjoy the cherry slash of the scarf Sarah had lent her, against the black of her coat.

Her mind drifted away to the wonderful clothes in the Springfield attic. She imagined shimmering green *crêpe de Chine*, rose-pink silk, and apricot taffeta; and felt in her fingers the softness of the fabric. They deserved to be brought out of their trunks again; to be seen, appreciated and understood.

Understood; for, as she and Sarah had sat up late the

night before, discussing Fashion-Aid, a framework for the show had suddenly become clear.

'You'll have to explain why girls wore stays,' Sarah had said; 'and why Dorothy was so desperate to attract attention.'

'You mean describe what the clothes say about the people who wore them? That'd be interesting,' agreed Gabriel. 'Sarah! Could I make it not just a story of clothes, but a story about how women saw themselves, and how they wanted to be seen?'

'Yes! Why not?' Sarah was eager too. 'It'd be good. The history of women through clothes . . . The history of feminism . . . Josie'd like it. What fun you'll have!'

They'd developed the plan as they talked. Gabriel could display a selection of the Springfield clothes, with accounts of their owners, and point out how they illustrated the jerky, but always on-going, process of the Women's Movement. From the voluminous dresses of the Miss Hardcastles – still, Sarah was sure, in their cabin trunk – they all indicated something about women.

'There might still be some of my old things in boxes up there,' said Sarah. 'White gloves, maybe; starched petticoats – though they'll be terribly limp by now.'

'Giving out "touch me not" signals,' said Gabriel.

'Yes, I suppose so. They were stylish at the time.'

'I shall end with a pile of old jeans and sweaters, and a kaftan or two,' said Gabriel, half seriously, 'to demonstrate sisterhood.'

'Don't make them too grotty. It'd be rather a shame,' said Sarah. 'And what about the way you dress, as an example of female independence? Iona and Lettice would never have got away with just wearing black when they were young, unless they were in mourning; and I bet you'd have had some frightful rows with Paul about it if we'd stayed married.'

Does Francis mind, Gabriel wondered. Surely he's different. Sarah seemed to pick up her thought.

'This Francis Ashwell – have you known him long?' she asked tentatively.

'No. We only met on Valentine's Day.' For the first time Gabriel realized the significance of the date, and she couldn't help laughing. Fate really must be taking a hand. 'Doesn't that sound corny?' she said. 'But it was really just chance. He's nice. I like him. D'you mind, Sarah?'

'As long as you're happy, darling.'

'Isn't it against your principles, going out with boys.'

'Oh, I hope not! There's no reason why feminists should always have to segregate themselves from men. Men can be OK, you know, and a lot of them have changed. There are plenty who want to be partners, not bosses.'

'You used to tell me not to give my heart away.'

'I just said – be careful.'

'I will be, if I can!'

'Do you know,' said Sarah, 'I think I'll come to your Fashion-Aid show. And it'd be a chance to see Dorothy too.'

'If you took her back to London afterwards,' said Gabriel, 'I could re-decorate her flat.'

'In black?' asked Sarah teasingly; but Gabriel remembered the words as she dressed next morning. For once, she felt oddly dissatisfied with her clothes. She wished she hadn't left her scarlet boots in Crosthwaite. There was a white shirt in her Warburton Street cupboard, which lightened things a little, but her coat would cover it up.

'Sarah,' she began, going into the kitchen, where Sarah was making breakfast, 'you know that cherry-coloured scarf of yours? D'you think I could possibly borrow it? Just till I see you again.'

Gabriel stopped off at Marlborough Street, to leave her suitcase, and walked on up Wortley Hill. Cloudy twilight was beginning to thicken about her, and a sharp little wind plucked at her bright scarf. The roads were empty, and she dreamed, as she walked, of Francis, and of the lost girls of Springfield – Iona and Lettice and Geraldine.

There was the house, a grey irregular mass, crouching under its gables. The trees, huddling round it, tossed their branches against the sky. She was coming home.

The sitting-room window, from which Deirdre had beckoned her, was a yellow square of light. Through it, Gabriel glimpsed people sitting by the fire. Lucy was stretched out on a sofa. Elizabeth's fair hair gleamed under a lamp as she turned to a boy in glasses, who seemed slightly familiar.

The Marlborough Street crowd! Suddenly, Gabriel's old aloofness rushed back. She didn't want to see them, to sit down and chat with them, tell them her ideas and hear theirs. She only wanted Francis and the clothes in the attic.

Francis wasn't visible. Maybe he was pouring tea or something. She could hear a faint rattle of cups. Quickly, furtively, she crossed the last few yards of the drive and slipped into the porch. Shadowy Miss Hardcastles rustled past her, unfurling their umbrellas. It's my home too, thought Gabriel. She opened the door and stepped down into the hall where the flagstones lay hard and cold under the coloured carpet.

'It'd be nice to use that hat with the satin roses,' she heard Lucy say, beyond the closed sitting-room door. 'I rather fancied it.'

'Me too.'

'Yes, you looked gorgeous in it, Liz.'

I can't just gossip about the clothes, thought Gabriel. She whisked past the door, up the steps of the panelled staircase, and on to the attic.

Clothes were strewn everywhere. They dangled out of half open trunks, and fluttered from the slanting lids over which they had been draped. A white glove flowered on the dark floor; satin roses glistened from a striped hatbox. How ghostly they were in the dim light, yet how real too; as if the people they belonged to had laid them down, only to slip into the next room. They whispered of dances and parties, of laughter on the sloping landing, and footsteps pattering down the stairs.

And love. Yes, thought Gabriel. She picked up Lettice's grey-green chiffon, as delicate as moth's wing, and laid it against her cheek. She felt the other girls circling round her, brushing her lightly with their dresses. Harp strings twanged gently as they moved.

'Well, I don't know what's happened to Gabriel,' said Lucy, 'but I'm afraid I'll have to go. I promised Emma I'd meet her before church.'

'Could we get a bit more done?' Robin asked Elizabeth.

'I've plenty of time, if you have,' said Elizabeth, happily consigning her week's essay to some unspecified later moment.

'Wasn't it lucky Gabriel told you she was going to do Fashion-Aid?' said Lucy to Francis. 'It's a weight off my mind to know she'll need the hall.'

'Maybe she stayed in her room, doing sketches for it, when she got back this afternoon,' suggested Elizabeth.

'No. She definitely said she was coming here,' replied

Francis. He couldn't give up hope, not publicly. But where was she?

'We left all those clothes out for her. I might just have time to tidy them away, if you'd like me to,' said Lucy.

'It doesn't matter.'

For suddenly, he only wanted them to go. They were all right – but they weren't Gabriel. He almost pushed them out of the front-door, and watched from the hall window as they vanished down the drive, between the trees. Then he turned away and began running upstairs. He had a strange feeling that he might be closer to Gabriel in the attic.

The door creaked a little as he opened it. Through the gloom he saw a white shirt, a pale face and the glint of a silver earring. A slim girl was bending over what seemed like an armful of cobwebs.

'Gabriel?' he said, half questioningly, for she might almost be a ghost. But she looked round. He saw her smile.

'Oh, Francis! I didn't tell you I'd come. I just didn't feel like talking to everyone, so I crept up here by myself. D'you mind?'

He only wanted to put his arms round her, kiss her, touch her hair.

'I sort of feel I belong here,' she whispered.

'So you do,' he said.

Her hands lingered momentarily on the fragile chiffon, reluctant to let it go.

'There was a letter yesterday,' he said, 'from my Oxford college. They're letting me go back next term.'

He saw the consternation in her face and rushed to reassure her.

'We've plenty of time before then. And do you remember how I told you about the College Ball? It would be marvellous if you could come to it with me.'

'Oh, yes!'

The silks and satins gleamed and rustled around her, and suddenly, with no conscious effort, the picture of another balldress began to form in her head. Not Victorian; not Edwardian; a perfect Klavir design.

She stiffened, terrified of moving in case it faded away, and gazed at the image. She saw a bodice of close-fitting lace, and a taffeta skirt with narrow stripes of red and black, as tight as a sheath in front, but billowing out behind into a waterfall of deep, extravagant, ruched flounces. Every detail, every stitch, was clear.

'Gabriel!' exclaimed Francis. 'Are you all right?'

'I'm fine. Just a minute.'

She still had a block of paper and a pencil in her bag. She pulled them out and, leaning on the windowsill, she began to draw, while the leafless trees outside sketched shawls and crinolines against the windy grey sky.